Dead in a Mumbai Minute

Madhumita Bhattacharyya wrote for *The Telegraph* newspaper in Calcutta for a decade, interrupted by a stint in the non-profit sector. She is currently working as a freelance writer and editor. After some fairly crazy hopping around over the past few years, she has landed in Bangalore with her husband, beautiful baby and manic dog. Her debut work *The Masala Murder* was published in 2012. This is her second novel, also featuring detective Reema Ray.

Also by Madhumita Bhattacharyya

The Masala Murder

Dead in a Mumbai Minute

Madhumita Bhattacharyya

PAN BOOKS

First published in the Indian subcontinent 2014 by Pan
an imprint of Pan Macmillan, a division of Macmillan Publishers Limited
Pan Macmillan, 20 New Wharf Road, London N1 9RR
Basingstoke and Oxford
Associated companies throughout the world
www.panmacmillan.com

ISBN 978-93-82616-17-7

1 3 5 7 9 8 6 4 2

Typeset by Glyph Graphics Private Limited, Delhi 110 096
Printed and bound in India by Replika Press Pvt. Ltd.

For Ishani, Bappa and Nemo –
companions through a crazy year

ONE

It seemed I did love trouble – at least of a certain kind.

How else could I have ended up back on the *Titania* on the open water somewhere in the vicinity of Mumbai? With my head in a bucket, and with Shayak playing pirate and hitting the waves with more force than I was sure was necessary; breaking, if there was one, the nautical speed limit?

I steadied myself and stood up in the tiny bathroom attached to the stateroom – both more pleasant than anything I could have imagined stuffed into the dimensions of a linen cupboard. If only I could enjoy the finer points of interior décor and space management with my stomach in my oesophagus. But I was determined: I could – and I would – get out of here.

I did my best to clean up the tear-streaked face in the mirror. I had started the month of September in Calcutta, wrapping up loose ends after closing the two biggest cases of my career as a struggling private eye in August. I had got on a plane with nothing more than the clothes in my cupboard and, after a brief doze, when I woke up on the ground, my life changed irrevocably. In a Mumbai minute. I was part of the Investigations team of the mighty Titanium, a security agency started by Shayak Gupta, rumoured to keep safe the who's who of the nation. In my brief time in the city, I had begun to suspect that was just the tip of the Titanium iceberg; I could only guess at what lay beneath the surface.

And now, here I was, headed for an island I had never heard of till hours ago when I was awoken rudely by a phone call from Shayak way too early in the morning and told I would be accompanying him on a murder investigation. I had gleaned precious little from him since then: the island was 50 acres and had roughly twenty residents, all attached to the same household belonging to Kimaaya Kapoor, Bollywood's reigning queen. Much in the manner of the Queen of England, if you asked me, overstaying her welcome with sheer tenacity and great genes. And generous help from her best friends Botox and butt lift (Kimaaya, not the queen). She was a good actress, even though her recent performances reeked of the desperation of youth slipping through the fingers.

There was a dead guy on that island. But according to Shayak, that would be just the start of our problems: we had, give or take, two hours before the media would catch wind of it and, after that, we could expect to be on the receiving end of unrelenting attention from every player in the twenty-four-hour news cycle. It would be impossible to beat it, but we had to try to get ahead of it, and in Titanium's capacity as security minders of the island, manage it.

Meanwhile, Shayak was acting so strange about the whole business that I had no choice but to accept that even my new boss, reputed to be the man providing a safe night's sleep to every top-billed star, might have a little bit of a crush on the comely Kimaaya. How else to account for his stony-faced silence?

I ignored a fresh wave of nausea and headed resolutely out of the bathroom and up the stairs, holding on to the railing, the wall, the light fixtures – whatever was at easy distance – trying to stay upright as my head reeled and my innards whirled.

As soon as I got out on to the deck and breathed in the salt air, I felt my head clear and my stomach settle. What would make me feel even better were words with Shayak.

I walked to the helm, where he stood. Even the water stretching in every direction as far as the eye could see failed to soften me. 'Got up on the wrong side of the boat this morning?'

'How are you doing?' asked Shayak. I could see the concern in his eyes, and it suddenly occurred to me that the choppiness of the ride might have nothing whatsoever to do with him.

'Is it always this rough?'

'This isn't rough.'

'Will I get used to it?'

'Maybe, maybe not.'

'Great. And you say I'll have to make this trip again?'

'Unless we can solve this murder case in a day, yes.' Shayak reached into a cabinet to his left and pulled out a strip of pills and a bottle of water. 'Take one of these.'

'What is it?'

'It'll help with the seasickness.'

'How long will it take to kick in?'

'It's pretty much immediate.'

'Why didn't you give it to me earlier?'

'I tried, but you bolted rather quickly, and as you can see, there is no one else to steer this thing but me. I couldn't exactly go chasing after you.'

I did as I was told, feeling sick as the liquid hit my stomach. 'Don't you feel it?' I asked. It didn't look like he did – fresh as a glass of cold, mouth-puckering lemonade in crisp white shirt and blue jeans.

'I've got sea legs on me to do an admiral proud,' he said with his first smile of the morning.

'And yet you don't seem happy.' In the face of Shayak's dourness, I continued. 'You still won't tell me what's wrong?'

'I do not enjoy people being murdered on my watch.'

'That's not all.'

'You'll find out soon enough. Why don't we just enjoy what's left of the trip? You seem to be doing better now.'

It was true. Being above board seemed to have helped much sooner than any meds could have possibly started work. If I hadn't descended into the bowels of the ship – beautiful though they were – maybe I could have avoided the upchuck altogether. Yet another thing to blame Shayak for. If he hadn't been so bristly, I may not have felt the need to flee and would have bypassed the bucket.

'Maybe you could tell me why you are annoyed with me,' I said.

Shayak looked at me in surprise. 'Not with you.'

'Then? Why the foul mood?'

'It's complicated.'

'When isn't it? Try me.'

'It's Kimaaya.'

'Kapoor?'

'Is there any other?'

'I am sure there are many – even if you have eyes only for one of them.'

Shayak laughed.

'You should eat something,' he said, looking more pleased than he should be, all of a sudden.

'I don't know if that's such a good idea.'

'Being on an empty stomach will only make it worse.'

'But the kitchen is downstairs. I can't go back there again.'

'Don't you remember my stash up here?'

Of course. My first time aboard the *Titania*, when it was safely and comfortingly docked in Calcutta, on the relatively still waters of the Hooghly, Shayak had produced a veritable buffet of world cuisine stored in a cooler somewhere up here.

'There's a smoothie in there for you,' said Shayak, pointing in the direction of a chill chest disguised as a table.

I opened the top and saw a tall cup with a thick straw protruding from it.

I took a sip. It was delicious. I could taste blueberries, mango and smooth, creamy yoghurt. My stomach gratefully received the offering. 'Thanks.'

'I think I have cracked the secret to making you happy.'

'And what's that?'

'Keeping you fed. At all times. The better the food, the less likely you are to fight me and anyone else you find in your way.'

Easy as that made me sound, I couldn't argue with his logic, even though the tension simmering between us this morning seemed too large to be done away with by a blitz of fruit and dairy, no matter how restorative.

'It won't be long now,' said Shayak.

I scanned the horizon for anything that might betray life. 'I don't see anything.'

'It's a small island, and we're still about fifteen minutes away.'

I drained my cup and set it down.

'So what are all these buttons and things for?' I asked, taking in the formidable console before us.

Shayak talked me through the main controls, and I tried to display more than a cursory interest in what was clearly his favourite toy. We were being guided by a GPS system, but it seemed as though Shayak knew his way well enough without it.

'You want to have a go?' he asked.

'At what?'

'At driving this big old jalopy.'

'First of all, even I can tell that this ain't no jalopy. And second of all, no.'

'Why not? It's easy-peasy.'

My mind went into montage mode as I imagined Shayak – the wind in our hair, sun glinting off sparkly white teeth, his hand over mine – teaching me how to steer his boat.

'Maybe later,' I said, taking a seat.

The sun warmed my face and soon I actually found that I was enjoying myself. Before long, I saw a speck emerge. 'Is that it?'

'Yes,' said Shayak, grim once more.

'It doesn't seem very large.'

'It's not.'

'It's a closed-door murder,' I said, a vein of excitement finally taking over from the gloom of the morning.

'Sorry?'

'It is an isolated island. The murderer might still be hanging around.'

'It's too early for assumptions, Reema. And this isn't one of your detective novels: Mumbai, as you have just discovered, is only a boat ride away. The murderer may well be on his way out of the country by now.'

'Still, having a crime scene so contained can be a good thing.'

'That might be true, but don't expect anything about this one to be straightforward,' he said, taking a deep breath. 'Let the show begin.'

Shayak guided the yacht into what passed for a dock, right beside a smaller yacht and a speedboat. The whole arrangement was far more ramshackle than I had expected on the private island of a leading Bollywood star not known for discretion in her ways.

'This is the temporary dock,' Shayak explained before I could ask. 'The main one is being renovated.'

'Is that Kimaaya's yacht?' I asked.

'No. I imagine it must belong to a guest. The speedboat is hers.'

'I would have thought a yacht was a necessary accessory if you owned a private island.'

'She had one till recently.'

We disembarked, and I was surprised by how well Shayak knew his way around. Of course, Kimaaya was a client, a very prominent one, and he must have worked on the security plan for the island. From the little I had learnt about Shayak's activities in the time I had been with Titanium, I knew he was hands-on with most of his biggest clients. It was, I had been told, his personal commitment that made him so sought after among the rich and famous. Now a murder had been committed here, and I couldn't help but wonder whether heads would roll.

A man in plain black uniform waited for us, one of Titanium's security staff. He saluted Shayak.

'Have the police arrived yet?' Shayak asked.

'No, sir.'

'Good.'

We had walked to a golf cart, and Shayak and the guard took the front seats, leaving me to climb into the back.

'Sa'ab, I don't know how this happened. I was at my station the whole night,' the guard said. I heard the quiver in his voice.

'Where exactly was the body found?'

'You want to go there now, sir?'

'Just tell me what you know.'

'It is not far from the old dock.'

'By the construction site?'

'Not very close to that either; it was on the other side. Around 300 metres away.'

'None of the workers reported any disturbance?'

'It was away from the quarter, sir. And there is reduced staff strength right now.'

'The site manager found the body?'

'Yes, this morning, at around 5.30. He came to the house and I spoke to you immediately after.'

'Whom does that other boat belong to?'

'I don't know, sir, but a number of guests from last night's party came on that.'

'Party?' Shayak shook his head. 'How many people?'

'Not many – I would say no more than eight.'

'Are they all still here?'

'Yes, sir. All except one who left last night itself.'

Shayak didn't ask any further questions, and the guard volunteered no more information.

The island was lush – far more untouched than I had expected. I could see the house in the distance and, as we drew closer, there was more landscaping – a small waterbody, with a pagoda connected by a bridge, hedges of flowers and a curved driveway with a couple more carts parked on it.

We came up to the house – and I would call it that only loosely. It resembled a spa resort in Kerala or Bali more than a home the likes of me would know. Tapering wooden pillars held up a tiled roof with fluid lines. Flowing curtains and plants provided a veil from prying eyes – not that there could be many unaccounted-for peepers on a private island in the general scheme of things. But this was now the scene of a murder, and the openness of Kimaaya Kapoor's home could only spell trouble for the security-minded.

Shayak turned to the guard as we disembarked. 'I'll sit with you and the other man on duty later.'

The guard gave a nervy salute.

I followed Shayak into the house. There was no door, and consequently no bell, and I found myself standing in a magical, welcoming foyer sort of space, with low seats and a sunken fish pond. There was a wooden divider separating it from the main living area, giving the impression of openness without leaving the inhabitants completely vulnerable.

We walked through to a living room where we found Kimaaya Kapoor, in a strappy top and yoga pants, talking to another woman. She turned to watch Shayak as we approached. The face I had till now only seen larger than life at the cinema seemed far more vulnerable and mobile before me. She was even more beautiful and delicate, the flirty, self-aware smile that had sold many a film ticket and tabloid was now replaced by a look of dismay.

'Oh Shayak,' she gushed, stepping towards him. 'What a nightmare this is!'

He watched her with a curious mix of anger and exasperation.

'What will we do?'

'I will do what I always do, which is to pick up after you,' he said. 'You will do your best not to get in my way.'

Kimaaya didn't seem to mind the cold words, except that they were uttered in the presence of a stranger. She turned her attention to me, starting at my feet, encased in black ballerinas, moving slowly up to take in my jeans and black top, before finally resting on my face with an icy smile.

'Kimaaya,' said Shayak, 'this is Reema, my newest, brightest recruit. She'll be lead on this case.'

I was as surprised as Kimaaya at this.

'What do you mean? Where will you be?' she asked.

'Don't worry, I'm here too. But it is critical I keep some amount of objective distance.'

'But Shayak ...'

'No buts. I don't want to be seen too close to this business or they will be all over us like a swarm of locusts.'

'Still afraid, I see.'

Shayak shook his head.

'Don't forget that this is my failing. We are here to investigate, but before that I need to find out how this happened, and ensure you aren't left so exposed ever again, at any location.'

'Hard on yourself, as usual.' There was a softness to Kimaaya's words, which left me wondering.

'Don't worry, I blame you equally for this mess.'

'What do you mean?'

'You shouldn't have been here, Kimaaya. You weren't supposed to be here with such little security, and you just wouldn't listen.'

'But after my South Africa schedule got cancelled, what did you expect me to do? Hang about uselessly in Mumbai, waiting to become tabloid fodder?'

'You could have given me time to clear the island of the construction staff and up the security to an acceptable level.'

'Well, there's no point blaming me now.'

'You and me both.'

'Either way! Tell me what's happening.'

'I'll be here for now,' continued Shayak, 'for as long as I need to be. But after that you are in Reema's hands. Give her what she needs. Be nice. Try not to suck her into your vortex.'

Kimaaya looked from me to him and seemed to decide it was time for her 500-watt smile. 'Shayak,' she said, stepping up, snaking her arms around him and planting a full kiss on his mouth, 'only from you would I tolerate such talk on a day like today. It's been horrid – just horrid! There is a dead body on my lawn that happens to be of someone quite important to me! And had you been there last night like you promised, I'm sure none of this would have happened!'

She buried her head in his chest. I could almost see Shayak counting to ten before he took a deep breath and looked at me.

'Reema, meet Kimaaya Kapoor, my ex-wife.'

TWO

I had hit the ground running from Day 1 in Mumbai, and had come up against a brick wall pretty damn fast.

If Titanium had been a mystery to me before I had joined, one month into working there it was even hazier. What did it do? Who were the clients? Who were the directors? What was I doing there? Questions, questions, questions which no one was willing to answer. Least of all, Shayak.

If I had been worried that it would be difficult to work alongside him after all manner of fireworks had gone off during the Calcutta investigations into Prakash Agarwal's murder, it didn't take long for me to come to the conclusion that I had been wasting my energy. Shayak was missing in action when I got to Mumbai, and I had barely even seen him.

On my first day of work, with so many butterflies in my stomach that I imagined them flying out of my mouth if I tried to talk, I hunted down the offices of Titanium Securities. I say 'hunted down' because the building was completely inconspicuous. Just off a busy Worli intersection, it was a seven-floor, simple whitewashed structure. There was no sign heralding it, nothing to advertise the nature of the activities inside.

It didn't take me long to realize that there was a reason for its unremarkable looks: Titanium was hiding in plain sight. If you saw it from a distance, you might notice a large number of satellite dishes on top of the building. Close up, at street level, all of that was lost. But if you got *too* close, you'd be stopped by a guard who made sure you knew he was carrying a rifle and that you couldn't get any further without good reason.

On my first day, my name had been given at the gate to let me in. The second day onwards, I had a swipe card to open the standard-issue wooden door, within which was a room that made the security check at the most thorough Indian airport seem like a breeze. Climate-lock containment, body scan, bag scan, quick swipe for suspicious particles – all without physical contact, thank you very much. Though I had some warning in the form of the mile-long confidentiality clauses in the contract sent to me which I had gone through with some degree of alarm, it was still a bit of a shock to the system knowing I would have to go through this rigmarole every day.

And it made me wonder even more what kind of world I had really stepped in to.

Once you made it inside, it was less intimidating. There was a refreshing amount of natural light and plants, common spaces and conference rooms. It was a different universe from my tiny, unpainted, ancient office in north Calcutta, where I had spent the past few years passing the time and waiting for my big break.

No, I definitely wasn't in Calcutta anymore.

Beyond the no-nonsense exterior, I knew what to look for. It did not take me long to deduce that hanging on the mundane skeleton of the building, much was fake – ceilings, windows, doors, even floors. There were rooms within rooms and walls within walls.

There weren't many people in the offices that you could see. Senior personnel were on the top floors. Plebs like me were on the first and second floors. Our access cards restricted us to those levels.

On my first day, I was greeted by Archana, the HR manager who was in her late thirties, smartly outfitted in white shirt, grey trousers, black heels and a veil of efficiency. She walked me through the formalities, handing me my key card and laptop. Finally, she took me to my department and introduced me to the man in the glass cubicle, presumably my boss, Pranav Adlakha.

'Shayak is out of town and expected to return in about a fortnight. Till then, you can speak to Pranav or me about anything you might need,' said Archana with a smile before departing.

I felt bereft. I had expected to see Shayak today, had looked forward to it. Instead, my welcome committee was a forty-something investigator, who was apparently all there was to the department I had been recruited into. The rest of the desks were empty.

'Good morning,' I said.

'Hello,' he replied, giving me only the most cursory of glances. And then, when he realized I wasn't going away, he shot me a look from above his thick, black-rimmed rectangular frames.

'Settle in. We'll talk in an hour or so. Have a look around, then go up to the second floor to the tech department and get your user ID, etc. sorted out. Without all that, you are useless to me.'

I headed to my workstation. It was an open office setting, but my desk was roomy, with partitions high enough to give me some semblance of privacy even if there were people occupying the other spots. It was a far cry from my grey-walled hole in Calcutta that I had been forced to abandon. But then, that had been my own.

I resisted the urge to roam the halls on my way to find the tech team, which turned out to be a bunch of guys who looked like they were barely out of high school. I was directed to Rishi, who was typing so fast that his fingers were almost a blur. He was very pale, with black spiky hair, an earring, jeans and tee, and canvas shoes.

He was engrossed in whatever it was on his screen, and I stood there for a minute before he finally looked up at me, his light brown eyes lingering on my face before he spoke.

If at Titanium I had entered a man's world, in these cubicles where technology ruled, I had infringed on its sanctum sanctorum.

'I'm Reema,' I began, surprising myself with my nerves. 'I've just joined Investigations and Mr Adlakha asked me to speak to you.'

'Take a seat,' he said, pointing to the chair across the table. 'I received a note from Archana a couple of days ago, and as far as I know, it's all been set up.'

Rishi made a call and scribbled on a piece of paper, thrusting it in my direction. 'Your username and password for the Intranet and your office e-mail ID. Both are active. First thing you must do is log in and change the passwords. Have you ever used an Intranet before?'

'In college,' I said.

'Chances are, it wouldn't have been anything like this. When you have some time, come across and I'll show you around. It's a great system.'

I thanked him and walked out. I could feel his eyes boring into my back, but the sound of his fingers dancing across the keyboard didn't falter.

Back at my desk, I turned on my laptop and logged into the Titanium system for the first time. There was an e-mail waiting for me. It was from Shayak.

Dear Reema,
Welcome to Titanium.

I am sorry that I can't be there to introduce you to the team and take you through the formalities, but I hope your first days on board are pleasant. You must have met Archana and Pranav Adlakha by now. Archana is your go-to person for all personnel and HR matters. I have had a word with Pranav and he will take you through some current cases, brief you about how the department functions and get you started.

I hope to be back before long, after which there will be a more complete briefing on the company, and your role within it.

Archana will also inform you as soon as your accommodation is ready. Once again, apologies for the delay on that front. As you know, the guesthouse is available for you at any time you may require it.

Feel free to contact me over e-mail if you have any questions.
Best,
Shayak

I was surprised at the formality of his tone. We had been in touch now and then since he left Calcutta; it had always been brief and work-related but still friendly. Was this my introduction to Shayak's formal boss persona? Did my refusal to be involved with him mean that we wouldn't even be friends?

I looked around the empty office, and the sudden stab of loneliness that I felt surprised me. I dismissed it with a reminder to myself that, for years, I had been treading time in the solitary confinement of my private practice, and had not been bothered by isolation then. In fact, I had revelled in it. There was no reason why now, surrounded by so many people, it should be a problem; no matter how small a fry I was in this very large pond.

I would feel more settled once I had my own place, I told myself. There had been a temporary glitch when it came to the accommodation that was part of my package: the flat Titanium was providing me had only just been vacated by the previous occupant, and it was currently being spruced up. I had gone to see it once, and was happily surprised. By Mumbai standards, it was palatial: a large, stylish one-bedroom apartment on the twenty-second floor, with nothing separating it from the sea. Large windows made the small space seem roomier than it was. I had been asked if I had any preferences when it came to paint colour, and I told them to strip the walls of the strange lavender they currently were, in favour of pristine white. In the meanwhile, I was staying with one of my friends from school, Sohana, and her boyfriend, Dhruv.

Finally, after over an hour of doing nothing, Pranav Adlakha called me in to his room.

'Welcome to the team,' he said. Not exactly the smiling welcome I may have wished for, but better than before.

'Thank you,' I said.

'I am not sure how much you know about Titanium's Investigations department.'

'Not a lot.'

'It is small, as you can see. Shayak prefers to use freelancers when necessary, who have so far been sufficient.'

I felt once more like I had strayed in where I did not belong, and I couldn't help but conclude that it was precisely the effect Adlakha was going for.

'Shayak tells me you impressed him with your work in the Prakash Agarwal matter.'

Did I see the hint of a smile? I didn't care; I flashed him one of my brightest. I wanted to start on the right foot; a little grumpiness wouldn't put me off. 'Thank you,' I repeated.

'But that doesn't help me much,' he said. 'What Shayak has in mind for you, I can't really say. And unfortunately he is not here. So what do I do with you now?'

The smile dropped off my face like a dead leaf from a branch in winter. 'Shayak said that you had a couple of cases to brief me about,' I said.

'He did, did he?' Adlakha watched me through his thick glasses, tapping his fingers on the table.

The helicopters returned to do sorties of my stomach, but I wasn't going to flinch.

At last, he swung around in his chair and pulled some files out of a drawer.

'Here are two matters that need looking into. Go through the paperwork and get back to me with your … thoughts.'

I took the files and left without a word.

I fought the growing feeling of dismay as I opened the first file. It was an infidelity case. The very sort I had been fleeing from, the very reason I had been willing to give up my practice in Calcutta, my freedom. Such as it had been.

Admittedly, the stakes in this business were higher. The husband, the client, was a star of the corporate world – Pratap Puri, self-made tech maven: driven, handsome, and now, obscenely rich. Why would any woman cheat on him?

Poonam, the wife, was a socialite, who ran a high-end boutique in Colaba but spent most of her time working with a number of charities.

The second case was straightforward enough: background checks on five new hires of a company; the company's name was not deemed relevant – or withheld for security reasons.

I could go about both the matters in my own way, but I was sure in a place such as Titanium, things would be done differently. I knocked on Adlakha's door.

'I think I'll start with the background checks. Are there any systems in place for such investigations?' I asked.

'You will find some forms and guidelines on the Intranet. If you need any logistic assistance, call Archana.'

'And the infidelity matter?'

'We seldom take on such cases. But I believe that is the kind of thing you excel at, so you are free to ferret out filth in the manner in which you are accustomed.'

I took a deep breath. I would not let him get to me. Not this fast. 'Could I ask why we've taken the case then?'

'Pratap Puri gives Titanium a lot of business through the year. And he's a friend of Shayak's.'

'May I know what resources are available for surveillance?' When I was working on my own, stakeouts were decidedly low-tech: for the most part, it was my eyes and my camera and my ass seated somewhere, watching and waiting. As unglamorous as it gets. But here, I had visions of satellite imaging, hacks and honey traps.

'Puri has made it clear that he doesn't want anything invasive.'

'Yes, I saw that in the file. No bugs, no phone taps. Nothing that can be traced back to us – or him. What about cameras?'

His eyes finally betrayed a hint of amusement. 'There you will not find Titanium wanting.' He got up from his seat. 'Follow me.'

He stepped outside the glass cubicle and used his swipe card to open a wooden door. We walked into a large storeroom, shelves burgeoning with untold treasures. 'On the right is all the standard forensic gear you may need. For more advanced items, you'll have to get in touch with Titanium's specialized forensics team, which is the best in the country by some distance. They are on the fourth floor and you will need clearance to go up there. Here,' said Adlakha, pointing to a shelf in front of us, 'you'll find all sorts of electronic tools. Much of this is out of bounds on this case, but there are many other toys you could play with. On the left are the more old-school aids, such as wigs, costumes and props.'

'I can use whatever I want?' I said, a little more wide-eyed than I would have liked.

'As long as you send the requisition form to Admin. Once you are done, you return what you have taken to them. They will check it, sanitize it and put it back in the cupboard.'

Half an hour later, I had to tear myself from the buffet of goodies. There was nothing 'standard' about the forensic kits, as far as I could see. There was the best in fingerprinting material, plasters and moulds for shoe prints, pastes for gunshot holes, reagents to detect blood and gunshot residue, evidence collection bags, tweezers and the like. And then there was the fun stuff: all manner of hidden cameras – on pens, handbags, brooches and tiepins. Phone taps, wiretaps, jammers and recorders: it was Bug Central. Finally, tools of mass deception: wigs of every colour and style, prosthetic enhancements, glasses, sunglasses, coloured contact lenses, make-up, body suits, shoe insoles designed to alter gait. And it was all mine to play with, when the time was right.

Despite the lure of the super-spy supplies, I got down to work on the very mundane employee background checks. They were far more exhaustive than any I had done before. Credit history, family background, spouse checks, verification of academic and employment claims. There were a couple of great resources on the system: a contact directory which seemed to have every number you were guaranteed not to find in the phone book, and protocols for due diligence in identity verification. It seemed that this was an important part of Titanium's business. I spent the next couple of hours making phone calls and sending out e-mails, but before long, I was stumbling over the forms. Rishi over at Tech had been right: I had never used a system quite as elaborate as this, and I needed a primer. I headed back up to see if someone was free.

Walking through the IT department for the second time that day, I was intensely aware of at least twenty pairs of eyes on me. I felt as though I had walked into a boys' hostel.

'Hi,' I said. 'Reema again from Investigations.'

'I remember,' said Rishi.

'Do you have time for that lesson you promised me?'

'Bring that chair around.'

I wheeled a chair beside Rishi.

'Enter your username and password,' he said.

'I still haven't changed it.'

'No matter. But do it soon.'

Rishi quickly demo-ed the basic features I had already figured out: e-mail, messenger, file share. Then he came to the tools.

'This is where it really gets interesting. It is designed so that everything is handled electronically and seamlessly, and yet with a surprising amount of flexibility.'

He showed me the human resource tools first: leave applications, pay slips, expense accounts, car requisition. Then he moved on to departmental needs.

'Who you are and your level decide what parts of the system you get access to.'

'I'm starting at the bottom of the heap?'

'At Investigations, you are never really at the bottom. But yes, there are sections that can only be accessed by your boss or Mr Gupta himself.'

He showed me what I needed first, which was the material for background checks, then the surveillance guidelines and tools, equipment requisition, case report templates, cyber security checklists. The forms were also to be filled online, and made available to only those eyes that were meant to see it.

'The tools are exhaustive and growing all the time,' he said.

'Is all of this really necessary?' I asked.

'It helps ensure the same standards are followed across the board, no matter who is on the job, and reduce paper waste and potential security breaches. But it's all pretty user-friendly. You'll get the hang of it soon.'

I nodded. All these rules were sure to be helpful. It was just that for someone like me, used to answering only to myself, it was a fundamental change, and I wasn't sure how I felt about it.

'It can be a little overwhelming,' Rishi continued. 'So once a month or so, the boss usually has us hold a class for the freelancers.'

'What about staff?'

'Well, so far "staff" in Investigations means only Adlakha.'

'He doesn't come for your lessons?'

'Not really, no.'

'Well, I'll be there.'

I thanked Rishi and got back to the real work at hand.

It was the past records of the candidates that gave me my first clue. They all had a security background. A couple were from the army, three from private firms. Which got me thinking: were they going to be employed by Titanium? Even if they were not, it was unlikely that a more lax set of checks was performed before in-house recruitment. Was such a comprehensive check also done on me?

I remembered what my occasional ally from Calcutta, fellow investigator Terrence D'Costa, had told me not so long ago: Titanium is a highly secretive organization that has changed the way the security business is conducted in India. Of course they would have checked me out. Shayak probably had his office get all he needed to know about me even before our second meeting. And before hiring me they would have reduced my life to an easily digested file in their database, down to which breakfast cereal I preferred.

And I had been so impressed that Shayak had known who I was, that he had read my little film reviews in the magazine I had been freelancing with and that he had actually remembered them. Now, holding the intimate life history of five complete strangers in my hands, I felt more than a little foolish.

Sohana was alone when I got home. 'Where's Dhruv?' I asked.

'We're meeting him for drinks at Frodo's. Time to celebrate your finally getting your ass to my town.'

'Tomorrow's only my second day. A little too soon to be showing up with a hangover, no? Can't it wait till the weekend?'

'Nothing in Mumbai waits for the weekend. Get used to a little bit of sleep deprivation.'

I knew further resistance was pointless, so I quickly got ready. As I ran a brush through my hair, Sohana came in with her hands full of glittery things that I stared at cluelessly.

'You are wearing earrings,' she announced.

'My piercings are closed, I think.'

Her face contorted with disgust. 'Something for the neck then.'

She held up two options; with overt reluctance but recognizing when I was beat, I chose the less spangly one.

She put it around my neck and then, with all the dexterity of a make-up designer, pulled out a lip gloss from the back pocket of her jeans and handed it to me. I puckered up and applied.

'Was that really so bad?' she asked.

'Hey, I've been trying here! Haven't you noticed?'

'Yes, I am happy to see you have finally added some colour to your wardrobe. What came over you?'

'Devika had her evil way with me.' My fashion-editor friend had very stern things to say about me coming to Mumbai from Calcutta with the monochrome collection I usually stuck with. She had dragged me, kicking and screaming, with my grateful mother's credit card in hand, on a pre-departure shopping spree.

Despite my reluctance to party on an office night, when we headed out, I felt the day's weight lift. There was a comforting buzz on the streets. The air of the possible. The promise of a clean slate. Apart from Sohana, I knew virtually no one in Mumbai. There was no one from my past to come knocking on my door. There were no expectations to live up to in the comfort of its anonymity. No warring parents to contend with. Here, at last with the job of my dreams, I had no more excuses.

'I think Dhruv is bringing a friend,' Sohana said casually.

And so it began. 'A set-up?'

'Not really,' she shrugged.

'But he's single?'

'Yup. And cute too.'

'I'm not ...'

'Yes, yes, I know. You're not looking for a relationship. You're not ready. Blah, blah, freakin' blah. This doesn't have to be a relationship. It doesn't have to be anything, if you don't want it to be. Just thought it was time you lightened up a little bit. Got some action, you know?'

I thought of Shayak's arms around me aboard his yacht as we closed the case in Calcutta. His fingers in my hair. How hard it had been to push him away.

I wasn't going down that road again. A clean slate, I reminded myself. As squeaky clean as it could be. A no-strings-attached guy – a stranger, an age- and occupation-appropriate stranger – might just be the order of the day.

Thanks to Titanium's network of resources and contacts, I was able to finish the background checks over the next two days without even leaving the office, and send them to Adlakha.

He called me in as he went over the documents. 'These are very thorough,' he said. 'You can start with the Puri case now.'

And then he went back to what he was doing. I got the feeling that I had come about as close to a compliment as I would get with Adlakha.

I then headed off to meet Archana, who had asked to see me.

'Want to get a cup of coffee?' she asked.

'Sure,' I said.

'Let me grab these papers and then we can head to the rec room.'

The recreation room was the only part of the Titanium office where it seemed permissible to even contemplate chilling. I had used it a couple of times for its café, and had also scoped out the foosball and TT tables, and the very adequate gym for future use. I was missing my kickboxing classes, and was planning to sign up as soon as I managed to save some money. Till then, the facilities here would do nicely.

It was well before lunch, so it was rather quiet. Archana walked me through some paperwork for the flat. Once that was out of the way, she asked me how work was going.

'I might need some equipment for an investigation,' I said. 'But I was concerned about what happens if something gets damaged.'

The requisition forms carried all sorts of clauses and warnings. I was used to careful money management to make my small income go as far as possible in Calcutta, and now, even with a generous salary, I still hadn't left my fears of penury behind.

'I know what the paperwork says but overall, this is a pretty flexible organization,' said Archana. 'If there is one thing Titanium values, it is good faith. The systems are in place to keep everything running smoothly, nothing else.'

'Good faith in a security company? Isn't that an oxymoron?'

She smiled and shook her head. 'Clients and employees are equally important here, and the crux of many of our relationships is trust.'

It sounded like an HR spiel to me, especially since I had had a peek into the incredibly intrusive background checks these allegedly trustworthy employees had been put through. But it seemed to be an ideal opening for the question I really wanted answered.

'I'm sure I'll hear more about the company's vision when Shayak returns. Any news on when that might happen?' I had tried calling him a couple of times but hadn't managed to get through, and an email I had sent yesterday had also gone unanswered.

Archana gave a little shrug. 'Sometime soon, I know. He called yesterday to ensure you were settled in. He wanted me to double-check that you didn't need a place to stay. The guesthouse is still open for you.'

I shook my head. 'One of my oldest friends lives here and she's happy to have me till the place is ready.'

'That's fine, but for our office records, I am also required to keep your current address on file.'

Archana's smile didn't slip, and I both liked her too well and didn't know her well enough to tell her to do something rude to herself. I jotted down Sohana's address, because Archana's politeness notwithstanding, I didn't think I had much choice in the matter.

Back at my desk, I turned my attention to the Pratap Puri infidelity business, but found myself annoyed by both the case itself and by my conversation with Archana. To shake it off, I picked up the newspaper that had been sitting on my table since morning to read the big news of the day that had everyone talking.

Guns blazed outside a goods warehouse in Worli, in a very public shootout that has left two policemen and one civilian dead, and at least three assailants absconding.

The standoff lasted from 10 pm to 1.30 am on Thursday night, and was believed to be triggered by the confiscation of a drugs consignment earlier in the day. The gang is thought to have returned to try to steal it back from customs officials, an attempt that was foiled by the rapid action of the police. However, their efforts to apprehend the assailants may have been prevented by the superior on-ground knowledge and communication between gang members.

'The shooters had an intimate knowledge of the port area and managed to make an escape, or conceal themselves expertly. The search is on for evidence. Based on accounts from those caught in the crossfire, we have descriptions of at least three, possibly four men. However, they were masked and positive identification

may not be possible despite several eyewitnesses,' said an officer on the scene, not wishing to be named.

Though the cache was yet to be fully inspected, it was believed to contain synthetic drugs such as oxycodone, ecstasy and ketamine, products that are gaining popularity in India and have a ready market abroad. Sources say that given the high street value of the pills – which sell for over ₹1,000 each – it may be one of the largest drug hauls in recent times, though they were not willing to reveal estimates of its worth.

It was all they managed to get into the late edition of the paper. Once again, I found myself pining for crimes bigger and better than the ones I had been dealt. With a heavy heart, I turned to my latest 'Is she a Cheater?' investigation.

I had heard of Pratap Puri, of course. Who hadn't? He was almost a legend by the time I had finished college in the States, though he couldn't have been more than thirty at the time. He had made a fortune in the first dot-com bubble, got out before the crash and had become a consultant for some of the biggest tech firms in the world. He had subsequently returned to India to devote his time to mentoring start-ups. He had been bitten by the environmental bug, and was concentrating on sustainable energy projects.

'I've never believed in charity,' he said in a recent interview. 'I believe in making common-sense solutions for the underclass, from which they both benefit and profit.'

One of his companies had become a leading applicant for patents on small devices and appliances powered by the wind and the sun. The firm had worked on numerous innovations to power gadgets such as lights, fans, cell phones, tablet computers and blenders, completely off-grid. But unlike many other manufacturers that were using NGOs and rural marketing strategies to get goods to the people, Pratap Puri didn't believe in doing anything on a small scale.

And then there was Pratap Puri, the party animal. It seemed like hardly a day went by when he wasn't photographed at some benefit, show or party. He seemed a different man after the sun went down – one quite happy with a new group of friends by his side every night.

I moved on to the wife. She ran a fashion boutique with a partner, another society type. She too was seen prolifically about town, as the pictures revealed, though her parties seemed to be of a different nature: art exhibitions, concerts, balls – mostly for the benefit of some cause or the other. Poonam looked the part of a trophy wife, but she leaned more towards socialite-social worker. Though her husband professed a disdain for charity, Poonam had chosen it as her way to pass the time.

It felt like forever since I had worked on a straight-up infidelity case, but it couldn't have been more than a few months. For too long, tailing cheaters was a part of my fabric and it wouldn't be a problem getting back into the groove.

There was, however, one serious difference this time: I was sorely out of sync with the terrain. My knowledge of Mumbai was at best sketchy. I called Archana.

'I need to keep tabs on someone for a few days.'

'Ooh, sounds like there's a scandal afoot.'

'I don't know Mumbai very well yet. Is there a driver I could depend on? Someone who knows all the roads, and won't get all Schumi on me when I am following someone?'

'All our drivers are fairly solid and experienced with most sorts of cases handled by Titanium, but there is one in particular who I think might be right for you.'

Half an hour later, I climbed into a black sedan, its windows tinted just enough to obscure.

'Vinod Mansingh, ma'am,' the fresh-faced driver announced.

'Good morning, Vinod.'

'Where do you want to go, ma'am?' he said.

'Nepean Sea Road,' I said, giving him the address.

We crawled through the city to what even a newbie like me knew was one of the most posh addresses you could have in Mumbai. I tried to absorb as much as I could of the streets and landmarks. I wasn't used to feeling lost, and I didn't enjoy it. When at last we arrived, I found that the Puri residence was an independent home in happy white with green wooden windowpanes, palm trees tickling the side of the building, a lawn and a sweeping driveway. When you are a dollar billionaire – or at least a multi-multi-multi millionaire – you can afford a nice little house like that, in the choicest part of town, even when that town was Mumbai.

There was no parking spot on the street in this area, so I had no option but to get out of the car. If I wanted to keep an eye on the house, I would have to wait in the open – the worst possible situation – as it left me vulnerable, and was a disadvantage if I had to follow Poonam in a rush.

I strolled down the pavement lining the sea face across the street, and took in the sight of the water. It was dirty and stinky, but it was enough to lift this strip of Mumbai to beauty. I took a seat on a bench. An eye trained to catch mischief might wonder why someone like me might sit with her back to the sea, choosing the view of a line of buildings instead. I took out the camera I had taken from the Titanium cupboard of wonders, a small, tourist regulation point-and-shoot, to take pictures of the house, turning my attention to the surrounding buildings as well to avoid looking suspicious. I held it out and took a selfie.

In half an hour there had been no movement in the house, and I took a walk, always within sight of the premises, to the bhelpuri-wallah down the stretch and ordered myself lunch, with an extra dose of green mango.

'Do the people in these fancy houses eat bhel?' I asked the vendor as he chopped and tossed.

'Some do. They send out their servants to get it for them. Most don't bother with us anymore.'

'Why do you stand here then?'

'There are enough tourists who come here, like you. Try walking here in the evening or on the weekend, and you'll stumble over people gazing at the stars.'

The stars of the screen, I presumed, not the sky. 'What about that house over there?' I asked. 'That white-and-green one? It's very nice.'

He shrugged as he minced onion with a sharp knife against his thumb. 'Not from Bollywood. But they are also like all the others. Fancy car, fancy house. They are big people.'

'From what I hear, the woman who lives there does a lot of social work. She doesn't help people in front of her own house?'

He shrugged again. 'I think she might send some food and clothes to the kids who hang around now and again. Why do you want to know?'

'No reason. I've heard about her.'

'Most people who come to Mumbai only care about filmi people,' he said.

'Do any of them live here?'

'Of course. This is one of the most expensive neighbourhoods in Mumbai,' he said with more than a hint of pride. 'Sunny Sharma lives in that building there,' he said, waving his knife in the direction of a luxury block of apartments down the street. 'Vivek Vishnu lives there,' he said pointing to the next building. 'Kimaaya Kapoor stays in that flat over there,' he said, indicating another tower a few doors down from the Puri residence, 'when she is in town. But half the time she lives on that island of hers.'

He gazed out at the sea. We both stood in silent contemplation of the kind of wealth that buys you islands.

Just then, a gaggle of giggly girls approached. They looked like high-school students ditching class. My guess was that they were farther from home than they should be. They ordered three plates of bhel and shared it between six. Kids from this neighbourhood wouldn't have to scrounge. And they probably preferred burgers to bhel.

I left the man to his job and went back to my bench. It was a warm day, but the salty sea breeze saved me from discomfort. Anyhow, my wait was not long: soon, I saw the main door of the house open and a woman come out.

I called Vinod. 'Can you come back?'

'Of course, ma'am.'

'Quickly, please.'

Lucky for me, Poonam's driver seemed to be missing for the moment. So by the time she was seated and ready to go, Vinod had found me. Her SUV pulled out of the drive and Vinod eased out behind her.

'How did you get here so quick?' I asked. I had been watching the traffic crawl by and had assumed I was in for a wait.

'Don't worry about these things, ma'am. You are new at Titanium, so you don't know,' Vinod said with a smile.

'Don't know what?'

'That we don't have to bother with parking and one-ways and nonsense things like that.'

'Why not?'

'Because of sir.'

'Which sir?'

'Shayak sir. Mumbai is his city.'

That made him sound like a mafia don or a crooked politician, but Vinod seemed so infatuated that I dare not suggest it. But how exactly had Shayak Gupta become such a force to be reckoned with?

'How long have you worked here?' I asked.

'Ever since I finished school.'

'No college?'

'Sir helped me through college while I was working. I did morning class and came here later in the day. He always made sure I took leave before my exams, whether I liked it or not.'

'How did you get the job?'

'My father has known sir for a long time. He only said I should join.'

'And was your father also in this line of work?'

'No, no!' Vinod said with a laugh. 'My father was in the army. That is how he knows sir, na.'

'They served together?'

'Well, not together, you know, because sir was always such a big man. But for a while, they were posted in the same place. He was very fond of my father; very good to him.'

'You didn't want to join the army?'

'I did, when I was younger. But then I realized I could do so much more here.'

This confused me. How could Vinod do more as a driver at Titanium than by enrolling in the army? I resisted the urge to question. Our first meeting wasn't the right time to pry, and I would find out soon enough what his higher calling at Titanium was, if any. I could bide my time – I was beginning to think of it as one of my prime virtues as an investigator.

Poonam's car took a turn into a walled complex, and I was finally about to taste some action. 'Ma'am, what would you like me to do now?' Vinod asked.

'Can you wait outside? I think I should go in on foot.'

'Sure, ma'am.'

I walked into the compound to find myself at a residential school – an orphanage, the sign told me. Appalled by the lack of security, I walked in straight after Poonam, careful to keep a relatively safe distance. Three young girls ran up to her and threw their arms around her. I had seen enough. If Poonam was having a midday dalliance, it wasn't here.

I went back to the car, feeling almost as dirty as I had when I walked in on a couple doing their thing – as I had more times than I cared to remember. This is what it had come to: despite leaving my practice behind and joining a reputed firm, I was still snooping on potentially adulterous women. It was only their profile that had drastically improved. I had to remind myself that just because Poonam spent part of her time in a productive manner, caring for orphans and the like, didn't mean she couldn't be spending the rest of it bonking gentlemen other than her husband.

In this way, three days passed. Poonam went from home to home, interacting with children, attending meetings at NGOs big and small, supporting causes from conservation and environment to education and upliftment. While all the tailing helped me figure out the streets of Mumbai, aside from speaking to a handful of beneficiaries of Poonam's good works and hearing her praises, I had made no headway. I found no evidence of inappropriate or suspicious men dropping by in her husband's absence in my round-the-clock vigil.

Back in office, I got a call from Archana. 'Your apartment is ready as of last night. You can move in whenever you want. Come by for the keys.'

'Great!' I said. I had had enough of Sohana's futon, and her social life was beginning to take its toll on me. I was ready for a real bed for a change, and some actual sleep. 'I think I'll do it tomorrow.'

'I can have Vinod pick you up and help settle you and your luggage in,' Archana offered.

'That would be perfect! Before work is okay?'

'I'll send him to your current address by 8 am tomorrow. Take your time coming in, if you can afford to.'

I thought I should update Adlakha about what was going on, so I peered through his glass door. His head was back in place, glasses perched atop it. It looked like he was asleep, and I paused. But then I decided to give his door a good, hard rap.

He opened his eyes and signalled me in.

'Tell me,' he said, pulling his glasses down.

'I might be in late tomorrow as Archana informed me I would be moving into my place in the morning.'

Finally, a smile. 'Ah, you are being kennelled.'

I wasn't sure what he meant by that, but I continued anyway. 'I have to say, I am not making much headway on the Puri investigation.'

'What have you found?'

'Only that she seems more interested in charity than in cheating.'

'Precisely the sort of goody-two-shoes that I'd be most suspicious of.'

I didn't want to know what kind of friends Adlakha had, but I'd be happy not to count myself amongst them.

'Keep at it,' he advised.

'Without deepening the investigation, I don't see myself getting much further.'

'Give it a couple more days. We need to ensure we have exhausted all options that fit the client's wishes before getting back to him with a negative report.'

'Could I hack her e-mail?'

'No.'

'Bug her home?'

'No.'

'Infiltrate her house or office?'

'No and no. The client authorized only basic surveillance and that is what we are going to give him, at least for now.'

I left Adlakha's room with the beginnings of a plan.

I was sure Adlakha and Shayak would both blow a fuse if they found out I had eyes on the client instead of his wife. But if I happened to stumble on him at a party, who could blame me?

I requisitioned a car and drove home, crawling through traffic. When I finally reached Sohana's place and got dressed, my friend was back home. 'We are going out tonight,' I announced.

'Where?'

'To a party, I think.'

'You think?'

'Just get ready. I'll tell you more on the way.'

Sohana did not need much persuasion to go to a party, even a possible one. And when we pulled up close to the Puri residence, I was about 95 per cent sure that was where we would be landing up. When I gave her a pencil sketch of what I had in mind, her excitement mounted.

'What fun – I've never followed anyone before.'

'I hope, for your sake then, that he surfaces.'

I got out, casually strolling by the gate, and spotted a Jag in the driveway. 'I think he's inside,' I said, once I was back in our car.

'How do you know he'll leave?'

'Trust me,' I said with more confidence than I felt. 'I've been keeping an eye on this house long enough to know his habits. It'll be some time soon.'

I didn't have to eat my words: party boy Puri headed out in about half an hour. First stop: El Diablo, a new Mexican restaurant.

'I hope you're hungry, and I hope they'll put this on your expense account. This is one pricey place,' warned Sohana.

'We'll order the cheapest thing on the menu.'

'Speak for yourself.'

'I want to see what he's up to when he's prowling around,' I mumbled more to myself than to her.

We entered the restaurant and were seated quickly. Though it was a little away from where Puri was sitting with his friends – two women and an older man – I could keep an eye on them.

'So how is the job going?' asked Sohana. It seemed that none of my friends knew how to mind their own business. I was a private investigator; Sohana was a fairly hard-hitting city reporter; our friend in Calcutta, Shweta, was a lifestyle journalist and the one who had set me up with my food-writing gig that paid the bills when Steele Securities, my agency, had faltered.

'A little slow to start,' I said, 'but it looks like things are beginning to happen. What about you?'

'That shootout at the docks had me working all hours for a few days there, but now things are back to normal.'

'Have the police figured out what that was about?'

'I'm sure they have,' she said. 'But they aren't giving us any information. I can't imagine it being about anything other than the drugs, though.' And then she paused. 'This is a long shot, but you said your boss's name is Shayak, right?'

'Yes.'

'Tall, good-looking guy?'

'Yes.'

'I think he may have been at the scene.'

'How do you know?' She couldn't have seen his picture before – he was practically unphotographed, as I had learned when I was trying to figure out who he really was just a few weeks ago.

'The day after it went down was when I saw him; I heard someone calling out to him.'

'It could be someone else … it's not an uncommon name.'

'True. But he wasn't in uniform and he was working with a forensics team. I don't know much, but I do know that Titanium's relationship with the police is special. Not many have that kind of access.'

'I really don't know,' I said, in all honesty. I had no idea where Shayak had been over the past few weeks. Plus, my contract forbade me from disclosing anything I did know about an ongoing investigation to anyone, without express permission. So it was a good thing I was in the dark and could answer my friend honestly – except for the burning curiosity I was now filled with. And a new pang of resentment that I was working an infidelity case even though the company was in on such a major investigation.

'He really is quite hot,' Sohana said.

'Who?'

'Your boss.'

I smiled.

'He's not married, is he?'

'No.'

A wicked gleam shone in her eye. 'Hmm.'

'Sohana, don't go there.'

'Already a no-go zone? That was quick. What happened?'

'Nothing.'

'Meaning it was anything but nothing.'

I tried to concentrate on the back of Pratap's head, but Sohana was not to be swayed.

'When did we start keeping secrets from each other?'

'It's not a secret.'

'Then?'

'I'm hoping that if I don't talk about it, it might go away,' I shrugged.

'You are making it sound so hot that I will only imagine the worst – and the best – unless you enlighten me.'

'There was some tension.'

'What does that even mean?'

'One kiss. Then he offered me the job.'

'Against company policy, is it, to cavort with the help?'

I had to laugh. 'It's against my policy.'

'Why?'

'Our job is complicated enough without asking for more trouble.'

'And it is easier to ignore something that is there?'

'Sohana, drop it.'

'Okay, okay. Anyone else on the horizon?'

'Why is it that all my gal pals are determined to see me coupled?'

'Why are you so determined to stay single? You've kicked Amit's sorry ass in the best way possible. Now isn't it time for you to move on?'

My cheating ex-boyfriend was in school with both of us. He had come back to me for help when his wife – the woman with whom he cheated on me and left me for – was kidnapped. It didn't take me long to figure out that the whole business was a scam, though that did nothing to lessen my disgust with myself for being in love with a pathological liar for so long. 'I was not hung up on him.'

'Try selling that to someone who hasn't known you for as long as I have.'

'Well, in future I'm determined to not be hung up, if that is of any use.'

'Music to my ears. I'll have a list of eligible men for you by the morning.' Though Mohit, the friend she and Dhruv had introduced me to, was a wash, she was not one to be foiled by a minor setback. 'I'll believe it when I see it.'

Just then, Pratap saw someone he knew over by the bar, which was behind Sohana's seat. He chatted with a young man for a few minutes. Then his eyes wandered to mine. I looked away immediately, but when my gaze strayed back, there he still stood, talking to this man but watching me, a smile at the corners of his mouth.

Sohana began to turn her head.

'Don't look,' I hissed.

'Geez, Reema. Is your mark standing there?'

'You've been watching way too many crappy movies. He's not my "mark".'

'Is he there or no?'

'Yes.'

'And, let me guess, he's ogling you?'

I said nothing.

'For someone who claims to hate fashion, you've bought a killer LBD.'

I looked down at the black dress, way out of my comfort zone with its plunging neck and sky-high hemline. 'You think I picked this? It's all because of that meddling Devika. Is it too much?' I asked, mortified.

Sohana waved away my squeamishness. 'This is Mumbai, Reema. Only stark naked would be too much.'

Pratap walked back to his table and we lingered till he and his friends finished their meal, before following them out. The car was already waiting outside the restaurant, and we got in and trailed Pratap to where he had parked a little further down the street. Then we followed him a few blocks, till he stopped at yet another upscale address, this time a nightclub of the sort the two of us would never visit, left to our own devices.

Sohana hadn't even let me pick up her tab at the restaurant. 'Just one drink,' I said. 'This one really is on me.'

The bouncer didn't stop us. Single women were always welcome and, anyhow, the new number I had added to my cupboard was really very little, and Sohana was always dressed to stop traffic. We walked into the dimly lit club where it didn't take me long to find Pratap. He was working the room like a pro, and just about everyone there seemed to know him.

Our eyes met again. A moment later he was walking over to us, and I cursed myself.

'Damn,' I said under my breath to Sohana.

'What did you think would happen in a dress like that?'

Chalk it up to the Calcutta girl in me that I didn't realize that even a man of Pratap Puri's stature would have no airs about talking to a stranger. But it was too late to beat a retreat. I would have to tread carefully; whatever else happened here, this man was a client of Titanium, and no lies must be told.

'Weren't you ladies at El Diablo just now?' he asked.

'We were,' I said.

'Pratap,' he said, holding out his right hand.

I took it. 'Reema,' I said. 'And this is Sohana.'

'Let me get the two of you some drinks.'

While Pratap headed off to the bar, Dhruv arrived, summoned there by Sohana's text. He'd been stopped at the door and Sohana went out to get him.

'What are we doing here?' he asked, when they made it back. 'And how did we get in? This place is impossible unless you know a member.'

Sohana grabbed him by the arm. 'Why don't we get lost? Reema is working, which apparently includes allowing herself to be picked up by a gorgeous gazillionaire.'

Dhruv raised an eyebrow in my direction. 'You turned poor, lovestruck Mohit down for this sort of stunt?'

I attempted what I hoped was a fetching pout. 'Reema Ray, crime-fighter by day, high-class escort by night. That sounds about right.'

They disappeared and, a moment later, Pratap reappeared with two glasses of wine. 'Where did your friend go?' he asked.

'She met someone she knows. I think they are on the floor.'

'I would have guessed that the two of you are new in town.'

'You're not far off. I've just got in, but Sohana's lived here for a while. But how could you have possibly known that?'

'That's easy. Don't get me wrong – I love Mumbai and everything about it,' he said. 'But you don't have the dead-in-the-eye look that most women here have.'

'What do you mean?' I repeated.

'Look around,' he said, scanning the room. 'Everyone has this glazed expression, like nothing interests them anymore or is worthy of their attention.'

'And I am like a baby with a shiny new toy?'

He laughed. 'Like the world still matters to you. That you might even care about the person next to you, even a stranger in an anonymous nightclub.'

It took me a while to spot it; this was nothing more than an elaboration of the 'you've-got-gorgeous-eyes' variety of pick-up line. For now, there was no harm in playing along.

'And what about you? Do you care about the world and the people in it?'

'Passionately.' He raised his glass to his mouth and I noticed he wore no wedding band.

'What do you do about it?'

Pratap flashed me a grin. 'I could tell you, but it might take a while.'

At least about this, I knew he was not lying. I fiddled with my glass with one hand and, reaching into my handbag with the other, discreetly gave Sohana a missed call. I hoped she would interpret it for what it was: an SOS, for I knew what was coming next.

'Why don't you try me?' I said.

'I'd love to, but over dinner sometime, perhaps?'

If Pratap Puri had been the target of my investigation, he'd just have stepped into my honey trap. But unfortunately my real task was a fair bit harder to crack. 'I'm travelling from tomorrow.'

'When are you back?'

'I'm not sure. It's a work thing. Could take a while.'

'What do you do?'

No big lies, I reminded myself.

'It's a new job, so quite honestly, I'm not really sure myself!' I said with a laugh. Just then I spotted Sohana approaching me, Dhruv a discreet distance behind her.

'There's Sohana,' I said. 'Your wine is waiting for you.'

'Thanks, but we really should be going,' she said.

'So soon?' asked Pratap.

'Meeting early in the AM,' she said.

'That's a shame.' He pulled a card from his pocket and handed it to me. 'Call me,' he said.

I smiled and gratefully followed Sohana out of there.

THREE

The next morning, I headed for my new home. I had visited the flat as soon as I had arrived in town but since I hadn't got my bearings yet, I had not been able to appreciate the rare wonder in Mumbai of a ten-minute commute. If the weather was good, I could walk to work on a daily basis.

The complex was relatively new and modern, with a gym and pool, everything pretty much on call. What you'd call luxury anywhere in the world, except that since it was Mumbai, the living space at my disposal was what most people would consider a walk-in closet.

But when I opened the door to the flat, I forgot all that. It had been remodelled since my last visit, and it was perfect. Or it would have been perfect, had I been the size of a Barbie doll.

What had been a one-bedroom apartment had been changed into a studio. The kitchen had become a kitchenette, the living and dining spaces merged into a bedroom, once tight enough to squeeze a bed and nothing else. Space had been created out of thin air and ingenuity.

A low, grey sectional sofa would be a snug fit for three, with a small black ottoman doubling as table and additional seat. At first, I couldn't find the bed. Then I took a close look at the walls. Finally, I spotted it above the sofa, a tiny lever. I gave it a pull and was amazed at the ease with which a double bed descended, fitting over the sofa. All I would have to do was remove a couple of cushions. The sofa could also be moved for a guest with whom I wasn't interested in co-sleeping. A short, thin sort of a guest. The beauty of it all made my minimalist heart sing.

The bathroom had a tiny shower stall, a tiny sink, a tiny window and, thankfully, a normal-sized toilet. It was a triumph of design, with sleek storage for toiletries hanging from the walls over the basin and in the shower area. If you had long arms, your elbows wouldn't be happy by the looks of it, but it would be enough for me.

The kitchen was even more impressive. Tucked away in the corner was a narrow L-shaped counter with a basin at one end and a wall-mounted dish-drying rack. At a right angle was a slim table in dark brown wood, with two high stools. If I needed more prep space, which I would, the table would do nicely. There was a small fridge, and a limited amount of storage for pots, pans and provisions. Also mounted on the wall, above the counter, was a microwave oven and the most indispensable part of my kitchen arsenal: an oven. It was small but it would do, for a half batch of cupcakes or cookies, a small lasagna or grilled meat and fish. I opened the door and found a piece of paper inside. Thinking it must be the manual, I pulled it out. On it were just three words:

Welcome home.
Shayak

I began unpacking my possessions, discovering hidden nooks and crannies for storage tucked all over the apartment. Luckily I didn't have much, so what I did have fit with room to spare in my spacious closet that I revelled at, hidden away beside the bathroom.

By 10.30 am, I was ready to head out when the doorbell rang. It took me a moment to recognize it as my own. When I answered it at last, there stood Shayak. A stubble – no, almost a beard – of black flecked with grey covered his face. In his eyes, deep and dark as ever, there was a hollow look.

'Welcome to Mumbai,' he said with a half smile.

'It looks like I could say the same to you. Did you get lost in the woods somewhere?'

'It feels like it. May I come in?'

'Of course,' I said, backing up. 'I moved in just now.'

'I know.'

'Keeping tabs on me?' I asked.

'Something like that,' he said with a smile.

'You look like shit.'

'Thanks.'

'Could I get you some coffee?'

'Screw that,' he said, taking a step forward, blocking out my light as he put his arms around me.

I was surprised enough that I didn't try to draw away though I had made it clear – to both Shayak and myself – that if we were to work together, involvement of a more personal nature was strictly off the table. But this was different from the last time I had been in that embrace; I could almost taste his exhaustion, his tenderness, his relief. Gone was the frenzy of longing and desire; there was only warmth, and a search for calm.

By the time Shayak released me, I didn't need to be a detective to know that something very serious had happened between our last meeting a little over a month ago in Calcutta and now.

'Sorry,' he said, when he let go. 'I know you have rules about such things.'

'Want to talk about it?'

'Your stupid rules?'

I turned away and walked towards the kitchenette. 'Coffee it is, then. What happened?'

'I can't tell you,' he said, matter-of-factly. 'Most of it, at least. And what I can tell you, I'd rather not right now.'

'Well, that is helpful.'

'Sorry.'

'Something has obviously gone wrong.'

'It always seems to – and at the most inopportune times.'

'Why am I getting the feeling that there is much more to Titanium than I have been told?'

Shayak's grim face warned me against pushing the point just yet. I put the coffee on, and turned around to find him with his feet up and head back on my sofa.

'How have you been? Sorry I wasn't here for your initiation.'

'I haven't had reason to complain.'

'You might not have had quite so many unanswered questions.'

'So there are some aspects of this agency that I might actually be privy to?'

'Of course. You are on board, aren't you?'

'And since I have been cleared through about six layers of security, you know I am not a terrorist, a spy, mentally ill or a village idiot.'

'I see Adlakha has got you started on your first round of background checks.'

'You guessed it. It was fun.'

'You had to have known that joining a company such as Titanium would have entailed a few intrusions into your private life.'

'On the contrary, since you told me precious little before I joined, I am not sure I know what a "company such as

Titanium" is.' I had thought it was a private security agency. I knew it was high profile, and that its clients included the who's who of Indian business, Bollywood and sport, but I was getting the sense that its roots went deeper into some part of the establishment that was well away from public gaze.

'No one has filled you in since your arrival?'

'If you mean Adlakha, the answer is no. He seems to believe that all I am good for is infidelity cases.'

'Infidelity?'

'The curious case of Mrs Pratap Puri.'

'He passed that one on, did he?'

'Yes.'

The only sign that Shayak was not pleased was a sigh – and I was certain the only reason he let that slip was because he was so tired. 'I should have warned you about Adlakha. He can be a bit … prickly.'

'I've deduced that by now.'

'When I'm back, I'll sit with the two of you.'

'Aren't you back now?'

'This is only a pitstop. I won't be in office for at least another three days. I request you to put up with Adlakha for the time being – and not mention to anyone that you saw me.'

I looked at Shayak's exhausted, lined face and felt a pang of remorse for carrying on about my teething troubles, when he clearly had so much more going on.

'The apartment is lovely. They really did a great job fixing it up. Thanks.'

'Glad you approve.'

'Archana lives here as well?'

'We have a number of apartments for employees here.'

'On what basis are they allocated?'

'Various parameters.'

Was this a good time to bring up the security cameras in the hallway? I couldn't resist.

'I was a little concerned by the CCTVs here.'

'It is unfortunately an occupational hazard.'

'So every employee's flat is monitored?'

'Those who have housing privileges are those with sensitive information.'

'Trying to sniff out double agents?'

'I know you have a Cold War fetish, but it is nothing as dramatic as that. The information you may come into possession of makes you a potential target. We like to keep you safe.'

'Tomato, *tomahto.*'

'Your theory implies a lack of trust. The truth is that these measures are for your own protection. Come over to my place and you'll see the same thing.'

Shayak got up and walked around the tiny kitchenette, crowding me, reminding me that breathing had always been a little difficult with him this close.

'Will this oven be enough for your prolific baking habit?' he asked.

'It's perfect. I honestly did not expect so much.'

'Good, I will wait for the first batch of cookies.' He drained his cup abruptly and got up, leaving me to regret pushing so hard. 'Thanks for the coffee. I'll see you next week.'

I got up.

'Don't bother,' he said. 'I'll let myself out.'

It was my first weekend on the job. With the no-surveillance equipment policy on the Puri case, I had no choice but to continue my stakeout. If Poonam was having an affair, there was no reason she couldn't tryst on a Saturday.

But Saturday too came and went without significant change. She stayed in for most of the morning. She lunched with a couple of gal pals, went for a movie and spent the evening at home again.

I had spotted Pratap Puri leaving with luggage the previous evening, but I couldn't be sure he wouldn't make a quick return, so I kept a safe distance from the house.

When I saw one of the Puri drivers hanging about outside the main gate, I thought Vinod might be able to help.

'Can you go and ask him a few questions?' I asked.

'Of course, ma'am,' he said.

'His boss' name is Pratap Puri, and I need to know when he will be returning to town.'

'Anything else, ma'am?'

'If you can find out what Mrs Puri's plans are for the weekend, it would be great. But why don't you see where the conversation takes you?'

I watched as Vinod walked across the street. I could tell that this wasn't the first time he had been sent on such an errand. He approached the driver, lighting up a cigarette, and started talking. In about five minutes, he was back. He got into the car and pulled out into traffic.

'To make it look natural.'

'Yes, good,' I said.

'He said Mr Puri is out of town for the next three days. And that Mrs Puri has given him leave tomorrow, though when his boss is out of town he usually does his wife's duty.'

'She has another driver.'

'She has given him an off too.'

'From when?'

'Tonight. Both drivers.'

'Excellent work, Vinod.' It sounded to me as though Poonam was going somewhere she didn't want anyone else to know about.

The next morning, I rose with the sun. I wasn't sure when – or if – Poonam would be heading out, but I didn't want to lose her. I set to work with supplies from office that I had brought home.

The hardest thing for me to hide was the corkscrew curls. I stood in front of the mirror and pulled my hair back as tightly as I could, tying it into a bun, smoothing it down with styling product. Then I opened a box that held the key to my disguise: a high-quality prosthetic nose. I put it on, gluing on the side with liquid latex. It transformed my face drastically but, since this wasn't the movies and I would quite possibly come within close distance of Poonam, I put on a pair of glasses so my excess of camouflaging make-up didn't give me away. There. Not even my mother would recognize me in a crowded room.

I had instructed Vinod to take a car other than the one we had been using, just in case Poonam had noticed us before, and meet me near the house. I hailed an auto and got there on my own. The added precautions may not have been necessary but I didn't want to take any chances. If I was right, Poonam was up to something; if I got too close to her, there was always the chance that she'd remember me later, and it was early days yet in the investigation.

I got to the Puri residence when the sun was still low. Both cars were in the driveway. Vinod was parked at a distance in an SUV and he scrutinized me with care before cracking a smile. He then raised two fingers to his forehead in a salute.

The guard wasn't around, and I peered through the gate again and saw movement on the upper floor. A curtain had shifted.

I went to the car.

'Morning, Vinod.'

'Ma'am, excellent disguise. No one will know you.'

'You knew me.'

'Only because it had to be you, ma'am. And you are so tall.'

'In this city of actresses and supermodels, I am still tall?'

He laughed. 'Where are we going today, ma'am?'

'As usual, I don't know. We'll see.'

Our wait was shorter than I had hoped – just a couple of hours after we arrived, Poonam left. This time, her destination was an inconspicuous coffee shop in Bandra. She parked her car and I followed her in. It was deserted aside from us. Poonam took a window table and I grabbed the one beside it, choosing a seat from where she could see mainly my profile.

A waiter came by to hand me a menu. I glanced through it. Some breakfast – or a lot of breakfast – would not go amiss; Belgian waffles with maple syrup and fresh fruit sounded about right, with a cup of coffee.

I heard Poonam order an egg-white omelette and multigrain bread and almost lost my nerve. But I stuck by my choice. I had been virtuous enough since coming to Mumbai, with the baking down to zero and incessant stalking making sandwiches de rigueur. My former food-writer self was telling me it was time for something that didn't taste like cardboard.

A few minutes later, the door opened and a man walked in. He was about 5'6" or so, slightly thick around the middle, hairline beginning to recede, clean-shaven. Average in every way. He carried a slim black case in his right hand.

The chitchat that followed puzzled me: it was strained, nervous even, and yet they persisted. Could this be a first date? It seemed most unlikely – if Poonam, an attractive woman herself, was cheating on her good-looking, obscenely wealthy husband, why would she pick this guy?

I worked my way through the waffles as I listened to what was being said. The only thing that was suspicious about it was the fact that these two people, who seemed to have little of interest to say and didn't seem to be work associates or relatives, were having breakfast together at all.

I wished I could take a photo. But in the confined space of the café, I couldn't use my cell phone camera without attracting notice. And anything more had been forbidden by the client.

Then the man left – without the case he had brought in. Poonam then called for the cheque, as did I.

I cursed my luck – and my gluttony. I should have followed Poonam's date but by the time the bill came, he was long gone. So I stayed with Poonam, and much of the rest of the stakeout proved as tiresome as the past week. After a few errands, she headed back home and we waited at our spot a little down the road. Vinod snoozed in the front seat as I read, sourced bhel and made a few calls. Aside from a servant who went out to buy vegetables there was no activity at all, until about 4.30 pm when Pratap came home.

'Wasn't he supposed to be gone for longer?' I asked.

'That's what the driver told me,' said Vinod.

And then again there was stillness till 5.30 pm when one of the drivers arrived.

Vinod sat up in surprise. 'But they'd been given the day off.'

'Maybe, with Pratap coming home earlier than expected, he called one of them in,' I said.

Half an hour later, their Audi exited the gate, and we followed. We were within sight of the Gateway of India when they pulled into a distinguished old colonial building.

'Do you know what that is, Vinod?'

'That's the Mumbai Yacht Club, ma'am.'

I had heard of the institution, one of the most prestigious in the city. To be a member meant that you were seriously old money or that you had newly arrived, and that you either owned or aspired to own a boat at some point in the future. I'd bet Shayak was a member.

'There is a problem, ma'am,' said Vinod.

'Tell me.'

'The security here is so high that I won't be able to park on the street.'

'Then I'll get out.'

'I'll wait somewhere close.'

'I'll call if I need you. Thank you.'

I'd had it easy so far, lounging around in the comfort of a car. But stakeouts weren't designed for comfort. At least, I told myself, I had one of the best views in the city.

I sat on the wall near the Gateway. It was a relatively cool evening, and tourists were out in numbers. I was hungry, and I stopped for my first vada-pav since moving to town. I knew the Mumbai classic deep-fried aloo burger was much maligned in some quarters but it satisfied all my criteria for comfort food, and comfort was what I was in search of.

As I took my first bite, Pratap and Poonam left the club premises on foot. They crossed the road and seemed to be headed towards me!

I hoped my disguise was decent enough to fool Pratap, since he might recognize me from the nightclub. I tried to play it cool by focusing all my attention on my snack. But they walked right by me, down a little gangway to a speedboat. The attendant took them to what looked like the biggest yacht in the harbour, statelier than Shayak's. I watched them sail away into the one place I wasn't equipped to follow them – the vast expanse of the Arabian Sea.

I was fast asleep when my phone rang. I looked at my glow-in-the-dark alarm clock – 6.05 am – before groping around for my phone. It was Shayak.

'Hello,' I said. The crack in my voice was solely because of the hour.

'How fast can you get ready?'

'What's going on?'

'Answer the question.'

'Twenty minutes?'

'Fine. Meet me outside your building.'

'Where are we going?'

'I'll brief you on the way.'

'What am I getting ready for?'

'A murder investigation.'

My heart pounded in my chest, waking me right up.

'And I hope you don't get seasick,' he said abruptly, before hanging up.

I did, but I'd only find that out an hour later, on my way to Kimaaya's island.

FOUR

For the first time in my life, there was a dead body at my feet.

I had come close to death before – a few family funerals; Pathology 101 in college – but never in the course of an investigation.

This, as Kimaaya Kapoor had told us back at the house, was Ashutosh Dhingre, her one-time agent, now a Bollywood nobody. How had he fallen from such heights? She only said something vague about disagreements over the kinds of roles he was getting for her. It was all years ago, she had said, and she couldn't even remember the last time they had met.

'What do you see?' Shayak asked.

Even now he was in training mode. It was just the two of us, with minutes, maybe a half hour, to go before the police arrived.

I saw a man, throat split open, on his back.

I struggled for composure. 'Male, middle-aged, possibly early fifties. Wearing grey trousers and a white-and-blue striped shirt, both intact though the shirt has a large amount of blood on it. Dyed hair, moustache au naturel. Looks to be about 5'7", 75 kg. Shards of broken glass around his head, quite a bit of blood. There is a jagged, penetrating wound to his neck, caused by something sharp. It looks like this could be the cause of death and the source of much of the blood. There is another visible wound to the head, to the right temple.'

'What about the glass?'

'It is a translucent green and quite thick, it has shattered unevenly and there seem to be pieces of a label which could probably be read off some of the larger fragments.'

'And?'

I bent over. 'It definitely looks like a red wine bottle – I can see some traces of it on the glass. There doesn't seem to be any serious amount of foreign liquid mixed in with the blood, so I would say it was either completely or mostly empty when the blow was delivered.'

'You feel the bottle was the weapon?'

'It would appear so. The blow to the temple could have been inflicted by the intact bottle, and the irregular wound to the neck by a shard of it once it had broken.'

'What about signs of a struggle?'

'Difficult to say without taking a closer look at the body.' I peeked at Shayak's face. His grim expression was tempered by a glint of approval.

'Good. Hopefully Forensics will tell us more.'

'Police forensics?'

'It's a collaborative process. We have an informal arrangement on some cases.'

Just then the guard returned.

'Kimaaya ma'am is calling you. She said to tell you it is urgent, sir.'

We were headed to the golf cart when Shayak stopped midway. 'Reema,' he said, 'come here. Look.'

I followed his line of sight to the gazebo not so far away. There was a body – it seemed to be a man – curled up in a honeysuckle hedge.

'Another victim?' I asked.

'Let's find out.'

Once we reached him, Shayak kneeled over and felt for a pulse.

'He's breathing. Pulse is strong,' he said, standing up and pulling his cell phone out of his pocket and dialling. 'Sir, there is another man on the island, alive but unconscious. I'm having him airlifted to the hospital.'

The commissioner of police? The chief minister? Who was it that Shayak called at a time like this? Who was it that he called 'sir'?

He hung up, then dialled again.

'Archana, how soon can you have the chopper here? Half an hour is not good enough. As fast as you can. Yes, to the island.'

And then he started examining the body.

'Can you tell me what just happened?' I asked.

'First call to the commissioner. He knows we are here and are investigating, but I needed clearance before moving this man.'

'And they are fine with all of this. Why?' If there was one thing I had learnt, the police were a territorial species. Private investigators were seldom on their list of favourite collaborators.

'Who knows better than them that their resources lag far behind the ideal? How long would it take to get this man to the hospital, and who is to say what his condition will be at the end of it? How much evidence could be lost in the meantime, with an insecure scene like this?'

I nodded my agreement, but my curiosity was piqued by the realization that I knew very little about the influence Shayak wielded over the highest offices of law enforcement. I could not begin to imagine what he had done to get to this position. I remembered what Vinod had told me, about his prior life in the armed forces. That might be part of the reason for such unfettered access.

'Wait here,' said Shayak. 'I'll get the first-aid kit from the boat.'

I watched Shayak jog towards the buggy and, like I had with the corpse, I tried to get a feel of what may have happened.

I could see no signs of a struggle. The man's clothes – expensive – were intact and appeared clean except for the soil that clung to him. His gelled hair was still in place, and his peaceful expression seemed ludicrous given his current location. I couldn't help looking at his hands: manicured, with the sheen of a recent buff.

We had no idea who this man was for the moment. Kimaaya or someone else at the party should be able to identify him.

And then his eyes fluttered open. He stared at my face, poised over his. I straightened up and looked in the direction of the path, suddenly nervous. There was no sign of Shayak, or anybody else. What if this man was our murderer?

He groaned.

'Don't move,' I said. 'You might be injured. Help is on its way. Do you feel any pain?'

'In my head.'

'Do you know your name?'

'Viraat Khanna.'

'Do you remember being hit?'

'No, but I remember drinking a lot.'

Great. A hangover.

'Where am I?' he asked.

'What else can you remember?'

'I don't know.' He thought for a bit. 'Being at a party. A boat. Am I at sea?'

I didn't point out that he was lying in dirt. 'No.'

'That's right,' he exclaimed, 'I'm at Kookie's place!'

Kookie – Kimaaya's nickname reserved for her friends and every tabloid reporter in the country. I heard someone approaching and turned around to see Shayak.

'Our man has awoken.'

'Is he hurt?'

'If you count a bad hangover.'

'How do you know Kimaaya?' Shayak asked.

'She's a friend,' Viraat said with a smirk.

'What were you doing out here?'

'Don't know.'

'Was anyone with you?'

'Can't say.'

He was beginning to sound like an indecisive survey respondent.

'Do you know Ashutosh Dhingre?'

'Who?'

Finally, Shayak pulled out a syringe. 'I'm going to take a blood sample.'

'Why?' said Viraat, more than a little squeaky at the sight of the needle.

'Because it might be pertinent to the investigation.'

'What investigation?'

'There has been a murder.'

'Whoa dude, what are you saying!'

'Since you have been found a few metres away from the body, it is only natural that you will be a person of interest.'

'Murder,' Viraat repeated in a daze, sitting up and trying to shake off his stupor.

Shayak's jaw clenched.

'Who are you?' asked Viraat.

'My name is Shayak Gupta. I am investigating the death that occurred on the island on behalf of Kimaaya.'

'And the hottie over there?'

Shayak looked at me with a raised eyebrow.

'She's with me.'

The helicopter arrived shortly with two members of Titanium's forensics team. The chopper rushed Viraat to the hospital, less one vial of blood.

The forensics team, under Shayak's supervision, collected samples from around the crime scene and from where Viraat lay – holding off on Dhingre's body till the police arrived.

They did arrive at last, over two hours after we did. A uniformed man, whom Shayak identified as DCP (Detection) Ajay Shankaran, via a coastguard speedboat, with two paramedics and two junior officers.

'They really sent out the big guns for this,' I said.

'This sort of case doesn't take place every day.'

'Not even in Mumbai?'

'A murder on a remote island involving a Bollywood A-lister? No, not even in Mumbai.'

Shayak and I were there at the makeshift jetty to receive them.

'Ajay,' said Shayak, offering his hand.

'Gupta,' replied the officer with a smile. But then I saw a flash of something else in his eyes, brief and fleeting, but less welcoming. 'Where is the body?'

Ajay, another officer and I boarded the buggy, and Shayak took the wheel. I observed them both from my seat: two powerful men, both of who carried themselves well. Shayak wore his authority lightly, Ajay with more gravitas, due in no small part to the uniform, but mostly because of an intensity that emanated from within.

'A suspect has been removed from the scene?'

'Yes, one Viraat Khanna. I have got word that two of your men have received him at the hospital.'

'Anything else I should know?'

'We've collected trace evidence from where Khanna was found, which will be sent back to our lab. The commissioner has said he will be sending someone to oversee that, as well as our investigation into the evidence from the autopsy and trace from Dhingre's scene.'

It did not seem as though Ajay Shankaran had much time for trace evidence. But when he examined the body, it was clear that he wasn't going to allow Shayak to commandeer the post-mortem.

'Get the gurney from the boat. Have him taken away,' Ajay told his man. The Titanium forensics team, having done its job, also left with the coastguard boat.

Satisfied, Ajay then headed back to the buggy. 'Let's get to the house.'

Once again, Shayak took the wheel.

'The suspect who has been taken to hospital was a guest of Kimaaya Kapoor, I am told,' said Ajay.

'Yes, one of her friends. He was found not far from the body.'

'In what condition?'

'Unharmed externally but unconscious – or possibly simply asleep – on the ground.'

'Drunk? Drugged?'

'The blood work should tell us soon enough.'

We reached the house and followed Shayak in. The foyer was deserted, and Shayak sent the housekeeper to fetch Kimaaya.

Ajay strutted around the living room. 'Trust the Bollywood crowd to have a lie-in, even when there might be a murderer amongst them.'

Kimaaya emerged at last, fresh out of the shower with damp hair, in a coral shift. She looked lovely and, for a moment, I could see that even Ajay's scorn was disarmed.

In her second appearance of the day, Kimaaya filled the room, just as she filled the movie screen. I had seen her so many times, in love, in fear, in sadness and in pain. And yet none of those Kimaayas had the power of the one to whom all eyes had turned. Without make-up, without a script, in the face of real danger, she seemed lost. And, in her vulnerability, much more beautiful.

She walked over to Shayak. 'I was waiting for you to come back. The servant told me something about Viraat being taken away? Why?'

'We'll get to that. First you should meet DCP Ajay Shankaran.'

She turned to face him. I had seen her in police uniform in at least two films. 'How can I help you?'

'By telling me exactly what you know about last night's events.'

'I know nothing. I was having dinner with friends, that's it, and this horrible thing happened!'

'What is your relationship to the deceased?'

'Ashutosh was a cross between a manager and an assistant in the early days of my career. I met him after my first film. I was overwhelmed at the time and, as an industry outsider, I badly needed help. He had contacts, and he helped me negotiate the thorny landscape of the industry. We worked together for the better part of ten years.'

'When did you part ways?'

'Over two years ago.'

'Why?'

'I had stopped needing his services for a while, and had only kept him on because he was a good person, you know? But producers and directors were approaching me directly, so I no longer needed that kind of an assistant. I needed more of a PA, someone to handle my appointments and endorsements and press, and Ashutosh was too old to learn new tricks and too set in his ways for me to make him run around doing those sorts of jobs.'

'He must have resented being cast off like that.'

'He made a lot of money off me over the years. He had no cause to complain.'

'What was Dhingre doing here last night?'

'I certainly hadn't invited him and I have no idea why he was here.'

'Are people typically allowed to roam on your private island?'

'Of course not. He must have snuck on, or the guards would have seen him.'

'How did you learn of his presence here?'

'The supervisor at the construction site stumbled on the body. Quite literally, I am told.'

'Did you go out to see for yourself?'

'Why would I do something like that? The supervisor found Auntie Clementine – Mrs Pereira, my housekeeper – who informed me.'

'What *did* you do when you found out?'

'I called Shayak.'

'Why not the police?'

'As far as I am concerned, Shayak is the police.'

I could see that this rankled. 'Ms Kapoor, a murder had been committed. You did not think it was important to inform the authorities?'

'I was not trying to hide anything. Shayak is in charge of my security. He also knows every policeman in town. I knew he would do what was right.'

'As the man in charge,' said Ajay, turning to Shayak, 'do you have anything to add to this?'

'We were understaffed due to a last-minute change of plans on the island. I will be questioning the guards at length later and you are welcome to join. They will be going through the security footage in the course of the day and we will have a report for you soon.'

'Tell me about the party,' said Ajay.

'There were six guests: Viraat Khanna and his girlfriend Afreen, Pratap Puri, Shiv and his sister Sandhya and my old school friend Carol D'Roza.'

My heart thumped rudely in my chest. 'Pratap Puri? You mean the sustainable energy guy?' I asked.

'Yes,' said Kimaaya.

'He is setting up an off-grid energy solution here, to reduce dependence on generators,' explained Shayak.

'Currently the only source for power is the generator?' asked Ajay.

'Yes, seeing as how we are in the middle of the sea,' said Kimaaya.

So this is where Pratap had come last night when I followed him to the boat! But surely his wife should be here too, in that case? I remembered the guard mentioning the guest who left last night. Was that Poonam?

And this also meant that I would meet him sooner or later. If he recognized me from the nightclub, I was screwed. I tried hard to think what I had actually told him. I had done my best to evade the truth, I remembered, but hadn't actually lied.

'How did they all get here?' Ajay asked.

'Shiv, Sandhya and Carol came with Viraat; Pratap arrived separately.'

'We only saw one yacht, in addition to your speedboat,' I said.

Kimaaya nodded. 'That is because Pratap's wife Poonam had come – was supposed to be there for the party – but had to leave all of a sudden.'

'What time was that?'

'They were the first to arrive, around seven. She left at about nine thirty.'

'Did she say why?' asked Shayak.

'Nothing to me, but you could try asking Pratap that,' she said. 'Anyway, they were all here by 9 pm. We were lounging by the pool, having a few drinks. At about 11.30, I sent the servants away. We continued till about 2 am. Then we – or I, at least – went to bed.'

'Do you know what Viraat might have been doing outside after that?' Shayak asked.

'I didn't even know he went outside.'

'We found him by the gazebo, fast asleep.'

'He was a little drunk. Who knows? Maybe he just needed some fresh air,' Kimaaya said with a shrug.

'Did he know the deceased?' asked Ajay.

'Not that I was aware of.'

'Did any of the other guests?'

'Again, I am not aware of any connection, but you really should ask them.'

'Could you ask them to come here?'

'All of them?'

'Let's start with Viraat's girlfriend,' said Ajay.

'Sure,' said Kimaaya, leaving the room.

Shayak turned to Ajay. 'There are between twenty and thirty people on this island at the moment, apart from the guests.'

'So many?'

'At least ten of them are attached to the house: cooks, maids, gardeners, the housekeeper. There are two Titanium security guards. And then there is construction going on at the southern part of the island, so there are a number of workers there.'

'What construction is this?'

'A luxury resort.'

'I thought this was a private island.'

'It is. The project is Kimaaya's. And I think I should mention that I am an investor and Titanium is in charge of the construction.'

'Really?' asked Ajay. 'You are now in the hotel business, too?'

'We have a number of investments that aren't a part of our core business. I can have a list of all the staff sent to you.'

'Fair enough.'

Afreen entered with Kimaaya. She was about the same height as the star, but less slender. She wore a skirt and halter top and, though they looked pricey, she carried them in a way that made clear she was not used to gatherings such as this. She had a pretty face, but one I would not remember in a crowd.

Ajay seemed almost not to notice her at first. 'Ms Kapoor, I need a list of all the household staff with their addresses, years of service and what they do here,' he said.

'Okay,' she replied, sitting down on the sofa, taking out her phone.

Ajay gave her a long look. Was he going to ask her to leave? He should have, given that he was questioning a possible suspect. But such was the effect of Kimaaya's status that even the unsmiling officer let it pass, turning his attention instead to Afreen.

'What is your relation to Viraat Khanna?' asked Ajay.

'He is a friend.'

'Friend or boyfriend?'

'Whatever. Does it matter?' she said.

'Ms Afreen, this is a murder investigation. Everything matters.'

'Fine. Boyfriend.'

'How long have you known each other?'

'A couple of weeks, maybe?'

'And what is your occupation?'

'Actress.'

I caught a glance of Kimaaya's face – I knew she had the acting chops to conceal her disdain better than she did. She just didn't feel it was necessary.

'Tell us what happened last night.'

'We were at the house, having dinner and drinks by the pool.'

'And?'

'And nothing. We went to bed at around 2.30 am. We slept.'

'When did you realize Viraat had left the room?'

'I didn't – not till the housekeeper woke me this morning.'

'You expect me to believe that? You were sharing a bed, I presume.'

'It's the truth. It was late – I totally passed out. We had been drinking, man.' She looked away with the insouciance of a spoiled child. The deadness in her eyes never lifted. I thought of Pratap Puri's words to me in the bar, that Mumbai did that to you over time. But it was not an attitude that sat easy with Afreen.

Ajay looked at Kimaaya for confirmation. She just shrugged.

'Do you have any idea when he could have left the room?'

'Viraat got into bed first. It was another fifteen to twenty minutes till I was changed and joined him. He was fast asleep by then, and it took me a while to doze off, so I would say the earliest he could have got up would have been 3 am. I woke up at 7.30 am and found him gone.'

'That was before he was discovered on the grounds. Why didn't you alert anyone?'

'I had gone downstairs in search of him. The housekeeper told me there had been a murder. I thought he must be out and about, finding out what had happened.'

The flat-on-his-back Viraat I had met hadn't struck me as a man of action, but it wasn't an implausible explanation.

'You weren't concerned?'

'Not really. Why should I have been?'

'There had been a murder and your boyfriend was missing.'

'As I have said, I didn't think he was missing. He could have been doing anything. He could have been in the gym, or in the bathroom taking a dump for all I knew.'

'You don't seem overly bothered, even now.'

'I don't know him that well.'

'You slept together last night.'

'So?'

'Yet you don't think you know him well?'

Afreen shrugged. Ajay stared her down for a while but when she didn't betray any emotion, she was dismissed.

Ajay turned to Kimaaya. 'Is there anyone else – perhaps a member of staff, a security guard – who may have seen Viraat's activities, or what happened on the grounds?'

'I really don't know who was awake at that time.'

'The service quarters and guards' rooms are not far from where we found him this morning,' said Shayak. 'One of the guards on duty told me that neither he nor his colleague had heard anything. But I am yet to speak to them at length. And there is still the video footage.'

'I'd like a copy of that.'

'Of course.'

Kimaaya then summoned some of her key staff members: an elderly lady, a younger woman and a man.

'That's Nimisha Shah, Kimaaya's assistant,' Shayak said to me softly, pointing to a pleasant-looking woman in her late thirties in skinny jeans and a red top. 'The other lady is the housekeeper, Clementine Pereira.' She was spotless, in a grey dress and white apron, like something you might expect to see in a 1950s movie. 'The man,' he continued, 'is Raj Rathore, though it's safe to assume that's not his real name. Resident dietician and fitness instructor.'

It was clear from his tone what Shayak thought of Rathore, who was handsome in a lumpy, fair, B-movie sort of a way. He had taken great care with his hair though I noticed, as he ran a hand through it, that he didn't spend as much time on his ragged nails. He might be an aspiring actor. So might Nimisha, for that matter: she was by no means unattractive but at her age, such aspirations must be a thing of memory.

Ajay started with Rathore. 'Where were you at the time of the murder?'

'What time would that be?'

'How about you tell me everything you did last night instead of asking questions.'

'It was my day off.'

'But you were here on the island?'

'Not till around midnight.'

'How did you return?'

'Speedboat.'

'You have a speedboat?'

Kimaaya stepped in. 'It is mine.'

'You let the help use it? What do you do in case there is an emergency here?'

'Like what?'

'Say a medical emergency, or a murder.'

'Really, DCP, it is not like dead bodies turn up every day. And I suppose I would call Shayak if they did.' She turned her chin up – it seemed she was beginning to enjoy rubbing her closeness with Shayak in the policeman's face at every opportunity she got. The edge between the two men was palpable, and she was happy to play on it.

'He is the answer to everything around here?' It was the first overt show of hostility, and Shayak was as surprised by it as I was.

'When I agreed to sell my yacht a few months ago, one of the conditions was that he would lend me his whenever I wanted it. It's part of our contract.'

'Is it now?'

Ajay turned around to give Shayak a look.

'That must be a little tedious.'

'Not really,' said Kimaaya. 'I haven't needed to be rescued so far. And it's not like I spend all my time here. Only the longer breaks between shooting schedules; and often I come with friends who have their own yachts. The rest of the time I am in the city.'

I remembered the bhelpuri-wallah outside Pratap Puri's house mentioning that Kimaaya was a famous resident of the vicinity, making those two neighbours as well as friends.

'What about food? I'm sure there's no local market here.' I wondered if this sarcasm was a response to Kimaaya's jibes about Shayak, or part of his method.

'Are all these questions really necessary?' asked Kimaaya.

'Excuse me if I seem inquisitive, but murders aren't committed on isolated islands every day. I need to know if anyone else comes and goes – vegetable-wallah, dhobi, electrician. No matter how irrelevant it seems to you.'

Mrs Pereira cleared her throat with a discreet cough. 'Before we come to the island, I stock up on all the essentials. We also grow quite a lot of vegetables here.'

'I am a vegetarian and only eat organic,' said Kimaaya.

'What about arrangements for the party?'

'As I said, we are well stocked,' said Mrs Pereira. If need be, trips are made back to the city by speedboat but on this occasion, for such a small group, we had everything we needed.'

Ajay turned his attention back to Raj. 'What did you do when you got back?'

'Went to my room and hit the sack.'

'Alone?'

Raj scowled.

'Answer the question.'

'Yes, yes,' he snapped. 'Alone.'

'Did anyone see you?'

He shook his head. 'I don't think so.'

'What about the guard?'

'I don't think he was near the jetty when I came in.'

'Did you see or hear anything?'

'I heard voices, laughter coming from the pool, but nothing that stands out.'

'Were you acquainted with the deceased?'

'No.'

Ajay seemed to have heard enough from Raj, and turned his attention to Mrs Pereira. She spoke with a quiet dignity that even the prickly Ajay did not feel the need to take on. Her monologue was delivered in an even, calm tone.

'I started my working day in the garden, picking vegetables and herbs for the dinner that had been planned. There were meats to be marinated and vegetables to be grilled. We've had a particularly lovely season this year. I got the kitchen started out and then supervised the cleaning of the pool, which had not been used in some days. The rest of the house runs well usually but since we were expecting the first lot of houseguests on this trip, I ensured their rooms were ready, and then got busy with the floral arrangements. By the time the guests arrived, in the evening, the house was looking its best.'

'And later on?'

'I ensured that the salads and cold dishes were ready. Madam requested the meats to be left for her guests to barbecue. She mentioned that Mr Puri was handy at the grill. I knew it would be late when they ate, so once the starters had been served, I instructed the kitchen assistant Jana to be at hand to lay out the food and clear up, then I went to bed.'

'Do you usually go to bed when there is a party on?' asked Ajay. I saw Nimisha tap her red nails on the table. Impatience? Nerves?

'There was a time, sir, when I would stay till the last guest had retired, but I am getting on in years and find late nights leave me struggling the morning after. I have been forced to delegate, with Madam's permission.'

Finally, Ajay moved on to Nimisha. 'Please tell me, ma'am,' he said, sarcasm back. He had seen the tap-tap too, then, and didn't look upon it kindly.

'I'm sorry?' said Nimisha.

'You seem to be in a rush.'

'Only because I have a number of calls to make. You do realize the press will be all over this as soon as the news is out.'

'I am sure the news is already out, Ms Shah.' For a change, Ajay seemed to sympathize.

'Then you understand my worry.'

'The quicker you can answer these questions the faster you can go about your business,' said Shayak.

She gave a curt nod.

'Dhingre was your predecessor in Ms Kapoor's service?' asked Ajay.

'You could say that. Though he left a few months before I was hired.'

'You never crossed paths?'

'He was already gone by the time I joined. Dhingre was so far out of the scene that there was no way I could have met him otherwise. None of the producers, directors and stars Kimaaya now works with really has anything to do with him.'

'Could you tell me why he is so out of favour?' The question was addressed to Kimaaya as well as Nimisha, and the actress answered with a little shrug.

'As I said, it has been years since we met. You should ask these questions to people who know him now.'

'We are talking about a time when you did know him. Why was he so irrelevant?'

'Speaking for myself,' said Kimaaya, 'as my career matured, I was working more and more with people who had become my friends. There simply was no need.'

'But some young star trying to make a name should have been happy to hire him.'

'My best guess is that fresh talent wouldn't want to work with him because he was close to an old crop of filmmakers. With new blood coming in and more corporate houses, things have changed, grown more professional,' said Nimisha. 'But who knows?'

'If you have nothing to do with him, as you claim, what was he doing on your island?'

'That, DCP Shankaran, is what I was hoping you could tell me.'

After the interrogation, we split ways with Ajay. Shayak spoke to the guards and took stock at the construction site, instructing the exceedingly contrite supervisor Kaustav Arora – a Titanium employee – to make a list of all the workers. Once time of death was more specifically established, questioning would start.

Arora apologized for just about everything he could think of – for not preventing the murder, for not hearing anything, for not knowing where all the employees were in the dead of the night, though he was certain none of them had left the workers' compound.

'Kaustav, don't worry. We'll have a look at the surveillance video and then we'll get back to you,' Shayak said. 'You didn't touch the body when you discovered it, did you?'

'No. Unfortunately, I have seen my fair share of bodies in the construction business, sir, and I know a dead man when I see one. I also know better than to get too close.'

And then Shayak said it was time for us to go back to the city. We hadn't met Shiv, Sandhya or Carol yet, or any of the other staff.

'You don't want me to stay here?' I asked.

'The DCP has the island in lockdown. None of the guests are leaving right now. We need some answers before we can ask the right questions.'

Shayak called Kimaaya to tell her we'd be leaving, and then we headed back towards the boat. Another vessel had arrived at the makeshift jetty: a woman and a man carrying a camera bag were disembarking.

'Who are these people?' Shayak asked the guard.

'Sir, I don't know. They wouldn't tell me.'

Shayak intercepted them before they got very far.

'May I know who you are?'

The woman looked flustered. 'Meera Verma,' she said.

'And you?' he said, addressing the man.

'Srini V. K.,' he replied.

'You are here for ...'

'Work. We need to meet Kimaaya Kapoor.'

'You are journalists?'

The woman gave a reluctant nod.

'Ms Kapoor does not receive uninvited guests on her private island.'

'But sir, please, if you could let me pass. If she refuses to meet me, I'll leave.'

'I'm sorry that you took the trouble to come all the way, but you have to go back now. When Ms Kapoor wishes to address the media, you will hear from her. In future, I'd advise that you make an appointment.'

I felt almost sorry for her. She seemed shattered, unable to say a word in the face of Shayak's firm yet polite stand. I had been on her side of the fence, and I could imagine her trying to explain to her editor why she had come back empty-handed. She should at least be satisfied at having got farther than any of her colleagues were likely to get in the future. As soon as Shayak saw them safely on the water again, he turned to the guard.

'Never again should a journalist get on land. I want a barricade of some sort put up around here. Find bamboo, wood or anything else and get the men from the construction site to help you put it up, and also to be on standby in case anyone tries to force themselves through. From now on, two of you are always to remain on duty. One of you must be at the jetty, and must communicate names of all visitors before letting anyone disembark. I'll send a list of people allowed to pass as soon as I am back in office. Another team will be arriving soon to help.'

The guard looked crestfallen.

'Don't worry,' said Shayak. 'This was not your fault. But it will only get worse from here, so be prepared.'

FIVE

Back on the yacht, Shayak handed me a pill and a bottle of water from the cooler. With my stomach drugged pre-emptively into submission, I found my body calm but my mind troubled.

'How did the guards not hear anything at all?'

'There is just too much ground to cover, and the two of them have been horribly overextended as it is. There are usually four guards working shifts but, with Kimaaya's unscheduled return, this was the best I could do on no notice. Reinforcements would have arrived in a couple of days.'

'You are blaming yourself even though Kimaaya doesn't see it that way?'

'She insisted on coming here despite the reduced staff, against my advice. But it is my job to protect the island, regardless of the idiosyncrasies of the owner.'

I shook my head. 'You want to tell me what I am getting into here?'

Shayak sighed. 'Where would you like me to start?'

'How about India's most successful actress of her generation, *the* Kimaaya Kapoor, being your ex-wife?'

'If you think it is relevant.'

'You don't?'

'As far as I am concerned, she is a client in trouble thanks to a security breach Titanium should have prevented.'

'That's it?'

'What are you implying?'

'No need to get so defensive. Just pointing out that perhaps you are too close to this.'

'Just as you were when your ex-boyfriend's wife got kidnapped in Calcutta. Didn't stop you from solving that case.'

'This is not the same thing!' I was appalled that Shayak had brought that messy business up now.

'Why?'

'Because my relationship with Amit was in the open. As was the fact that it was over. Here, your entire marriage is under wraps, which makes it far more loaded.'

'Loaded? Sorry,' he said. 'I just don't see why my prior relationship should be a problem. While it gives me extra insight into her life, there is no evidence so far that this crime has anything to do with her.'

'The murder was committed on her private island.'

'Where there are over thirty other people at the moment.'

'None of whom appear to have anything to do with Ashutosh Dhingre.'

'With a suspect being found unconscious in the hedges not 500 feet from the crime scene, that might be a premature conclusion to draw.'

'Maybe so, but I think your deliberately obtuse attitude right now makes it especially important to know the backstory.'

Despite himself, Shayak cracked a smile. 'Deliberately obtuse? That's what you call your boss on the third week at work?'

I shrugged. 'If the shoe fits.'

He drew a deep breath and then began. 'I have known Kimaaya since we were both about five years old. We were in school together. We were friends till high school, after which we decided, stupidly, as teenagers often do, that we were in love. When we were still too young to know any better, we married. Within two years we were separated, and soon after that, divorced.'

'The separation was, what, fifteen years ago?'

'Give or take.'

'And no one knows about it?'

'It is a well-kept secret.'

'Why?'

'You may have noticed that movie stars – especially female ones, in our country – usually wait till their time has more or less come and gone to tie the knot.'

'That is why your marriage ended?'

'That is why our marriage ended quietly. In the industry, no one knew that we were married in the first place. Very few did outside it, either.'

'Oh, come on. Something like that must have been hard to hide.'

'It was a different time. It all happened before Kimaaya's first hit, in an era well before the twenty-four-hour news cycle and paparazzi. When I was away from Mumbai forty-five weeks of the year.'

'Doing what?'

'I was in the armed forces. Don't tell me my brightest young detective didn't know that?'

If his praise was an attempt to distract me, I wasn't about to let it succeed. 'There still must have been some people who knew – after all, friends and family must have found out about it. These things have a way of getting out.'

'Friends and family, yes. But only close ones. Some others probably did at least suspect a relationship of some sort. But information about our marriage was not in the public domain. And you forget – at the time it happened, *we* were not in the public domain.'

'Why was it such a secret then?'

'I was leaving on a mission; I suppose we were both afraid that I might not make it back. It was practically decided overnight. Then I was gone a long time, almost a year. By the time I returned for any significant period, and our families were planning to have a reception to make the marriage public, both of us realized we had made a mistake.'

'Fair enough, but you don't think someone like, say, Dhingre, Kimaaya's first agent, might have had an inkling?'

Shayak's face was stormy, but his silence gave me my answer.

'What do you think Ajay will do when he gets to know?'

'He doesn't need to know."

I started shaking my head even before the words were out of his mouth. How could I be the only one seeing this? 'If he goes digging – which he might, despite your partnership with the police – and finds out, it will be far worse than if you told him.'

'I am sure there are plenty better motives to kill Dhingre than the secret of a marriage a decade and a half old.'

'You may be right. But motive is still motive, and it will need to be pursued.'

'So you are implying that Kimaaya did this to keep Dhingre quiet about her marrying her high-school sweetheart?'

I didn't say anything, but Shayak guessed what was on my mind. I saw a hint of anger creep into his gaze. 'No, that's not it, is it? You think it gives *me* motive.'

'It's not about what I think. It is much more important what Ajay Shankaran thinks. That you and Kimaaya are still close, and work together intimately in various fields, may prompt a deeper look into your relationship. What is essentially harmless when revealed voluntarily looks very different when concealed.'

I thought Shayak was about to say something, but he held his tongue.

'She is having financial problems?' I asked.

Shayak nodded. 'She has mismanaged her fortune epically.'

'And you are helping her get out of the hole? Building the resort, selling her yacht?'

'Happy to see nothing gets past you.'

'I'd think it would be a quality you'd value.'

'Kimaaya has always been short on friends.'

'Doesn't look that way.'

'Those aren't friends,' said Shayak. 'Not really. Except for Auntie Clementine.'

'The housekeeper?'

'More like surrogate mother.'

'You never did say why you weren't at Kimaaya's party last night. She clearly was expecting you.'

'I don't recall being asked.'

'I'm asking now.'

'You know I have been out of town.'

'You called me at an obscene hour to tell me to get my ass moving. I'm assuming you were in Mumbai at that time.'

'I was. In my flat. There is security footage to prove it. I got back late last night.'

I half expected him to remind me he was my boss. When he didn't – not that he would have stopped me, just slowed me down – I continued.

'And have you had any association with Dhingre since the split?'

'No, nor before it. I've never met the man.'

'But you have been friends with her through it all.'

'For the first few years, it was strained. I was very busy, frequently away, and her star was on the rise. It is only more recently that we have become close again.'

'Okay,' I said, 'suppose for the moment that you are right – that no one in the film industry or media knew about the marriage. What about the paparazzi now? You think they won't go digging into Kimaaya's past after this?'

'This is India – the gossip rags are thankfully still immature and there is only so far they are willing to go to dig up smut.'

'Things have changed in the past few years. Don't you think you are being optimistic?' I asked. Naïve was the word that had come to mind, but I thought better of spelling it out.

'Realistic. As opposed to paranoid.' Shayak turned away from me, fixing his eyes on the placid waters ahead, signalling the end of the conversation. I thought better of pushing him any further for the moment so I went below deck, prepared to battle a new bout of seasickness rather than listen to his continuing refusal to admit what was, to me, blatantly clear.

It was past 4 pm when we were finally back on dry land and seated in the car, with Vinod at the wheel. He had come to pick us up from the coastguard jetty, where Shayak was allowed to anchor his vessel, for reasons I did not know but was beginning to guess at.

It had already been a long day, and there was no end in sight. I closed my eyes and felt my head reel. I hadn't eaten anything since that blasted smoothie in the morning. When I prised them open, we were in standstill traffic. Beside us was a filthy grey wall, brightened by a line of film posters. Kimaaya Kapoor's gamine face was all I could see, and I felt a twinge of something unexpected. Anger? Jealousy? I brushed it away.

Shayak finally spoke. 'Of course you are right. I am too close – which is why I need you.' He looked out of the window as he continued. 'Give me time to think about what to do with the information I have. For things to crystallize. Can you do that?'

He was asking my permission? 'Shayak, the call is yours to make.'

'No, I need you to stay focused on the big picture. Even when it seems difficult.'

'What do you mean?'

'There will be a lot of distraction in this case. The media. The number of witnesses. Kimaaya herself.'

'Why Kimaaya?'

'She's a star, Reema. She can't help but make everything about herself.'

There was no time for him to elaborate, for we had pulled out in front of a greying building.

'Welcome to the state forensics headquarters. Even if you can't depend on anyone in the system, these guys are impeccable,' said Shayak.

'So why is Titanium needed here?'

'The men are good, but their machines are prehistoric. What makes ours an especially potent synergy is that they turn to us for help, ready and willing, thanks to our superior resources. You'll see how it works.'

We walked in to the lobby, where we were met by a putrid smell.

'Is that …'

'The smell of death,' said Shayak. 'The morgue facilities were last upgraded fifty-odd years ago. I am working on it now.'

'What do you mean?'

'I am trying to convince the bureaucrats in charge to let Titanium install a new one for them.'

'Why would they turn down such an offer?'

'Do you really need me to answer that?'

No, I didn't. The answer was sure to be something about official malfeasance, with a liberal dose of unofficial corruption on the side.

We entered a lift that looked like it had been there for a century, and creaked up to the fifth floor, the smell of rot our constant companion. We got out and Shayak led me down the hall to an unmarked door.

'Have you seen an autopsy being conducted before?'

'Yes,' I replied.

'You were okay with it?'

I nodded, and we walked in. I saw a man in white lab coat and gloves reaching into the cavity of a body – no doubt, Ashutosh Dhingre's. He looked up and smiled at Shayak.

'What a pleasure!' he said, pulling out what looked like a liver.

'This is my colleague Reema Ray,' said Shayak. 'Reema, this is Dr Sudhir Mishra.'

'Welcome, Reema,' he said, teeth still very much on show.

I may not be as squeamish as most around death, but I didn't think I'd be smiling if I were elbow-deep in a man's entrails. I tried to return his warmth, but failed.

'What do you know so far?' Shayak asked.

'Murder, for sure. Nothing accidental about this one. Have to establish whether it is the blunt head trauma or the sharp trauma to the neck that actually killed him.'

'Any idea about time of death and weapon?'

'Time of death appears to be between 2 am and 4 am,' said Dr Sudhir. 'Weapon, it is too early to say.'

'Could it be a glass bottle?'

'I had heard something about a bottle at the scene, and the lacerations do fit that scenario,' he nodded. 'But contrary to what they depict in the pictures, a bottle isn't your usual murder weapon. Many people are hit over the head and walk away with only superficial damage.'

His words conjured images of unsuspecting people randomly being whacked about with glassware. In Dr Sudhir's world, perhaps.

'What if it was a thick, heavy bottle?'

Dr Sudhir gave this some thought. 'Hit at just the right spot, where the skull is soft, it might cause serious damage, yes. I will have to examine the bone to give you a confirmation of that.'

'Could a shard from the same bottle have been used to create that neck wound?' asked Shayak.

Dr Sudhir nodded. 'A glass fragment certainly could have been the culprit.'

'What about the trace evidence and other samples?'

'They have been harvested and are ready for you. You'll find Paresh in his office waiting for your arrival.'

With that, we returned to the screaming lift, going down a couple of floors. 'Paresh Parikh is Dr Sudhir's assistant,' explained Shayak. 'He is the leading expert in the country on trace. He's helped train the team at Titanium.'

Even before the grill gates could open, a man greeted Shayak like an old friend.

'Mr Gupta! We have been expecting you!'

From actresses to lab techs, everyone seemed to welcome Shayak.

Back at the Titanium offices, we helped Paresh take the collection kits and boxes out of the car. When we all piled in to the lift, I was stunned to see which button Shayak had pressed. The fourth floor. I was finally going to get a glimpse of the mysteries that lay within.

We walked into a small foyer, after which there was another door to clear with an additional swipe and a biometric scan. Shayak led us in.

When the doors opened, I had to try very hard to stop my jaw from dropping. It was as if I had walked in to a scene from a spy film. On my right was a glass-enclosed lab. Four white-coated techs were already at work. On the left was a series of doors, each with a swipe machine and a biometric scanner.

But I wasn't going to find out what was behind those doors just yet. We turned into the lab. I could see Paresh's eyes light up. Boys and their toys, I thought to myself, till I caught my reflection on one of the room's shinier surfaces and saw the glazed look that I too wore.

'Sorry to bring you here like this. I had meant to give you the tour first,' Shayak said to me.

I couldn't care less that he was laughing at me. I was dazzled. Our college lab had been adequate and I had seen some equipment on visits we had made to professional establishments. But in the past few years, the only piece of machinery I had at my disposal had been a computer, phone and fairly decent camera.

And now I suddenly found myself in a toyshop worthy of a couple of Os and a seven.

Paresh knew his way around the lab. He got straight to business, unpacking his kit. Vials, envelopes and plastic bags emerged. Some I had seen the techs collecting at the scene, such as the soil samples and scraping from the victim's shoes, while others had been brought in directly from the morgue. Blood, hair, microscopic evidence of where Ashutosh Dhingre had been and what he had been doing.

'There was some sort of substance under the victim's nails,' said Paresh. I knew this could be crucial: if there had been a struggle, these scrapings may contain DNA of the assailant.

'There are glass fragments from the wound,' he added.

'And the glass collected from the scene?' asked Shayak.

'All here,' said Paresh, pointing to a plastic collection box. 'Reema, do you want to get started on this?'

I stared at him. Handle evidence on my own in this lab?

'Someone will help you with the equipment, of course.'

I nodded, and Shayak summoned one of the techs who had been at the scene.

'Kaushik, this is Reema, from Investigations. Will you help her reassemble this mess of glass, please?'

Kaushik seemed rooted to his spot, befuddled by this unexpected conversation with the boss. He took a minute to recover, and then nodded. Darting a furtive glance in my direction, he led me to a corner of the room.

'Hi,' I said.

'Hello,' he replied. His whole body was stiff and it seemed an effort for him to speak to me at all. Was this Shayak's residual effect, or was it the impact of seeing a woman in the lab?

I waited for him to begin but when he didn't, I opened the box. 'It seems to be a wine bottle,' I said.

'Right, and we should try to reconstruct it. It shouldn't be difficult estimating its circumference.'

'I am not sure about the age of the bottle. Judging from the thickness of the glass, it might be quite old, meaning it might be of unusual size.'

'Okay.' Kaushik put on gloves and began to sort out fragments. He was picking out the larger ones first.

'If you could give me an idea of what you are looking for, I could help,' I said.

'I would like to create a 3-D model of the bottle. But unless we have some idea of the dimensions, it will be time consuming. I am sorting pieces that look like they are from the main body and others which appear to be part of the neck or base.'

'What if we first try to assemble this label? If it is an old bottle of wine, it is likely to be well known, and we should be able to find some reference images online.'

I could see Kaushik approved of my suggestion. We started sorting out the pieces with bits of paper stuck to them. The label, once white or cream, was red with either wine or blood or both. But the letters were still legible and, as they came together, I flushed with excitement. It was a Chateau Lalou, 1899.

On the table right there, the shards of glass had transformed into motive. The bottle would easily be worth more than a crore. To a collector, it would be priceless.

We looked online for images; the Internet and especially eBay was full of pictures of Lalous, many of them probably fakes. I finally found a reliable source and pulled it up for Kaushik.

'Okay, I should be able to proceed much quicker with this.'

Kaushik took large fragments from various parts of the bottle. The base had more or less broken off in one large chunk. Then he measured the arc of various large pieces from the body and neck, and entered the values into a computer programme. Soon we were holding a 3-D recreation of the Lalou's internal dimensions. Then Kaushik painstakingly photographed each piece of glass, examining them for evidence that the state forensics lab may have missed. We then began assembling the pieces, jigsaw puzzle-like, around the model. It came together beautifully, except for a gaping hole from around the shoulder of the bottle.

'Could the crew have missed some pieces at the crime scene?' asked Kaushik.

'Does the Titanium team usually miss things?'

'Not often.'

It was more likely removed by the killer. The perpetrator had had the presence of mind to carry away the murder weapon – the piece of glass that had been used to slit Ashutosh Dhingre's throat. It could now be anywhere. The logical choice for disposal, given the circumstances, being the bottom of the Arabian Sea.

Kaushik took out a brush and handed it to me. 'Would you like to do the honours?'

It was time for fingerprinting. This was a process I was familiar with, so I took it from him without hesitation. There were numerous prints on the bottle. I took a small plastic sheet and carefully pressed it over one, and it came off cleanly; I then repeated the process with the others.

Kaushik took the prints from me. 'I'll start running these to see if we have any hits in the state database. Do you know if any suspects have been printed yet?'

'As of this morning, no.'

As soon as he had scanned them, he turned to me. 'I can tell you right now that these aren't from the same hand. There are two sets of prints here, but one is not as clear as the other. You'll show sir the bottle?' Kaushik asked.

It took me a moment to figure out who 'sir' was, and I nodded. Kaushik turned back to the scanner.

When I couldn't find Shayak in the lab, I went to his office and peered in. There was a small reception area where his assistant was seated.

She looked up at me and smiled.

'Is Mr Gupta in? I'd like to see him, please,' I said, introducing myself.

She made a call and waved me through another door, behind which I found Shayak at a desk significantly smaller than what I had expected on the fourth floor.

'What do you think?' Shayak asked without preamble.

'It's like stepping into an episode of *CSI*.'

'And?'

'There can't be many facilities like this in India.'

'How do you feel being a part of it, now that you've been here for a few weeks?'

In the light of the morning's events, I wasn't sure where to begin. 'I think it is a little early to say. As I've said before, there is a great deal about the company that I don't know.'

'Ask away, then.'

'Are you sure this is the time? I have a lot of questions.'

'A preliminary forensics report will be on my desk in thirty minutes. Till then, I might as well bring you up to speed. Things are likely to only get busier in the days to come, and I don't want you to have any doubts.'

'Fine.' But where to begin? 'What exactly does Titanium do?'

'We are a security solutions provider. In every sense of the term.'

'What does that mean?'

'We ensure that our clients, their homes and their businesses are free from external or internal threats of any kind. Our process often starts with a detailed risk assessment, and then we provide a strategy to address any weaknesses we find. That might include your run-of-the-mill equipment installations, security guards, bodyguards, IT solutions, intelligence reports. In short, whatever it takes.'

Much of this I had heard already. 'And who are these clients?'

'The bulk of our business comes from large international corporations in India, prominent businessmen and government agencies. We also do security details for politicians, and people you might call celebrities, such as cricketers and film industry personnel.'

I wondered how Kimaaya would feel if she heard herself described as 'personnel'.

'And that's it?'

'Not enough for you?'

'Something is not adding up.'

Shayak nodded. 'Once again, you are right. There is a component of our work that I am not at liberty to discuss. Most of it is for governments.'

Governments, plural. Was Titanium a security contractor working with the army? If so, whose army? And what was the nature of this work? I was imagining secret missions and authorized assassinations.

I was revisited by the feeling that I was being left out of Titanium's most exciting assignments. But Shayak said he couldn't talk about it, and that meant he wouldn't, let alone involve me in it. 'Where do I fit into all of this?'

'Our investigation team is critical to our process. That is why, after years of operating mainly with consultants, I felt the need to develop our in-house capabilities further. Though we don't typically take on stand-alone investigative cases, most of our clients require intelligence reports at some stage of their relationship with us.'

'Such as?' I felt silly asking now; shouldn't I have cleared this up before I joined? Instead, I was won over cheaply, on a boat, by a speech. And perhaps a kiss?

Shayak smiled. 'I think we'll need some coffee if you want me to get into all that.' He picked up the phone and called for a couple of cups.

Food, I suddenly remembered. But now seemed hardly the time to bring it up.

'When a client approaches us for the first time,' Shayak continued, 'we begin with a risk assessment depending on their needs. If we are called in for an external security threat, we try to understand where the organization's weaknesses are, who may have made the threat, how serious it is and so on. There is obviously a need for investigators there. If there is an internal breach, we begin by sending in forensic accountants to examine the books. Most often, the money tells the story. The next level involves digging deeper into the private lives of suspects. If the client is an individual, the requirements are often more straightforward – checking out stalkers, for instance or, in certain instances, accidents and other unforeseen events.'

'Like the murder on Kimaaya's island?'

'It's called Maaya.'

'Cute, if a little narcissistic.'

Before Shayak could respond, the door opened and two cups of steaming coffee were brought in by a liveried man. I was grateful to see a tray of muffins and croissants along with it.

When we were alone again, Shayak pointed to a muffin. 'Eat,' he said.

I was too hungry for pride, so I helped myself. I forced myself to chew like a human and not swallow like a greedy puppy.

'We'll come back to Maaya Island – cute or otherwise – on our way over tomorrow.'

I took a sip of coffee. 'Why am I the lead on the investigation and not Adlakha?'

'Any reason you shouldn't be?'

'No, it's just … unexpected.'

'I am not big on hierarchy. Didn't think you'd be.'

'It's not an objection, merely a question.'

Shayak responded by taking a long sip of his coffee.

It didn't seem as though I'd get anything more out of him. 'So this infidelity case I am looking into now is not the usual sort of case I'll be dealing with?'

'Absolutely not. Sometimes our clients come to us with this sort of request, and we prefer not to turn them away. Usually we'd outsource it but as Pratap is a friend and had very specific instructions on how he wanted it dealt with, I thought it best we keep it in-house.'

It seemed a reasonable enough explanation. 'Thank you,' I said.

'What for?'

'Humouring me.'

'I'm not humouring you.'

'You answer all questions from highly demanding employees?'

'Some are more demanding than others, but I would like to think I hear everyone out,' he said with a smile.

I remembered that I still hadn't told Shayak about the bottle. I briefed him now about what the label had revealed, the estimated value of the bottle and the fact that it seemed as though we had a couple of usable prints from it.

'We need to ensure all the guests at the party are fingerprinted,' I said.

'The cops have that covered,' nodded Shayak. His phone rang, and he stood up as he answered.

'Viraat is awake and ready for questioning,' he said, hanging up. 'Lucky for us, I have it on good authority that one of the businesses his daddy has set up for him is wine import,' he continued as we got moving. 'In fact, he is one of Mumbai's leading importers. Though he reportedly loses more money than he makes.'

'Not surprising,' I said, 'if he polishes off bottles worth crores on a regular basis.'

When we reached the hospital where Viraat Khanna was being examined, we found the police on guard outside. The officer on duty cleared the way for Shayak and me.

'There you are!' Viraat said as soon as he saw me. 'I've been telling the cops I need to speak to you. Where's my watch?'

'Uh, how would I know that?'

'You were there when I woke up. I assumed you must have taken it for evidence or something.'

'No I didn't,' I said. 'In fact, I didn't notice a watch on you at all.'

Viraat slapped his forehead. 'Shit! Someone must have stolen it.'

'Do you remember when you last saw it?' I asked.

'I know I had it on last night.'

'Could you have taken it off, forgotten about it?'

'No! And it isn't in the room or anywhere else in the house. I asked Kimaaya to check. I'm telling you, someone must have stolen it, man!'

'Was it valuable?' I asked.

'Hell yeah! It's almost an exact replica of Rafael Nadal's watch! I need it back.'

'A man was killed here,' Shayak said. 'I think that might be more important than your knock-off watch.'

'That was no knock-off,' Viraat snapped. 'It was made by the same watchmaker who made Nadal's. I paid, like, over 2 crore for it.'

What planet had I stepped on to? Wine and watches worth crores? In most parts of the world, each of those would be motive in themselves. It still was a possibility: though it might be spare change for the guests on the island that night, 2 crore would always be inducement for murder in my book.

'Did you mention the value of the watch to anyone?' I asked.

'I might have.'

'Last night?'

'Puri asked about it.'

'Who else heard?'

'Everyone, I think. You don't think one of them could have taken it, do you?' He looked incredulous. 'They are all, like, loaded. All except …' he trailed off.

'Now that you have had some time to think, can you remember anything else from last night?' continued Shayak.

'I think I got there around 9 pm or so. I had a bunch of people coming with me. I'd already had some to drink and when I got there, I had some more.'

'Could you tell me what drinks were being served?'

'Dude, what kind of a question is that? It was an open bar. Kimaaya had everything a good bar would stock.'

'Wine?' he asked.

'Sure.'

'Okay. What next?'

'Soon after I got in, Poonam left. She like said she had a thing early in the morning at one of the orphanages she works at. But Pratap stayed,' he said. I saw his eyes cloud over for a second, and evidently so did Shayak.

'Did something happen with Pratap?'

'Not really, but the dude seriously has trouble keeping his junk in his trunk.'

I had visions of Pratap Puri flashing everyone at the pool party.

'Why do you say that?' Shayak asked.

'It's like he wants to do all the women in the room. Even Kimaaya was getting pissed.'

'What about your girlfriend?'

'Who?'

'Afreen.'

Viraat let out an unattractive snort. 'Oh, her! Dude, she's not my girlfriend.'

'Whatever,' said Shayak. Was that a flash of irritation? 'Did Pratap say anything to her?'

'You know. The usual. Nothing too bad or I would have socked him.'

'Why, if she wasn't your girlfriend?'

'She was for the night.'

'Did anyone confront him about his behaviour?'

'Not really. He was a guest, and a friend of Kimaaya. Though she looked like she might.'

'Anything else of note?'

'No, man. It was a really chilled out night, for the most part. We grilled some meat, hung out by the pool, drank.'

'Seawater was found on your shorts, Viraat,' said Shayak. 'Do you remember anything about that?'

Viraat's eyes widened. 'Duuude.'

We waited as he struggled to recall his actions.

'Dude, that's right. At some point I think I went to the yacht. I vaguely remember taking a dip. Thought it would be cool.'

'Were you alone?'

'Don't remember. Think so.'

'What were you doing on your boat?'

'I think I went to get a bottle of Scotch. Yeah, that's it. Kimaaya knows nothing about the stuff, so I went to get something decent from my personal stash.'

'Is that the only trip you made?' he asked.

'Huh?'

'We have reason to believe a bottle of Scotch isn't the only thing you brought from your bar.'

Viraat squinted in concentration – it seemed to be a novel attempt for him. And then enlightenment.

'Duuude,' he said, almost a whisper. 'Not *that* bottle. Please tell me I didn't touch *that* bottle.'

'Could you tell me what you mean?'

It was infuriating, but I knew Shayak didn't want to lead him in a rush to get answers.

'A bottle of wine. I had acquired it for a client. I had to pull serious strings to get it, and it cost a bomb.'

'Was it a Chateau Lalou?'

'How did you know?'

'We found it at the crime scene. It was used to murder Ashutosh Dhingre.'

As Viraat cradled his head in his hands, I quickly did the math. Between the watch and the wine, he had lost at least 3 crore in one night. It had turned out to be a seriously expensive party for him.

Then, in a moment, Viraat clammed up, insisting he didn't know anything about it, and that he wanted a lawyer.

It was past 9 pm when we left the hospital. 'Let's go home,' said Shayak.

Seated in the car, Shayak scrolled through the forensics reports that had been sent while we were out.

'Preliminary blood work came back from the lab. Viraat had flunitrazepam in his system.'

'The date-rape drug?' I asked.

'Yup.'

'That explains him passing out and the patchy memory.'

'But not much else. What was he doing out on the grounds? Who gave him the drug? Why?' he said. 'It is possible that he is a recreational user. There were also traces of cocaine in his system.'

'You still think he is connected with the murder?'

'His wine bottle is now confirmed as the murder weapon. Even without the gash to the neck, Dhingre would have been a dead man from the blow to the head, it just would have taken a little more time.'

'Everyone at that party had access to that bottle, and there is no connection between the deceased and Viraat.'

'So he says. We still need to corroborate that.'

Shayak handed me a piece of paper. 'This is Ashutosh Dhingre's address. I want you to go there tomorrow morning. Mrs Dhingre is expecting you at 8.30 am. Pack your bags tonight because the car will bring you directly from there to the boat, and we'll head back to the island together.'

'What do you want me to ask her?'

'Let her talk. See what she says. You have a way with people.'

We drove into my complex and Shayak and I got out, then the car pulled away. Was he planning to come up?

'Good night, Reema. Call me if you need anything.'

'Are you going to walk home?'

'Of course.'

'How far?'

'Twenty steps away,' he said, pointing to another building in the same complex – the fancier one.

'Let me guess – the penthouse?'

'It does have the best view,' he smiled.

'Good night,' I said, shaking my head as I walked away.

I didn't know how I felt about Shayak being my neighbour. Between the boss next door and security cameras in the hall, it did seem as though, like Adlakha said, I had been kennelled. What happened if I brought a man back to my apartment? Would the whole office get to know? Would Shayak get to know?

I walked into the flat, and my eyes went to the TV. I turned it on for the first time. It took me a while to figure out the channels; it had been so long since I had owned a TV that I still remembered them as idiot boxes and not as a canvas hung on the wall like art. When I reached the news channels, Kimaaya's face was everywhere.

Whether this murder was about Kimaaya or not, she loomed large over every aspect of it.

The cameras captured no footage of the crime scene itself – Shayak's guards would have seen to that – but there were plenty of chaotic images of people coming and going from Maaya Island – the police, the Titanium crews. They must have arrived in greater numbers after we departed. Then there was a news conference with Ajay. He kept it down to the facts: the victim's name and relation to the actress, the location – thankfully vague – of the murder.

'Is Kimaaya Kapoor a suspect at this time?' asked one reporter. Ajay didn't even justify that one with a 'no comment'; he simply moved on.

'Any suspects?' another journalist asked more judiciously.

'Too early to say, Swapan, you know that.'

'Is the murder in any way related to Kimaaya?'

'As soon as we are prepared to reveal these details, we will release them to the press,' he said, before leaving the room. I was impressed. Ajay did not dodge the media, but he did not kowtow to them either. It seemed the sensible route: this was Bollywood and this was the most shocking crime to happen in connection with an actor in some time. On the other hand, Shayak's determination to pretend the media would just go away seemed of little real value.

And then I flipped to a channel showing a special feature about events at Maaya Island. 'Though they have never admitted to any animosity publicly, sources say that Kimaaya Kapoor and Ashutosh Dhingre's parting of ways was anything but amicable. One industry insider claimed Dhingre had been dismissed because of his disapproval of her on personal issues. Though it remains to be seen if that was a factor in his murder, it is definitely a mystery as to what he was doing on the private island of a film star whom he had had nothing to do with for some years.'

I switched off the TV, unable to keep my eyes open anymore. I didn't even bother to pull down the bed; I set my alarm, kicked off my shoes and trousers, curled up on the sofa and soon was dead to the world.

'For the past month we would have been hungry, had it not been for the help from my daughters. That is why my husband was trying to get in touch with Kimaaya ji. How long can we expect our sons-in-law to tolerate this?'

I was seated in Ashutosh Dhingre's flat, speaking with his wife as she wiped her tears with her sari pallu.

You wouldn't think the Dhingre family was living hand to mouth. The two-bedroom apartment was not in a posh part of town, but they owned it. It was sparsely furnished, and yet there were photos of stars sitting shoulder to shoulder with those of the children and dead forefathers. The walls were clean, though they hadn't been painted in a while. This brand of middle-class poverty was clearly new to the Dhingre family.

'How did things get so bad?' I asked.

'We had been falling back more and more on our savings, but with three daughters to marry off, whatever we had finally ran out after the wedding of our youngest one last year. It has been getting harder and harder ever since he lost his job with Kimaaya ji. Finally it was down to one old producer who would give him small jobs from time to time. But he died so, for the past few months, there had been no work at all.'

'Where are your daughters now?'

'In their homes. They have married into families like ours only. By God's grace, all are good.'

'And your son?'

'Finishing school this year. Now, whether he wants to go to college or not, he will have to find some work to support us.'

'Mr Dhingre didn't want to sell the house?' With property rates being what they were in the area, the proceeds should have been able to buy them a comfortable rental and peace of mind for some time.

'It is all we have to give our son. My husband decided not to sell it till there were no other options. It's my son's decision now. Since it is only the two of us, maybe he will rent this out and we can go live in some small room somewhere. He'll have to wait till he is settled himself to get married since we can be of no help at all,' she said, wiping her face once more.

'Do you know why Mr Dhingre had gone to the island that night – and so late?'

'No. He would never tell me such details of his daily activities,' she said. Her mouth was a twist of withheld tears. 'I think he just had enough and went to demand his due. We have no food on the table, eating only dal and roti, while that woman owes him her whole career, all her crores, all her houses. Couldn't she do anything to help?'

'He had tried to contact her before?'

'Yes. Over phone. Always that Nimisha would answer and make some excuse or the other as to why Kimaaya ji couldn't talk to him.'

A fact they had both neglected to mention. 'Do you know why they stopped working together in the first place?'

'He never told me, but he didn't have to. I know how these women are. Kimaaya ji became too big for him. She said she didn't need an agent anymore. Why pay someone when you keep it all to yourself?'

'Is that it?'

'Must be, no? In the past few months, sometimes, when he couldn't take my nagging, he would shout at me and say that it wasn't so easy going to her for help. Finally one day, a few weeks ago, he gave me some nonsense about how Kimaaya ji had been walking a dangerous road which he had objected to; that if he went to the media, her career would be over; and a disagreement about that is why he had to leave her in the first place.'

It didn't sound like Dhingre had been referring to Kimaaya's secret wedding – that could hardly be characterized as dangerous. 'But your husband finally decided to go in person to Kimaaya.'

'It looks that way.'

'Did you notice any change to his schedule in the past few days?'

'He had been leaving the house early in the morning, coming home late at night,' Mrs Dhingre said.

'Do you know where he was going?'

She shook her head.

'Did your husband have his cell phone with him?'

'Yes, he always carried it.'

And yet it wasn't discovered on his person. Either it was lost or it was removed by the killer. Perhaps because it contained possibly incriminating evidence.

'Do you have any papers, a computer perhaps, on which he worked?'

'No computer, but he had some files where he would put things.' Mrs Dhingre walked over to a rickety wooden chest of drawers and rummaged through it, pulling out a couple of cheap blue files. She handed them to me, and then pointed to a cupboard. 'His older papers are in there. But he didn't keep much. He would always say that in his line of work, it is about who is in your phone book more than anything else.'

'He still kept a phone book?'

'Yes. Old people like us can't suddenly change our habits, you know. Cell phones and all are fine but you just can't trust them, can you?'

'Could I see it?'

As Mrs Dhingre went in search of it, I flipped open a file to find a collection of newspaper clippings. They were mainly about Kimaaya. The most recent, dated two weeks ago, was about the film shoot that Kimaaya had allegedly dropped out of.

Mrs Dhingre came back with the phone book. 'Can I take these with me?'

Mrs Dhingre nodded. 'As long as you bring them back.'

'Of course,' I said. 'One final question, Mrs Dhingre. Did your husband have access to a boat?'

'Boat?'

'Yes.'

'He comes from a family of fishermen.'

'In Mumbai?'

'Oh no! In his native village.'

'How far is that?'

'It takes five hours by train.'

'Did he know anyone who owned a boat in Mumbai?'

'No!' she said, with a vehement shake of the head. 'He left his village because he was so afraid of the water after he almost drowned as a young boy. Why would he go near a boat here?'

'How is it that you get to dock your yacht here?' I asked Shayak as I climbed on board with my bag.

'One of the few personal favours I have asked for.'

We were at a small coastguard dock near Worli Sea Face, flanked by lines of warehouses.

'How does the arrangement work?'

'It is fairly casual. They like me, they give me space,' he said with a smile.

'How does it feel to be so full of yourself?'

'Surprisingly good. Light, with all that hot air keeping me buoyant.'

'You must have done someone important a favour to be allowed to park here.'

'We don't call it parking.'

'Wasn't the warehouse shootout a few days ago somewhere in this area?'

Shayak pursed his lips. 'Yes.'

'My friend thought she saw you there.'

'Which friend?'

'Does it matter?'

'Yes. And you know the rules about discussing your work with outsiders.'

'It was a journalist friend who was covering the shooting. I neither confirmed nor denied anything. And how could I, when I knew nothing about it?'

'Tell me about your meeting with Mrs Dhingre,' he said.

I gave him the update. 'It's beginning to sound more and more like blackmail to me,' I said finally.

Shayak's face was impassive. 'For now, we have to treat Viraat as the prime suspect. We need to establish his actions through the night. Apart from that, we wait and watch. We can't forget that our primary role is to keep the island safe. Ajay has seen to it that the guests are all there for another day at least, so we'll take the chance to speak to everyone while we still have easy access.'

'I would also like to question Afreen again,' I said.

Shayak's phone rang and, as he took the call, I realized that it had been some time since we had hit the water and my stomach was doing fine even without the meds.

When he hung up, he looked pensive. 'That was the surveillance crew. They have finished going through the security footage from around the time of death. We do have footage of Viraat exiting the house at about 12.30 pm, coming back soaking wet and carrying two bottles – one of whisky, the other our wine. '

'Nothing of Dhingre arriving at the scene?

'No.'

'Anything else?'

'There was no unusual movement at the construction site during our murder window.'

So the question remained: By what vessel did Dhingre arrive at the island? And what had happened to it? And if Dhingre could arrive and be killed and not be picked up by the cameras, could our murderer also have been a trespasser that night? Could they have arrived together? 'Maybe the key to this is figuring out how Dhingre actually got to the island,' I said. 'How easy is it to get hold of a boat in Mumbai?'

'In addition to the navy, coastguard and police, plenty of civilians have access to them. Fishermen, tour guides, private yacht owners – the list is long.'

Physically checking all the boat operators would thus be highly impractical, even for an organization of Titanium's girth.

My phone was the next to ring, and I was surprised to see the name that popped up: Terrence D'Costa, my old associate from Calcutta. I had a feeling I knew what this call was about, but I answered anyway.

'Hello,' I said warily.

'Reema! How've you been?'

'Good, good. You?'

'Me too, me too. In your city, actually.'

'Mumbai?' I was still a long way from thinking of it as 'my city'.

'Yes. For a couple of weeks, probably.'

'What brings you here?'

'A case,' he said. 'Would be great to see you.'

'Sure, sure,' I said, trying to stay as non-committal as possible.

'Free tonight?'

'Er, actually I'm out of town.'

'Let me guess – Maaya Island.'

That didn't take long. 'How about I call you when I'm back?'

'Absolutely. Gosh, you took that job just in the nick of time. Big case like this. Good going, Ray.'

If you considered someone else's murder to be your good fortune.

'How's it been so far?'

'Terrence, you know I can't discuss this.'

'Right.'

'I'll call.'

I hung up. Shayak raised an eyebrow at me.

'Terrence, from Calcutta?'

'Yes, the detective who helped us with that video footage in Aloka's kidnapping.'

'I remember. He's of Goan extraction, right?'

'Yes. Why?'

'No reason. He's pumping you for information?'

'So it would seem.'

'You know that comes with the territory, right?'

'Yes.'

'And you can expect it from your journalist friends as well.'

'I can handle it.'

'It won't be their fault. They'll feel enough pressure from their bosses to make that call, despite their discomfort, just in case you can throw anything their way.'

I fought back a growing sense of irritation. 'You don't know these people. How can you assume the worst?'

'When you have done this for as long as I have, you'll know. Big cases like this are not easy on anyone. Just be prepared.'

Thankfully my phone rang again, cutting that conversation short. It was my mother, and ordinarily I would not have been so happy to hear from her.

'Darling, I saw the back of your head on TV!' she squealed.

'What?'

'This coverage of the murder on Kimaaya Kapoor's island! What were you doing there?'

So the TV crew Shayak had thrown out had run with whatever scant footage they had managed to get. 'Ma, it's work-related. I can't talk about it.'

'You are working on that murder investigation! How shocking the whole thing must be for poor Kookie!'

My mother was an actress herself, though on a completely different scale than Kimaaya. 'I am sure she doesn't remember me but I've met her, you know, at one of those film-festival parties. Such a charming girl. Very beautiful, of course.'

I listened to my mother rattle on about Kimaaya's many virtues, putting as much distance between myself and Shayak as I could without going below deck.

Finally, I could take it no more. 'How about I call you back, Ma? I'm in the middle of something.'

'Okay, Reema. But don't forget this time, okay? I worry about you. Try to remember that. It's been ages since we spoke.'

'No, Ma. It's been about four days,' I clarified, bidding a hasty goodbye.

Shayak gave me a smile when I returned to his side. 'You should invite her to Mumbai. Show her around the office.'

'Yeah, right.'

'Why not?'

'You don't remember her trying to thrust me at you?' For my mother, murder cases were all fine and well but not so compelling as marriage, despite the breakdown of her own. And she hadn't been shy about showing her enthusiastic approval of Shayak during their one accidental meeting.

Shayak didn't seem to be perturbed at having been treated like monsoon's first catch of hilsa. 'I do remember it,' he said with a smile. 'It was charming. She clearly recognizes quality when she sees it, which is more than I can say for her daughter.'

SIX

It was less than a thirty-minute ride to the island, and we were still five minutes away when I realized something was off. There were at least a dozen boats of various sizes and persuasions – speedboats, motor-powered dinghies, day cruisers – hovering about.

'What's going on?' I asked.

'The media circus has well and truly begun,' said Shayak, his mouth a grim line.

'What do we do?'

'Nothing. Between Titanium and the police, there is a team of ten additional men to ensure they do not make it ashore. The police have also issued instructions to the media that, as a crime scene, the island is off-limits.'

'Do you think that'll stop them?'

There were camera crews, reporters, photographers. I tried to cover my face, but this time it was likely that my mother would be seeing more of me than the back of my head.

Shayak reached into a compartment. 'Put this on,' he said, handing me a floppy sun hat. He pulled on a baseball cap.

'Keep your head down, wear your sunglasses. No matter what they say, do not respond. Not even a "no comment".'

I knew Shayak's zero-tolerance approach to the media glare for himself – and me. He had saved me once already in Calcutta. A low profile was critical to the work we do, he insisted. Rather difficult to maintain, I would imagine, with clients like Kimaaya.

We bypassed the gaggle. I followed Shayak's lead, amidst shouts to the security personnel.

'Why are you letting them onto the island and not us?'

'What business do you have here?'

'Are you with the police?'

'Get us an interview with Kimaaya and we'll go away!'

Once we hit the ground, two Titanium guards came to our side. 'No,' said Shayak, 'stay here.'

'Sir,' they said, falling back.

I had a hard time keeping up with Shayak till we found the golf cart, which Shayak drove way too fast to the house.

The party mood finally seemed to have been dampened somewhat, but that didn't mean the same thing to me as it did to the gang marooned at Maaya Island. The living area was deserted. We were met by Mrs Pereira. Shayak asked the housekeeper where everyone was, and we were told that Pratap and Afreen were at the swimming pool, Nimisha was giving Kimaaya a massage, and Raj Rathore was at the tennis court playing mixed doubles with Carol, Shiv and Sandhya.

Shayak looked at me. 'You want to head out?'

I nodded.

We walked through the swimming pool deck to the lawns at the back, at the far end of which was the court. The sea was visible in the distance.

'Why isn't the house on the beach?' I asked.

'Security. Can you imagine holding those hacks at bay if we had been right on the water?'

'You don't approve of the house.'

'It's a very beautiful nightmare. We are sticking with the same design sensibility for the hotel, and that will actually be on the beach.'

'Won't it be a bigger threat to have strangers on the island?'

'They will be very elite strangers. And most guests will only be permitted when Kimaaya is not here.'

'That is often?'

'When she's shooting in Mumbai, it's just not practical for her to live here. And so much of the year she is out of town anyway.'

We reached the hard court and waited on the sidelines. Raj and his partner Carol seemed to be in the lead. The foursome continued till the end of the game, when Carol came up to greet Shayak.

'Carol, it's been far too long,' he said, giving her a hug.

'The last time I saw you, you were still in uniform.'

Shayak nodded. 'We went for lunch.'

'Before you disappeared for god knows how long. And now to meet under circumstances like these. Kimaaya told me you are helping out with this nasty business.'

'Yes, and this is my colleague Reema.'

Carol looked at me with appraising, though not unkind, eyes. If she was Kimaaya's school friend, she might be one of the chosen few who had known about the marriage. Dressed in a fashionable tennis dress, she was petite and pretty, with cheeks flushed from the exercise and almost auburn hair. Raj had walked away, but she introduced us to the guests we had not met earlier: Shiv, who looked to be around his early thirties and his sister Sandhya, a couple of years younger.

'We'd like to ask all of you some questions, starting with Carol. Could the two of you come to the house in about half an hour?' said Shayak.

I followed Carol and Shayak inside, giving them space to catch up. Carol was saying how she was now a party planner, and her husband an investment banker. Their two daughters were in school. Shayak responded with polite answers to her questions, revealing little, murmuring something about working 'in security'.

Seated in the lounge, Shayak got down to business. 'Carol, we are trying to create a timeline for what happened here last night,' began Shayak. 'What do you remember?'

'I have run through it all so many times, and all I can say is that I really wish I hadn't had so many martinis! I got here with Viraat – Kimaaya arranged it – and some of the other guests,' she said. 'I have tried to remember anything that might help but for the life of me, I can't.' She repeated details of the party by the pool we had heard from the others, but could add little else.

'What about after you went to bed?' asked Shayak.

'I can't be sure.' The hesitation in her voice was unmistakable.

'Whatever you saw, or think you saw, you can tell us,' he said.

Carol hesitated. 'But what if I am wrong?'

'Without more evidence than your account, we won't be able to do anything. It will only serve as a starting point.'

She gave a little nod. 'I went upstairs and I wasn't feeling so great with all the alcohol in my system, so I decided to sit up for a while. When everything stopped spinning a little and I was getting into bed, I heard a noise. I went over to the window and saw Viraat leaving the house.'

'In which direction was he going?'

'He was crossing the lawn, which I thought was strange at that time of the night.'

'What time would this have been?'

'Around 3 am, maybe?'

'Was he alone?'

'As far as I could see.'

'Did he have anything with him?'

Carol frowned again. 'This is why I feel so bad – since I can't be sure.'

'What did you see, Carol?' Shayak asked gently.

'He was carrying a wine bottle.'

'Which room were you staying in?'

'One of the guest rooms on the first floor.'

'How well do you know the others here?'

'Oh, you know Kimaaya, always inviting a random assortment of people over. I had met Pratap and Poonam a few times, over at the Mumbai house, but no one else.'

'Poonam left soon after arriving.'

'I thought that was a little strange. She seemed a little distracted. Then she got a call and insisted she had to leave just then, that she had to be somewhere early in the morning.'

'Do you know whom she spoke with?' I asked.

'She didn't mention details. I got the feeling she wasn't particularly upset to leave the party, though.'

Then Carol left to send in Shiv and Sandhya.

'Do you know these two at all?' I asked Shayak. He shook his head.

When the siblings walked in, I noticed how much alike they looked. Both baby-faced and with an amount of good cheer inappropriate for a murder investigation.

Shayak turned to me. 'Reema?'

It was my turn to do the questioning. I felt more flustered than I liked, having never had an audience watch me work before.

'How do you know Kimaaya?' I began.

'We actually don't know her very well; we met her just a week ago,' said Sandhya, 'at my best friend's house, who was also supposed to come to this do. Then she got sick, but Kimaaya is so sweet, na, that she said we should come anyway, and even made arrangements for us to get here.'

Shiv nodded his head, silly smile stuck to his face. It looked like we had another fanboy on our hands.

'What do you do?'

'We are hoteliers,' said Shiv.

'Both of you?'

'It's a family business,' said Sandhya. 'Shiv looks after the marketing and finance side of things, along with our father, and I manage the properties.'

'Did you know Mr Dhingre?'

Brother and sister shook their heads. No.

'Tell us what you remember about last night.'

Sandhya giggled. 'I think I was the only one who would remember anything! Everyone else was so wasted!'

'You were not?'

'I am on meds, such a bummer. So I only had two, maybe three drinks over the evening. I would have stopped at one, but when Viraat brought out that insane bottle of wine, I had to try it!'

'Around what time was that?'

'It was late – must have been after 1 am. He came back drenched to the bone – said he decided to take a quick dip in the sea. Didn't seem to have sobered him up any.'

'What prompted him to get the wine?'

Shiv rolled his eyes. 'He was trying to impress Kimaaya all evening. First, he went on about that watch of his. And then he decided to get the Scotch, and came back with what he said would be the wine experience of a lifetime.'

'Did he mention how much it was worth?'

Sandhya giggled again. 'Yeah, like, only about five times.'

'Did everyone drink it?'

'Yup. Viraat uncorked it himself and poured it out for us all.'

'Did he decant it?'

'Yes. I helped,' said Sandhya.

'Do you know what happened to the bottle afterwards?'

'I think we just left it on the poolside bar.'

'How was it?' I had to ask.

'I've never had a wine like that, you know? It really set me thinking about our wine cellars at the hotels. It's like, I suddenly realized why some wines can be so frickin' expensive. It's because they are worth it. Not that anyone else noticed by that time. What a waste!'

'Hey, that's not true. I enjoyed that glass to the hilt,' said Shiv. 'Don't know how after you cleaned out the whisky.'

'Anything else that struck you as unusual through the evening?'

'Not really. But we didn't really know anyone there, so wouldn't be able to say what "usual" is.'

'Any tensions or arguments?'

'Not that I noticed,' said Sandhya.

'As I mentioned, Viraat was a loudmouth showoff,' said Shiv, 'but I'm pretty sure that is standard operating procedure for him. He and Pratap seemed to be having a bit of a pissing competition.'

'Did you hear or see anything after you went up to your rooms?'

'We are downstairs, so we don't have much of a view. And I, for one, was out like a light as soon as my head touched that pillow,' said Shiv.

'I may have heard something, but I don't think it had anything to do with the murder,' Sandhya said with a smirk.

'What did you hear?'

'It was nothing.'

'Why don't you let us be judge of that,' said Shayak.

Sandhya did not look pleased at being told off. 'Sex,' she declared. 'I heard someone having some pretty loud sex.'

'Where?'

'It sounded like it was coming from upstairs, but who knows?'

'Anything else?'

'No. With all the grunting and moaning, I got up to close my window.'

'I have one last question for you both,' continued Shayak. 'Before you came here, did you know that a hotel was being built on the island?'

Shiv and Sandhya exchanged a look. 'No,' said Shiv. 'No we didn't.'

But their expressions told a different story altogether.

After they left, I turned to Shayak. 'You think Shiv and Sandhya have designs on the hotel here?'

'It's possible. We are looking at a managing partner with experience in hospitality. Perhaps they heard that.'

'As for the sex, do you know whose room is above Sandhya's?'

'Yup,' he said. 'Kimaaya's.'

As I let this sink in, Shayak didn't miss a beat.

'That leaves Pratap,' he continued. 'We'll approach that a little differently – I know him quite well, and we may learn more by keeping the chat a friendly one.'

I really didn't want to face Pratap – not in front of Shayak – and this seemed the best escape route. 'In that case, wouldn't it go better if you were alone?'

'No need.'

'It's just that ...' I began.

'What?'

But it was too late. Pratap had already found us. I turned away and began to inspect a potted geranium as though my life depended on it.

'Shayak,' he said warmly, following it up with one of those one-armed hugs men specialize in.

'How have you been?'

'Frantic, man. I have to get to work and the cops have all but ordered us to stay here. I can't afford to lose any more time.'

'I've been hearing whispers about some deal you've been working on.'

'We hope to be announcing a big project sometime soon.'

'The power solution?'

'Yup, a much more ambitious version of the one we're setting up here. We've got a lot riding on it.'

'I'm sure it'll just be a little longer.'

'Can't you do something? Aren't you in charge here?'

'I am in charge of security, but the police have their own way of doing things, and I can't interfere with that. This is a murder investigation, after all.'

'Isn't it obvious that Viraat did it?'

'Why do you say that?'

'He was found under the shrubbery, for crying out loud, within shouting distance of where the guy was killed.'

'I'm afraid more than that is needed to make an arrest,' Shayak said. 'Why don't we go in and get a cup of tea or something. Reema?'

I was forced to turn to face them. My eyes went from a quizzical Shayak to a confused Pratap.

'Pratap, this is my newest recruit, Reema. She's an investigator.'

'Haven't we met before?' he said.

I could feel Shayak's gaze on me, but I stayed focused on Pratap. There was no avoiding it now. 'At the club the other night.'

'That's right! You didn't mention you were working with Titanium.'

'It's not the sort of thing we are supposed to advertise.' Logic I knew Shayak could not fault.

'A detective, eh?' he said with a smile. It didn't seem as though he suspected anything. But as we walked towards the house, Shayak shot me a look that warned me I hadn't heard the last of it.

'So why are you so convinced it was Viraat?' asked Shayak as we seated ourselves. As always, someone was at hand to take our order right on cue. Beer for Pratap, nimbu paani for Shayak and me.

'He was acting strange all evening, man. He arrived with this chick Afreen, but didn't seem to be interested in keeping her company at all. Poor thing didn't know anyone else there, and was obviously feeling like a fish out of water. Then he kept talking about money, and that stupid watch. Guess I can't blame him; he's from Delhi, right?' He laughed. 'But if he was trying to get into Kimaaya's pants, it didn't look like he was making much progress.'

'She wasn't impressed?'

'By that clown? Please. When he pulled out that bottle of wine, I was like, dude, it's your funeral. But now that I think of it, he disappeared for quite a while before reappearing with it. Couldn't he have bumped Dhingre off then?'

I knew the timeline was off on that one, but Shayak wasn't about to reveal more than necessary. 'We aren't ruling out any scenario at this point,' he said evasively. 'Do you remember anything else that might be useful?'

'For the most part, it was a pretty chilled out evening. I grilled some meat, Carol helped. Great girl, that Carol. We had dinner and probably a few too many drinks, but what's new about that?'

'Your wife had to leave early.'

He rolled his eyes. 'Yeah. Not that she wanted to come in the first place.'

'Do you know where she went?'

'You'll have to ask her that, man. She told me it was an emergency at one of her charities the next morning. She had to get there by 9 am, and she knew it wouldn't have happened if she stayed the night.'

'She was right about that,' said Shayak.

'How did she get back?' I asked.

'We have a captain. He took her, though she can sail better than I can.'

'Why didn't the yacht come back for you?'

'Didn't seem to be much of a point. Someone would have given me a lift back. Besides, with the renovation work, the dock seemed a bit tight for her.'

It took me a second to realize that the 'her' Pratap was referring to was his boat.

'She's a beauty, but she can't be easy,' said Shayak.

'And these bloody jokers just have to make it even more difficult and block every single effort to set up a private dock. You'd see the number of yachts in Mumbai double overnight with a half-decent facility. But I wouldn't give her up for the world. Last year we sailed to the Mediterranean, and she was a dream.'

'Cannes, right? Didn't Kimaaya go on that trip?'

'Yup, she, Deepak and Salman.'

'What about later that night, after you all went to bed? Did you see or hear anything unusual?'

He shook his head. 'I passed out. I'd been travelling non-stop and was dog-tired to begin with. Sorry I can't be of more help, man.'

'Not at all. Whatever you can tell us is important.'

Pratap took a sip of his drink. 'How's it going with the other investigation?'

Shayak looked at me. 'I've been keeping an eye on Mrs Puri for quite some time now, and I haven't found anything suspicious,' I said.

'She's up to something man, I just know it!'

'Mr Puri – '

'Pratap, please.'

'Could I ask you to reconsider your position on more in-depth surveillance strategies?' I said.

'I don't know,' Pratap said, shooting a glance at Shayak.

'We could try a phone tap, or a bug in your home,' he suggested.

'Dude, no way!'

'How about monitoring her financial transactions? Could you give us access to her records?' I added.

'Our joint ones, yes. But she has her own private accounts and that would be hard.'

'We could look into her electronic communication.'

'You mean hack her e-mail?'

'Yes.'

'Let me think about it.'

We left Pratap and, to make the most of the daylight hours, headed back to the crime scene.

'You want to tell me why you were following Pratap?' asked Shayak.

'Who said I was following him?'

'You are investigating his wife and you just happen to bump into him at a nightclub?'

'I didn't think it could hurt to find out more about them both,' I said.

'And what did you learn?'

'That Pratap's tabloid persona is an accurate reflection of his socializing style. He certainly is very happy approaching complete strangers in nightclubs.'

'You mean he hit on you?'

'Yes. While he is having us investigate his wife for supposed infidelity.'

Shayak didn't seem overly surprised. 'Even cheaters get cheated on.'

'Are we helping him get a comfortable divorce?'

'We are making an exception by helping one of our loyal customers on a personal matter. I don't judge beyond that. Neither should you.'

'Not judging. I'd like to know, that is all.'

'Let Pratap decide how he wants to proceed. For the moment, that is on the backburner anyway.'

'But maybe it is relevant here. Doesn't it sound awfully like Pratap wishes Kimaaya was more than just a friend? Couldn't he possibly be a person to watch?'

'She usually has that effect on men.'

I rolled my eyes.

'But at this point, we are watching everybody,' he said. 'Though I don't see how killing Dhingre could help him win over Kimaaya. Unless you think Kimaaya wanted him dead and wouldn't hesitate to use Pratap to get the job done.'

Shayak got behind the wheel of the golf cart, with me in charge of the field kit. We took another look around where the body had been found, and ensured all bases had been covered. When we got to where Viraat had been discovered, I lingered longer.

'Why would he be here in the first place?' I asked myself, standing in the gazebo for a little elevation. From there, I could see Shayak's yacht in the water; it wouldn't have taken more than three minutes to walk to it at a reasonable pace, perhaps five minutes for a careening, drunk man. He had gone to his boat to get a bottle of wine once; could he have returned for more? In his stupor, did he decide to make himself comfy in a hedge? If the drugs had knocked him out, he couldn't have taken them – inadvertently or otherwise – too long before. Maybe he went to the boat to dip into his secret stash. The yacht had been taken back to the mainland and the police had searched it. They hadn't found anything yet, but they could have missed something. But why would he be self-administering the date rape drug?

I moved closer to where we had found Viraat, and I could not see the spot where Dhingre's body had been. I crouched to the ground and spun around. From that vantage point, I could see the house. The ground floor was largely obstructed by trees, but a number of rooms on the upper level had windows looking on to this vista. Maybe someone apart from Carol had seen him?

A little further along the hedge from Viraat's makeshift bed, I saw the earth had been dug up, and the cavity had a very distinct rectangular shape. I felt around with my gloved hands. There was nothing there but I was almost certain that there must have been quite recently.

Shayak came up to me. 'Found something?'

'Doesn't it look like something was buried here? Something rectangular?'

Shayak pulled the camera from the kit and took some more photos. 'You're right. The team should have spotted this yesterday.'

I took the dimensions: it was about six by four inches, and three inches deep. I took a closer look with a flashlight and saw something glinting in the corner. I picked it up with a pair of tweezers. 'It looks like a shard of wood with some paint on it. Gold and blue.'

'We can send it to the lab,' said Shayak.

'Yes,' I said, 'but I think I know what this is.'

'Really?'

There was the hint of a paisley in that gold paint. 'I've seen this sort of thing before. It's one of those Kashmiri boxes you get in every gift shop in New Market in Calcutta. I've lost count of how many times I have bought them for people.'

'So it could have held anything?'

'I suppose. Most women I know use them for jewellery, but that doesn't mean anything.'

I bagged the fragment and labelled it. We then drove to the old pier, currently being overhauled and in a rather precarious state. Shayak got off and led me to the muddy pathway. 'There are footprints that start on the wooden planks that can be traced as far as the path running towards the house,' he said. 'The first ones were disturbed when the team made casts, but you can still see them here. It hasn't been confirmed by forensics, but on superficial examination they seemed to belong to the victim.'

'There are a number of other footprints as well.'

'All of them older. The household staff hasn't been here recently with the pier out of commission, and the construction crew was due to start work in this area only this week.'

'Why would Dhingre use the old dock?'

'He has been to the island before but not recently. Only someone who had been here in the past two weeks would know that it is not functioning at the moment.'

'And with no other fresh prints here, that means the murderer knew which pier to use – unless he was already on the island when Dhingre got here.'

Shayak nodded his head. 'Precisely.'

SEVEN

We continued to an annexe of the house, which had a line of rooms styled in a similar manner to the main building but enclosed.

'This is the service wing. There are a number of rooms here. The housekeeper has her own, so do Raj and Nimisha when they are around. The others are dorm-style for the rest of the staff. The gardener and the boatman usually stay in a small one-roomed cottage near the old pier, which is currently being used by the police.'

'Would you like me to interview the staff?'

'For now, I want you to have a look around, get a sense of the space.'

The quarters were well concealed from the house. They were single-storeyed, with a thick fringe of trees between it and the main building, which was angled away from it. There were paths leading to the grounds.

'Did the police search include the servant's quarters?'

'Yes.'

'Anything turned up?'

'Not that I know of. But the police tend to rely more on confessions than evidence, Reema. Don't expect them to be thorough.'

'Did the Titanium team search the premises? What about the other guests?'

'That, unfortunately, we could not do. Kimaaya will not permit it unless we find specific evidence implicating one of them. She said the police search was inevitable, but she wouldn't put her guests through further inconvenience.'

We were headed back to the house when we heard a ruckus in the direction of the pier. Getting closer, we saw that from among the media boats had emerged a larger cruiser. Shayak pulled up to one of his men. 'What's going on?'

'Sir, that is Bindu Bisht.'

'Why is she docking?'

'It is Bindu Bisht,' he repeated.

'So? No media. I thought I was clear about that.'

'Sir, Miss Kapoor herself asked us to let her on the island.'

'Just perfect,' Shayak mumbled, speeding off as fast as the golf cart would allow. 'Of all the vultures to invite into her home at a time like this, Kimaaya has to choose the worst of the lot.'

'Why is she here?' I asked.

Shayak shrugged, annoyance writ on his face. 'She has an all-access pass in Mumbai. No matter what she writes.'

'That bad?'

'She is the best connected because she is the journalist who is much more than a journalist. She is a socialite, a bestselling author, a trophy wife and effectively the most powerful gossip columnist in town.'

'I've read her column and I don't know that I'd categorize it as gossip.'

'She throws in substance now and again to keep people guessing, and she is careful never to trample the egos of those whom she likes, and those with true power. But make no mistake – Bindu Bisht is toxic.'

I turned around to see a woman being led off a boat, amidst shouts from the other reporters who had been camped out for two days.

'Why are you letting her on?'

'Tell Kimaaya to hold a press conference and we will all go away!'

The police officers on watch made it very clear that if they got any closer, there would be consequences.

Bindu Bisht arrived in her always impeccable skirt suit, her working uniform, as she called it, in the interviews she was so happy to give. Pearls in place around her neck.

At the house, she seemed to know everyone except Afreen, Shayak and I, air-kissing her way through the room, finally throwing her arms around Kimaaya with a sympathetic cluck.

'Poor Kookie! This must be so awful.'

Kimaaya closed her eyes and nodded. 'You'd met Ashu, right?'

'Who hasn't? He used to be everywhere back in the day.'

Kimaaya nodded again, and gave a delicate shudder. For the first time since I'd met her, she was in full performance mode.

'Are the police being ghastly, dear?'

'They tried their best and have practically held all of us hostage since the nightmare began, but thankfully Shayak is here to help,' said Kimaaya, with a flutter of eyelashes.

Shayak's jaw clenched as Bindu looked towards him. 'You two haven't met?' asked Kimaaya.

'I don't believe we have,' said Shayak softly.

'Bindu, this is Shayak Gupta, one of my oldest friends.'

She took a long look at Shayak before proffering a hand.

'And this is Reema,' he said.

Bindu turned her unerring grey eyes on me and I knew that this woman could not be dismissed as yet another Bollywood hack. I hadn't read any of her books on cinema – or the racy fiction it had inspired – but after this meeting, I thought I might.

We all proceeded to the formal dining room where a lunch buffet had been served. The sideboard was laden with salads and appetizers, while the main course was on the long wooden table. Kimaaya, Afreen and Bindu seemed to have an appetite only for salad. Afreen, in particular, picked at a few leaves and little else besides. The men, Sandhya, Carol and I made the most of the spread of poached salmon, spinach and ricotta quiche, honey-glazed ham and bread.

Bindu dominated the table. 'It is just appalling how they have made this into a circus. So crass. All those cameras out there should be towed back to the city.'

'I haven't turned the TV on out of fear. My assistant is keeping a watch. If they cross the line, I am taking them to court,' said Kimaaya.

'Line? What line, darling,' said Bindu with a laugh. 'They are making this murder about you and your lovely island, and may as well have forgotten about poor Ashutosh.'

I wondered who had paid for the speedboat that had brought Bindu here. The newspaper she worked for, perhaps?

'You knew Ashutosh?' I asked.

'As I said, I'd met him.'

'You must know everyone in Bollywood.'

She shot me a sharp look. 'Yes, that's true. And you mustn't call it Bollywood, dear.'

'Sorry?'

'Our film industry is not derivative of any other in the world. It is unique and deserves respect.'

I nodded, though I couldn't quite believe I had just been told off by the woman who had named her first novel *Bollywood Belles*.

'So where is the investigation now, Shayak?' asked Carol.

'It's only been two days. These things take time.'

'What happens next?' asked Sandhya.

'I, for one,' said Pratap, 'leave tomorrow morning. I am in the middle of a fucking deal and I can't be here indefinitely, just because someone happened to be murdered.'

Sandhya and Shiv instantly perked up. 'Can we go back with you?' asked Shiv.

'Sure. My yacht will be here first thing, and I need to be out of here by 8 am.'

'Have you run this by Ajay?' asked Shayak.

'He had made a request that we stay, Shayak. That's it. He can hardly expect us to give up our lives for this. I have millions on the line.'

'Just keep him posted is all I am saying. Pissing him off is in no one's interest.'

After lunch, the group broke up and wandered off towards their pursuits of choice. Afreen hung back, looking rather lost. It didn't seem as though she was in any particular hurry to go, though the only one who had paid her much attention since Viraat's departure was Pratap, and now he seemed keen to leave too.

'Have you heard from Viraat?' I asked her.

'I tried calling, but the police have his phone.'

'He's okay,' I said. 'We met him at the hospital.'

She smiled a little, as though she was happy to hear it but didn't really care very much.

'What are your plans now?' I asked.

'To do whatever the police want me to do. I am not important like the others here. I can't afford any trouble.'

'You must be impatient to get back home.'

'A little.'

'Are you working on any films now?'

'One. I haven't done any shooting yet so I'd rather not say.' Her pretty features were clouded by something more than uncertainty – it felt like fear.

'How did you meet Viraat?'

'Oh, you know, common friends,' she said with a shrug. Afreen appeared to be an old hand at evasion.

'What did you think of that bottle of wine he came up with?'

'I don't usually drink wine,' she said. 'I only knew it was a big deal because he said so.'

'Do you know what prompted him to bring it out?'

'Who knows with these people?'

'These people?'

'Sometimes I think it is unfair how much they have and how little they appreciate it.' She had me pegged as closer to her own social standing than the others at Maaya Island – and she was right.

'You must have some recollection of what happened, now that some time has passed.'

Once again that flash of panic. 'I don't think Viraat and Pratap like each other,' she said, speaking a little too fast. 'They were both showing off, trying to get the most attention. Pratap cooked, flirted and dove like a dolphin into the pool. Viraat talked about his boat, his watch, how much money he had just spent on this bottle of wine.'

'Did he mention that it was meant for a client?'

'Not that I heard. In the middle of it all, that fitness instructor came in and had a conversation with Kimaaya. He didn't look very pleased, though Kimaaya didn't pay him much attention.'

This was the first I had heard of it. 'Do you know what time this was?'

'It was after we ate. Around 1 am, maybe? Viraat knows him too, so he went over for a chat.'

'And you went to bed at what time?'

'Around 3 am.'

'When you went up to the room, was Viraat still wearing his watch?'

She frowned. 'I don't think I noticed. Why do you ask?'

'It's missing.'

'I don't know anything about that.'

'Are you sure?' I asked.

'Yes.'

'Did you see him take anything? A pill, perhaps?'

'No, why?'

'He had drugs in his system. As the last person to see him conscious, I thought you may have noticed something.'

'Well, I didn't.'

'You aren't used to circles such as this.'

'Hanging with A-list Bollywood stars? Yes, that's new for me. And look where it's left me.'

'Do you find it intimidating?'

'Only the women,' she said with a wry smile.

'And the men?'

'They don't judge. They are easier to handle.'

'And with intimate access to them, you can get what you want.'

'If you think I took Viraat's watch, you should come out and say it.'

'I can't ignore the possibility, since you were sharing a room.'

She shook her head. 'I thought you'd be different. But you are just as quick to jump to conclusions as the rest.'

'I'm only asking the obvious question. It has nothing to do with who you are and everything to do with opportunity.'

'Whatever,' she mumbled, walking out of the room.

I left in search of Shayak. I found him on the phone, and angry.

'Where is the hold-up?' he said. 'I expect it by the end of the day, no matter how late.' He turned to see me standing there.

'The forensics report is not yet ready,' he said.

'Why?'

'We need clearance from the state lab before we move on. They will tally our findings with their own, append the autopsy results and release them officially. Adlakha hasn't managed to get it done.'

'Nothing unofficial we can use?'

'The footprints at the old pier have been confirmed as Dhingre's.'

I nodded. 'How the hell did he get to the island?'

Shayak shook his head. 'A mystery.'

'Anything else?'

'Yes, but it will have to wait.'

I was surprised just how by-the-book Shayak wanted to play this. Surely the Titanium lab could send us the results to help us get moving before the official report came through?

'Why don't you question the staff at the house? I'll head down to the construction site,' Shayak said.

I was puzzled and annoyed. Cooperation with official actors was supposed to speed things up, not slow them down. Without timelines and specifics, our questions would be speculative and sloppy at best.

I walked away, distracted by my thoughts, quite surprised to find myself missing being my own boss quite so soon. I turned the corner towards the staff quarters, when I was assailed by the loud blare of a TV. The informal sitting room was separated from where I stood by a thicket of bamboo and curtains. Then I heard voices: female, hushed, angry.

'You haven't been taking his calls. He isn't happy.'

'What does he expect?'

'Your loyalty. He wanted me to tell you to remember what he's taught you. And to find your own way to the truth.'

'I have nothing to say.'

'That's convenient. Are you forgetting what he's done for you so soon?'

'No one told me that there were these kinds of strings attached.'

A laugh. 'There always are, sweetheart. You should consider yourself lucky.'

Then an ad came on and the TV blared even louder, leaving me straining to hear the rest. Before I could walk down the path to the room to try to get a glimpse of the speakers, Mrs Pereira appeared.

'Shayak sir sent me to help you with your staff interviews,' she said. If she had seen me eavesdropping, she didn't show it.

'Yes, thank you,' I said, tearing myself away from the voices.

EIGHT

After an hour spent with the household staff during which time I learnt nothing of note, I went in search of Raj Rathore.

I found him in the gym, in the middle of what appeared to be an intense circuit. I was getting ready to retreat so I could return at a less sweaty time, but he held up two fingers to tell me to wait.

The gym was equipped with just about every piece of heavy machinery a top-notch city establishment would have. Living on Maaya Island would not leave your pecs wanting, which made sense as Kimaaya had one of the most toned, athletic bodies in Bollywood, even though she was positively geriatric by the standards set for a leading lady.

'Are you here for a workout?' asked Raj, mopping his face with a towel.

'Uh, not now,' I said. 'I actually had a few questions for you.'

'I told the police what I know. You were there.'

'I have some additional queries.'

'As I said, it was my day off and was with friends in Mumbai. The police have their names and have called them already to check,' he said, stepping on to the treadmill.

'Thanks Raj, but I am more interested in knowing what happened once you returned.'

'Went to my room, poured a drink for myself, finished it, went to bed.'

'Anything else?'

'Not that I remember.'

'You don't remember joining the party?'

'No, because I didn't.'

'We've heard that you stopped by to speak to Kimaaya during the course of the evening.'

Raj seemed stumped at first, before realization struck. 'Oh, that. I was there for all of two minutes. Wouldn't exactly call that joining the party. I needed to speak to Kimaaya.'

'What about?'

'I wanted some time off. She wasn't supposed to be in town now – she was supposed to be away for months on location and then shooting in the city – and I had a bunch of things lined up. She's not my only client, you know. Suddenly she shows up and needs me back on the island, like, indefinitely? What's that about? It really put me in a spot, having to cancel everything else at the last moment.'

'What did she say?'

'That it wasn't the time or the place to talk, and that she'd see me tomorrow.'

'You were angry.'

'Annoyed, more like it.'

'She must pay you quite generously to be here.'

'I don't complain about the money.'

'You also had a brief chat with Viraat and Afreen.'

'Don't remember.'

'Sure about that?'

'Yes,' he said shortly.

'Did you hear or see anything else?'

'No, but I am stuck out there in the servants' quarters, which is quite far from all the action.' He seemed resentful about his living situation, though the service block was hardly shabby.

'Have you considered leaving?'

'Not till recently.'

'What's changed?'

'Kimaaya's not exactly at the top of her game anymore, is she? How much longer is she going to keep me around?'

'She seems to have a few good years yet.'

'Then why was she dropped from SRT's last film? Why did they take Priyanka Chawta instead? She's over the hill, man!'

'Why does that make a difference as long as you keep getting paid?'

'Because I either need another long-term gig or I need to open up my own place. I don't want to work for some two-bit star or some gym chain where my talent won't be recognized.'

'Coming back to last night, your quarters are not far from where Viraat was found. You didn't hear or see anything?'

'I went back to my room and fell asleep.' He turned up the speed of the treadmill, brisk walk becoming a flat-out run, making further conversation impossible.

I found Mrs Pereira tending the garden – rows of greens of different kinds, broccoli, cabbage, onions, tomatoes and peppers. She was on her haunches, giving instructions to the gardener as she filled her basket with produce.

I waited till she had finished and spotted me. She stood up and straightened her dress.

'Ma'am, how can I help you?'

'Please, call me Reema. It's a beautiful garden you've got here.'

Mrs Pereira smiled. 'It's the work of many years.'

'What happens to it when you are in the city?'

'The gardener lives here. The staff here eats much of the produce, and some is sent back to the city when people come and go for maintenance, which is fairly frequently. If there is anything left, I send it to my church for their charitable meal service. Nothing goes to waste. We compost the scraps here, and we generate enough to tend to most of the garden and landscaping. Everything here is 100 per cent organic,' she said proudly.

'You are very fond of these grounds?'

'I've spent all my life in Mumbai. I think you can see why a place so open and so beautiful would be precious to me.'

'How long have you been with Kimaaya?'

'I was hired by her father a month after her mother died. That was around twenty-five years ago.'

'Then you must have known Mr Dhingre.'

'Yes, I did. It is a sad thing. He was a good man. Not like many people in the industry.'

'What do you mean?'

'He had a notion of what it was to be a gentleman. He didn't try to use Kookie the way I see all the young men and women around her doing nowadays. He was respectful, punctual and had an old-fashioned way of doing things.'

'They worked together for a long time – and then he was fired. There must have been problems.'

'It's not my place to say.'

'Mrs Pereira, your discretion is admirable and I am sure Kimaaya really appreciates it, but this is a murder investigation. Anything you tell us might help us learn what Mr Dhingre was doing here and get to the bottom of his death.'

Mrs Pereira proceeded with reluctance. 'I don't think they had problems as such. Kookie just wanted a different sort of person as her aide.'

'In what way?'

'The industry has changed. Mr Dhingre was, as I said, a little old-fashioned, a little cautious in his ways.'

'Nimisha is definitely younger,' I said. She also seemed to have media savvy, and was possibly easier to push around. 'But I think there is more to it than that.'

Mrs Pereira closed her eyes, letting out a sigh that told of a deep struggle. 'They argued.'

'When?'

'Back then – before Mr Dhingre left. But don't ask me what it was about because I can assure you I don't know!'

'Thank you, Mrs Pereira. These are questions that have to be asked, unfortunately.'

'I know how it must look. Kimaaya hasn't always been on top of things in her life; she's made her share of mistakes, but I know she does her best to be a good person. She would have nothing to do with murder, even if Mr Dhingre tried to harm her!'

'Harm her? What do you mean?'

She looked into the horizon, at the endless blue of the ocean so close we could hear the waves lapping at the shore. 'I didn't tell the police this because I knew it would cause trouble, but you work with Shayak sir and I know he would never put Kookie at risk.'

Mrs Pereira paused, and I gave her time to compose her thoughts.

'Mr Dhingre had been calling the house phone ever since Kookie came back from her cancelled shoot. First he called the flat in Mumbai, and then here. I had instructions to tell him that both Nimisha and Kookie were busy. And that is really all I know.'

I left and apprised Shayak of what I had learned. 'Isn't it beginning to sound like blackmail to you?' I wondered.

'Let's wait till tomorrow morning, when we'll have more data. Then we can consider theories and have a chat with Kimaaya.'

'Fine, then,' I said. Why not speak to Kimaaya right away?

Irritation mounting, I didn't think I could sit through an evening of pointless pleasantries. As it was, I was sleep deprived enough to merit an early night. 'If there is nothing else then, I think it's time I turned in,' I said.

Shayak turned to me with a flash of concern. 'Of course,' he said. 'I'll show you to your room.' He led me upstairs; on turning a corner, we bumped into Kimaaya.

'Reema's beat, so I'm getting her settled in for the night,' said Shayak.

'You won't join us for dinner?' Kimaaya asked.

I shook my head.

'I'm sure food won't be served before midnight,' said Shayak. 'I'll have a tray sent up for her. In fact, I think I'll be calling it a night as well.'

Kimaaya looked from Shayak to me as though she were seeing me for the first time, and not liking altogether what she found there. 'What a killjoy you have become, Shayak. I'll get the food organized right away.'

'Fine. I'll be at the boat.'

'Why?'

'Even your sprawling home doesn't have quite enough bedrooms for us all. Besides, I love sleeping on my boat. Don't get to do it nearly often enough.'

Kimaaya pouted. 'You can sleep in my room.'

'Really? So where will you be tonight?'

The pout turned into a scowl.

'Good night, Kimaaya,' Shayak said, and I could hear him smile.

We entered the room, the sound of the sea welcoming me before Shayak flipped the switch. There was a gorgeous four-poster bed with a thick, inviting mattress and carved hardwood headboard. In the corner was a Victorian vanity table, an armoire and a chair with a lamp by its side. I saw my bag had already been brought up.

'You know I would be happy to sleep on the boat,' I said.

'All these enticing propositions in one night?' said Shayak.

'I mean that you should sleep here.'

'Don't be silly. Wouldn't want you staring into a toilet bowl all night. You'll have another long day tomorrow. Get some rest. Come and find me tomorrow when you surface. We can have a look around before the inevitable exodus.'

'Okay.'

'You did well today, Reema,' said Shayak, his dark eyes on mine filled with the exhaustion of the day. He looked as though he had something else to say, but then stopped himself. 'Your food will be up soon,' he said at last.

I nodded, and Shayak let himself out.

I kicked off my shoes and sank into the mattress, but that look had unsettled me and, instead of slipping into the slumber I so needed, for the longest time I listened to the waves, feeling more alone than I could remember.

At 7.30 am, I woke to a quiet house. I showered in the beautiful bathroom, complete with mini bottles of toiletries fit for a luxury hotel, the kind I never stayed at.

I headed to the boat, and the cool salt breeze blew away some of the confusion I had been feeling. There must be a cause for Shayak's caution, else he wouldn't be the foremost security consultant in the country, and it was time I discovered what it was. I got to the boat and, sure enough, he was standing on deck – hair still damp and curling from the shower, in a pair of blue jeans and a white shirt. I could smell coffee.

'You look like you need this more than me,' he said, holding out a cup. 'Come on board.'

He poured himself another and pushed the fruit basket towards me, which I rejected. He passed me a jar of biscotti instead.

'Who stocks this thing for you?' I asked.

'Can't believe I might be competent enough to keep myself fed?'

'No, I can't, and also where would you find the time?'

'Okay, I confess, my staff should get the credit. But as I have told you in the past, I am a very proficient cook.'

'Uh huh.'

'Drink up. You might be less crabby.'

'Not crabby. Just sceptical of unsubstantiated claims.'

'Let this nonsense get over and I'll cook you a meal to do away with your doubts. But for the moment, chew on this,' he said, thrusting a sheaf of papers in my direction. 'Forensics are in. They are still going through fibre samples and other trace, but this should be enough to point us in the right direction.'

Some of it we knew, more or less. Cause of death was confirmed to be the neck wound, inflicted by a missing shard of the wine bottle found at the scene. Footprints belonging to a male, size 10, found at the old dock were a match to Dhingre's.

Other information was news. For instance, the blood at the crime scene belonged only to the deceased. The trace under Dhingre's fingers came back to an unknown male. Fish scales of at least two different kinds were found on Dhingre's trousers.

'So we are definitely looking for a man,' I said.

'Not altogether a surprise. Not likely a woman could have launched the sort of physical assault that killed Dhingre. But we can't rule out a female accomplice.'

'The fish scales would indicate that Dhingre arrived by some sort of vessel used for fishing.'

Shayak nodded.

Then there was the buffet of drugs in Viraat's system: flunitrazepam was found in the largest amount, despite its quick decay, but in the background there were cocaine and Ecstasy.

'Where is Viraat now?' I asked.

'He's still at the hospital. The prints on the bottle were his, of course. Another set belonged to Sandhya, which matches what she told us. Not enough to establish anything, really, but the police are treating him as the prime suspect at this time.'

'Any explanation for how the drugs got into his system?'

'Not for the moment.'

'Wouldn't the flunitrazepam make him look more like victim than perpetrator?'

'Hard to say for sure. Flunitrazepam is used by some as a sleeping aid, or even recreationally. The cocaine and E suggest he is at least an occasional drug user.'

'Were any drugs found on his person?'

Shayak shook his head.

'Could he have got them here, on the island?'

'Nothing is impossible, but Kimaaya does have a very strict no-drugs policy.'

Shayak then handed me the victim's phone records. 'You'll see that there are a number of calls made to Kimaaya's cell, Nimisha's cell, Kimaaya's Mumbai landline and the island here. Just like Mrs Pereira said. Now is the time for your theories.'

'Blackmail of some sort is one possibility. We know Dhingre was broke and desperate. But there could be a more benign explanation. Mrs Dhingre had said her husband had tried to contact Kimaaya for assistance, for work. Perhaps it was that?'

'Rather too persistent, don't you think?' said Shayak.

I looked at the call records more closely. It started as a call every couple of days, for a few weeks. Then it escalated to multiple calls every day for the three days before the murder. 'Yes, you're right.'

'Now take a look at the last sheet there.'

I flipped forward to it. It was a scanned image of a piece of paper with three, hand-written dates on it: 26 February 1997; 13 July 1999 and 25 May 2012.

'During the autopsy, they discovered a small piece of paper in Dhingre's back pocket. It looked like it was torn out of a notebook,' Shayak explained.

'Any clue what these might mean?'

'I know what the first two are. The first is the date on Kimaaya's marriage license; the second on her divorce papers,' said Shayak, his face giving away nothing.

'How is that possible? You are still certain that it is not common knowledge?'

He sighed. 'We've been over this before, Reema.'

'Okay, however these dates were obtained, this lends weight to the blackmail theory.'

'Yes, it does.'

'What about this third date?'

'I don't know. I think it's time we had another chat with Kimaaya.'

Finally.

We headed back to the house and found Mrs Pereira there. 'Where is Kimaaya?' Shayak asked.

'Still asleep, I think, sir.'

'Can you call her for us?'

'Sir?' She clearly wasn't in the habit of taking requests like this.

'Tell her I said it is an emergency.'

'I gather Kimaaya doesn't like to be roused,' I said once Mrs Pereira was out of earshot.

'There is a reason they tell you to let sleeping dogs lie.'

Five minutes later Kimaaya wandered in, wearing a robe and bedhead. And she still looked beautiful. 'What is it that can't wait till a more respectable hour?' she said, stifling a yawn.

'We need some answers from you, Kimaaya, if you expect us to get anywhere with this investigation,' said Shayak.

'What are you going on about?' she mumbled, running a languorous hand through her hair.

'There seems to be a fair amount you are withholding from us.'

'I don't know what you are talking about,' she said, taking a sip from the warm lemon water that Mrs Pereira had brought in her wake.

'25 May 2012. What does it mean to you?'

This finally seemed to snap Kimaaya out of her self-absorption. Her eyes widened, but she had immediately composed herself. 'I have no idea,' she said.

'Answer the question.'

'It means nothing to me.'

'The truth, Kimaaya.'

'You have no right to talk to me like that,' she said, taking another sip. I watched her draw into herself, gathering the distress and tucking it away where no one could see it.

'You have no right to lie to me when all I am trying to do is help.'

Chin up, Kimaaya held her tongue. It was actress Kimaaya here, not the woman I had seen so far, unafraid of her cracks as long as Shayak was by her side. She had armoured up.

'Three dates were scribbled on a piece of paper found on Dhingre's body,' Shayak said. 'The first was the date of our wedding. The second, our divorce. The third, this.'

'There was no way Ashu could have known any of it. He joined me only after our divorce, and left before May 2012.'

'He worked for you for so long. He'd know where to find your personal papers.'

'Those documents stay in my safe at all times. Are you saying Ashu broke in? Need I remind you that Titanium set up that safe for me?' she said with a cold smile.

'Why didn't you tell us he had been calling you the past couple of months?'

She sipped her tea again, careful not to let the mask slip.

'Not mentioning those calls – do you know how bad it looks?'

'I'm not an idiot, Shayak!'

'What was it about Kimaaya, and why didn't you mention it earlier?'

'I … I was embarrassed, okay? He kept calling to ask for money. It was so humiliating for us both!'

'Blackmail?'

'No! It wasn't like that! A month ago, I finally spoke with him. He told me that he was in very bad shape financially, and needed work. I helped him out with some cash. And then I asked him not to call anymore because I didn't have any work for him, and he said he didn't want any more handouts.'

Shayak stood up and paced the room. 'You gave him money. Can't you see how that might look?'

'No, Shayak, I can't. Please enlighten me.'

'Like you had succumbed to a blackmailer – and had a very good motive for murder.'

'I had no idea then that he would die on my island, now did I! An old friend needed help and I stepped up. Most people would consider that a good thing!'

'Then explain why he would have these dates on him that night.'

'I don't know!' she screamed.

'And that's it?'

'That's it, Shayak, believe it or not! I am as shocked as you are.'

'A secret marriage, a secret divorce,' said Shayak softly. 'My parents, your father, Auntie Clementine and a handful of others knew these two dates; none of them would reveal what they know to Dhingre. And even if they did remember our wedding anniversary, why would anyone remember the exact date of our divorce? The only way someone would know those specifics was if they had the documentation. Is there anyone else who could have accessed your papers?'

'I'll have to check my safe in the city, but don't you have a copy? Couldn't someone have gotten hold of those?'

'No, but I'll still check as well. And I have no clue about this third date, which is why I feel it could hold the answer. What does it mean?'

Kimaaya closed her eyes.

'Whatever it is, it isn't as bad as you think it is,' said Shayak in a soothing tone.

She opened her eyes but avoided our gaze. When at last she spoke, the words were a whisper. 'It's the date I left rehab.'

I felt my pulse quicken.

'Jesus Christ, Kimaaya,' Shayak said, dragging his hand through his hair. 'Don't tell me you kept those papers lying around! You should have destroyed all evidence of that!'

Kimaaya's moment of weakness had passed. 'Not lying around, no. But it was the hardest thing I've ever done so you're damn right I kept a reminder. It's not like it was hanging on my wall or anything; it was in my safe which, by definition, is supposed to be safe!'

'Dhingre knew this?'

'Yes. But all I know is that he wouldn't use this information against me; it was he who had pleaded with me to get help. Who knows, I may not even be standing here if it wasn't for him.'

'That is why you fired him, wasn't it?' I asked. This was the cause of the fights Mrs Pereira spoke of.

Kimaaya buried her face in her hands. 'I shouldn't have, but I did. And when I got back from the clinic, I called to thank him for saving my life. But too much had happened for me to hire him back.'

As my mind went into free fall, Shayak persisted. 'Is there anyone else who knows this?'

'I suppose the rehab clinic people do, but they are absolutely discreet.'

'Anyone else?'

'No! You were the only one I ever told about it. And even then, after the fact.'

'You didn't mention any dates to me. Where was that place again?'

'Antigua.'

'And you are sure there couldn't be a leak at their end?'

'Positive.'

'Your basis for such trust?'

'It's how they get their business. It is owned by a celebrity who got himself cleaned up and now charges huge amounts to help others. Stars from all over the world go there; the paparazzi never gets to know anything. In fact, there was a Hollywood actor there when I checked in. No one heard a peep about that, even though the shit hit the fan for him with all sorts of scandals in the past few months. Why would they suddenly be any different with me?'

'Anyone else who might know? What about other patients?'

'I went incognito, and there weren't any Indians there. No one seemed to know who I was.' Kimaaya looked a little humbled by this admission.

'Wait a minute,' I said. I thought about the date again. That was about the time I was setting up my practice, when I was twiddling my thumbs waiting for clients. I had little to do but read the news, and everything else that passed for it. 'Wasn't that when your stalker situation went out of control?' I remembered following the case with some interest.

'Yeah, so?' asked Kimaaya.

'Could he have been tapping your phone? Hacking your e-mail?'

'We hadn't found anything to suggest it,' said Shayak. 'But an e-mail hack is difficult to catch.'

'Did you correspond with the rehab clinic over e-mail?'

Kimaaya nodded almost imperceptibly.

'That was before we stepped up your digital security,' said Shayak.

'But that bastard's still in jail!' said Kimaaya.

'He was let out after only a few months,' said Shayak quietly. 'I had him watched for about six months after that. He didn't seem a threat at the time, so I called off my men.'

'How could you not have told me this?' Kimaaya yelled.

'Was there any point in alarming you for no reason?'

'There is still no evidence that he is our guy,' I pointed out. 'But there are too many strands of this case that are no longer confined to this island. I need to get back to Mumbai.'

Shayak nodded grimly. 'We'll leave today.'

NINE

Madhav Pande was a final-year student of computer engineering when, without precedent, he failed his mid-term exams. His parents and friends urged him to continue, saying that the result was an aberration in an otherwise consistent academic career. However, he found himself unable to stay on course. One Friday soon after, he left his college in Pune, never to return.

Madhav then headed for Mumbai. Kimaaya Kapoor's biggest blockbuster till date had released the very day he arrived. The film was about a girl who chucks everything – an engagement, a family, a stable life – to live on the fringes of Mumbai and become a singer.

Over the next week, Madhav watched the film repeatedly, sometimes twice a day. He didn't want to be a star himself. But in the reels of that film, he found his dream – Kimaaya Kapoor.

Madhav got lost in his fantasy. On the laptop that once held all of his course work, he watched film after film, all starring Kimaaya Kapoor. He started keeping tabs on her public events, going to as many as he possibly could, even coming within arm's length of her once in a mall when she was promoting a new lipstick shade for a top cosmetics brand. He didn't ask for an autograph.

And then, Kimaaya Kapoor disappeared. When her next film released, she was nowhere to be seen. She did not appear for a single promotional event; the producer and director claimed she was away at a remote location for a shoot though everyone in the industry knew it wasn't so. When for three months there was no sign of her in the media, the gossip mill started working overtime. She had recently fired Dhingre and, with no publicist or agent to fill the gaps, talk of secret affairs gone wrong, suicide attempts and drastic weight gain grew everywhere like weeds.

But Madhav had been convinced that none of this was true. He waited day after day outside her house till she returned. He knew she would need his help to get by, and he made a promise to himself that he'd always be close at hand.

That was how Madhav Pande transformed from college boy to Bollywood's most famous stalker.

'Tell me how Madhav Pande was caught,' I said to Shayak, as once again we were on our way back to Mumbai. Afreen and Carol had hitched a ride with us and were below deck in the salon, the last of Kimaaya's guests to leave.

'When Kimaaya came back from rehab, she threw herself into public life with a vengeance. She was shooting two to three films at a time, doing appearances all over the country and ensuring the spotlight was firmly back on her. She hired Nimisha and did as much press as she could bear. Creepy fan mail wasn't anything new to her or any other star, but there was one guy whose letters began to concern her, so she brought them to me.'

But naturally, I thought, Shayak would be involved in this chapter too.

'She was right to be worried, for this fan clearly knew exactly what she was doing, in far more detail than he could have from merely tracking the news. When she left the house, what time friends were arriving to meet her, her workout schedule. In addition, he seemed to have guessed her secret: Kimaaya had been struggling with drugs for some time, and the disappearance that had everyone speculating was when she went to get cleaned up. He mentioned it in more than one letter.'

'Lucky guess?'

'I thought so at the time. Now, I have to reconsider that theory.'

'Someone must have known of her habit.'

'She was very careful about it. She would never use at parties or talk about it.'

Once again, I was surprised that a man of Shayak's experience trusted that secrets – especially such secrets – could be kept. 'She must have had a dealer.'

'We had checked him out – he is the least star-struck man I've met in Mumbai. Possibly owing to the fact he keeps most of Bollywood's famous faces high. Doesn't fit the profile of a stalker, and hardly one to risk his livelihood by blabbing to one.'

'If he was watching her so closely, he could have seen something.'

Shayak nodded.

'So what was Madhav after?'

'A chance to meet Kimaaya. Just one meeting, he kept saying over and over again, to prove that he was the one for her, the only one who understood the real woman behind the façade, etc. etc.'

'I am blurry on the details – what triggered the arrest?'

'There was an explosion in Kimaaya's building. In the chaos that ensued, Madhav Pande got inside, up to Kimaaya's floor and waited in the stairwell till she left the flat. He tried to grab her but luckily she wasn't alone – her friends who were following her out the door caught him before things got out of hand. He was arrested. That was when she hired us to look after her security.'

'And now he is out of jail.'

'Yes. He has appeared since on news shows, talking about the depression he suffered at that time, and how he needed the help of a mental health professional. He said he is being treated and is keen to go back to college and resume normal life. His family is fairly well off and has stood by him.'

'So what is our strategy now?'

'This is your case, Reema. You tell me.'

'Checking out Madhav Pande, for sure. His whereabouts at the time of the murder; his association, if any, with Dhingre. And digging a little deeper into this Viraat business. He is still looking like the best suspect.'

'True, though I am beginning to have doubts about that. We don't know that Viraat has done anything worse than take some drugs, drink his own wine, lose a watch and pass out where he shouldn't have. It is possible to see sinister intentions where there are none. Coincidence does exist – even in crime.'

The benefits of working for a company like Titanium were soon driven home to me. No more depending on hearsay or statements from unreliable sources; I went into office to find a file full of information on Dhingre and Kimaaya's houseguests gleaned from sources official and unofficial. The research and communications team as well as the tech guys had pulled up whatever they could over the past few days on Shayak's orders.

And now I needed more. The first thing I did on my return to office was to request the file on Madhav, updated for his activities since Titanium dropped the tail on him. Then I started with the sheaf on Dhingre.

Born in 1958, Dhingre grew up in a fisherman's village not far from the city and then, when he was fifteen, ran away to Mumbai. Living with an uncle who was an odd-jobs man around the studios, he started going to a slum school and, in his free time, would pitch in where he could – tea boy, assistant to light boy, shoeshine boy. After a couple of years and not much progress on the academic front, young Dhingre's enthusiasm and good temperament caught the eye of producer Buddy Mehta, who hired him to be at the beck and call of his stars. For over a decade he worked his way up through the ranks of the production unit till Savitri Sharma, a character actor, took him on as her personal assistant.

By this time, if Dhingre didn't know who you were, you weren't worth knowing in the film industry. Which is why Kimaaya, whose first film featured Savitri Sharma, didn't waste any time poaching him. He was in her service for about nine years, from her second film to her sixteenth, and he helped her navigate the dirty, difficult terrain to find her place in the spotlight.

And then, when Kimaaya decided he was no longer needed, he became redundant overnight. He had come too far to go back to working the floors, and none of the younger stars wanted to employ Kimaaya's over-the-hill cast-off. There was a sense that something had gone bad between the two of them, though neither spoke of a fallout publicly. A few old-timers gave him work and that was about it.

But before I delved deeper into the past – which might even involve taking a closer look at Kimaaya's role in the affair, despite what Shayak thought about it – I needed to look at the most obvious suspect first, and for that I had to find out what Viraat was doing on the lawn, in the dead of night, passed out.

That was when Adlakha called me into his room.

'I just got a call from Shayak,' he said, pushing his glasses to the top of his head.

He didn't look pleased, but then he never seemed to, if he could help it.

'The Pratap Puri case is now no longer your headache. You, apparently, have better things to do with your time.'

'Shayak has asked me to work on the Maaya Island murder.'

'And how, I wonder, did that happen.'

'I don't think I understand what you mean.'

'It is quite simple. How does someone who has worked here for five minutes get the assignment of the year?'

'I think you should ask Shayak that.'

'But I'm asking you.'

'I can't speak for him.'

'You can't even hazard a guess?'

'I try not to speculate.'

'Then let me offer you my explanation – and you can treat it as a friendly warning if you wish. I don't know what happened in Calcutta, but Shayak is hoping to capitalize on your relationship to ensure you toe his line with this investigation.'

'And why would he do that?'

'All I know is that Kimaaya is one of our clients Shayak keeps close to his chest. Maybe he has a little bit of a crush.'

I shrugged.

'And maybe he thinks you have a crush on him, which would make you very easy to control.'

At first I didn't think I heard him correctly. Then came anger. Following which, after a few calming breaths, my insecurities stepped in to take over. Could Adlakha be right? Was Shayak using my feelings for him – and my greenness – to keep this investigation as tightly under his control as possible? But it was his company – if he wanted to exclude us all and run the whole show himself, he was well within his rights to do so. Yet he seemed preoccupied and happy to pass the reigns of the investigation over to me.

None of it made sense. And either way, it had absolutely nothing to do with Adlakha.

'I will e-mail you my report on the Pratap Puri case,' I said, as businesslike as possible. 'I had an opportunity to speak with him at the island as he was one of Kimaaya's guests the night of the murder. Unfortunately, he still won't budge on his no-surveillance position.'

Adlakha just stared.

'If that is all, I would like to get back to work now.'

Adlakha dismissed me with a wave of his pen. He had said his bit and, unable to get a rise, was now done with me.

The quicker I sent my report on Pratap Puri to Adlakha, the sooner I would have it – and him – off my back, so I spent the next hour or so on that. Once done, I turned my attention back to the files on my desk, choosing the one on Viraat.

His father was a businessman of some clout in Mumbai, with roots in heavy machinery. Viraat himself, after an uninspiring academic performance, went to Australia to study, after which he seemed to have no desire to break from Bondi Beach and return home to join the family business. That is when daddy decided to start a venture more in line with Viraat's interests – an import outfit with a focus on Australian and New Zealand wines. Viraat seemed to know what he was doing, or had hired people who did.

But then he had begun to dabble in more risky ventures, investing crores in a vineyard in Nashik that went bust, buying a case of Bordeaux that was reportedly rescued from a 100-year-old shipwreck that proved to be a fraud, throwing grand parties for his friends whenever the fancy struck. And, on at least one occasion that I knew of, consuming wine worth crores himself, meant for a client.

I called the hospital and was told that Viraat had been released earlier that afternoon. I referred to the file again and found his home details. No answer on the landline or cell phone. I thought I might as well go over and see what I could find – perhaps he would be in a more cooperative mood now that he was at home.

When I got there a little after 4.30 pm I found the door open just a little bit, the lock smashed.

'Hello?' I called out. 'Anyone there?'

There was no answer.

I pushed the door and at once knew something was amiss. A chair was lying overturned, a vase had met a similar fate, flowers and water spilled onto the carpet. I moved gingerly through the living area, careful not to touch anything. In the dining room there was a large wooden table and a bar, behind which was a stool that had toppled over. As I got closer, I saw a sight that sent a chill through me – a pair of well-heeled feet, attached to a body, lying on the floor. I inched forward with dread, for I had seen those shoes before.

It was Afreen, eyes wide open, blood turning the blue silk carpet beneath her a glistening black.

I heard a noise and swung around, acutely aware of how exposed I was.

'What the hell happened here?' I heard a man's voice say. It sounded like Viraat.

With nowhere to go and nothing in sight that I could arm myself with, I stood my ground. Viraat turned the same corner I had a few moments before and saw me.

'What are you doing here?' he said, bewildered, shifty-eyed. He had shaved since I last saw him, and smelled like a duty-free store.

'I had come to meet you. The door was open. I let myself in and found … this.'

He followed my gaze, and peered over the bar.

'Duuuude! What the hell is this?' he said, more dazed than shocked.

I didn't know quite how to respond to that.

'Who is that lying back there?'

'It's Afreen.'

'What's she doing on the ground like that?'

'She's dead, Viraat.'

I saw his eyes widen. His pupils were dilated.

'I knew this would happen!' he screamed, running a jerky hand through his hair. 'I knew they were out to get me!' He sat down on a bar stool.

'Who is out to get you?'

He didn't answer.

'Why would they hurt Afreen?' I asked.

'Because they came for me and I wasn't home!'

'Whom are you talking about?'

Viraat could only shrug.

'Was Afreen staying here with you?'

'No!'

'What was she doing here, in that case, with you out of the house?'

'Who knows, man! Maybe she is one of them. Maybe she was here for more money.'

'More money for what?'

No answer. And then he raised an angry arm and brought it down on the bar. Two things happened – suddenly the surface came to life like a TV screen and next, when he lifted his arm again, he knocked over a glass that was on it, spilling water everywhere.

I gasped: we had contaminated the scene. I watched mutely as the water danced around the surface of the luminous bar. Luckily there was not enough to spill onto the floor. Viraat hardly looked concerned.

I pulled out my phone and dialled Shayak's number.

'Yes,' he said, curt.

'There's been another murder. Afreen's been killed at Viraat's house.'

I gave him a quick account of what I had found. Shayak swore. 'I'll tell Ajay to send a team out there. Do you have an evidence kit with you?'

'In the car.'

'Get to work.'

'Before the police arrive?'

'Try to get as much as possible before they do.'

What was going on here?

'Whatever they say when they do get there, tell them to speak to me.'

'Is there something I should know?'

'This is not the time for questions, Reema. Get moving. They may not want us working on this case for long.'

'But it has to be connected to the murder on the island! Afreen might have seen something.'

'Reema, be careful what assumptions you jump to.'

'Okay,' I said, trying to focus on the task at hand. 'What do I do about Viraat? He is here, contaminating the scene even as we speak.'

'He's wasted, isn't he?'

'Looks like it.'

'Keep him out of the way,' he said, hanging up.

I could not understand what was happening, but I had my instructions and they were clear.

'Viraat,' I said.

No response.

'Viraat,' I repeated.

'Huh?' he replied.

'I need you to go to the living room.'

'Sure thing,' he said, still sitting.

I pulled my phone out of my pocket and told the driver to bring the evidence kit – it was company protocol for the Investigations team to always have one at hand while on the job – up to the flat. I then led Viraat to the living room and stood guard. 'Try not to touch anything. Keep standing for the time being.'

No reply.

'Cool bar you've got there,' I said.

'Yeah? Thanks.'

'It's a screen?'

'Yeah. Our newest product. Pitching it to nightclubs as a way of integrating ads and stuff at point of purchase.'

It seemed like a good idea. I could see the booze companies jumping at a fresh way of advertising their wares, particularly with all the legal restrictions on their marketing activities.

'Well, it looks great.'

He nodded absentmindedly.

'Do you know why Afreen was here, or how she may have gotten in?'

'Nope.'

'Or who may have wanted to harm her, or you?'

He shook his head. No more mention of those who wanted money.

My kit arrived, and I quickly dusted for prints on a chair before asking Viraat to take a seat.

'What's happening?' he said.

'I need to take some evidence. The police are on the way and I am sure they will have questions for you.'

I went back to the body, starting out by taking photographs of poor Afreen.

Single gunshot to the chest. No signs of a struggle – her hands and arms were free of defensive wounds. Her clothes were not disturbed, and there were no obvious signs of sexual assault.

I moved to the living room with the camera, starting with the lock on the front door. I had just finished when I heard the lift stop at Viraat's floor. Out came Ajay and two constables.

'Reema, I'm afraid I'm going to have to ask you to leave,' Ajay said.

'Shayak said you should speak to him.'

'We have spoken already.'

I stared open-mouthed as the DCP and one of the constables entered the flat and the other officer took guard at the door.

It didn't seem as though I had much of a choice in the matter, unless I wanted to take on the Mumbai Police. I packed up my kit, took the lift down and waited in the lobby.

Fifteen minutes later, Ajay and his men left, leading Viraat away in handcuffs. Ajay turned to me.

'Shayak called again. Much as I would like to help, there is nothing for you here. I have told him as much.'

I watched his retreating back with frustration, unsure why this latest roadblock had presented itself. But there was no point in wasting more time. I flipped through my notebook and found Afreen's address, which I had made a note of at the island, along with the contact information of everyone present.

I cursed Mumbai traffic for the ninety-four minutes it took me to reach Afreen's apartment in a very unfashionable part of town. It was in a four-storey building, and I walked up a steep, narrow staircase to the top floor. Confronted by a standard-issue padlock, I put on my gloves, took the right tool from my kit and eased it open.

I stood outside the door, knowing that I was about to cross a line that couldn't be uncrossed. What was I doing here, in direct violation of orders from my boss and the police? Was I willing to lose my job over this? Perhaps even risk arrest?

And then an image flashed through my brain: of a girl, no older than me, lying cold at my feet.

Who was Afreen? Who would want her dead? Was it Viraat? Could she have known something about Dhingre's murder? Why were we being called off the case summarily?

I hadn't seen enough death to walk away from it. Maybe I would get to the point in my PI career that I could look at a lifeless body and be unmoved, but that would also be the day, I hoped, that I would have the courage to put the job behind me and move on.

I needed to know. I needed to know why, how, who. I needed to know that I had done my bit to ensure justice. I couldn't walk away from this anymore than I had been able to walk away from the Prakash Agarwal murder in Calcutta, and I knew it was pointless trying. If there were consequences, so be it.

I had to get into the flat before the police did, before Shayak had the chance to tell me to back off. So I pocketed my reservations and walked into the one-room apartment. To call it a studio would be to give it airs it did not possess. There was a bed, a cupboard, a little fridge and a table with an induction hob on it. It was tiny, though not shabby, and filled with the clutter of tasteful, even expensive items. I opened a cupboard and found it overflowing with clothes, bags, shoes, make-up – each one capable of making a sizeable dent in my pay packet.

Afreen had said she was an actress – a claim Kimaaya had been sceptical of – but she had told me that she had landed a role recently. It would have been her big break. Trying to make it in Bollywood was not easy, nor was it inexpensive, from what her designer wardrobe told me. Where was she getting all this cash? Nothing about her just slightly awkward deportment spoke of family money, and the size and location of the apartment only confirmed that. She was saving on rent.

I found a little diary with a number of appointments written in it. Names, places, phone numbers. Men called Vicky and Rocky.

I rifled through drawers and shelves and found little else to tell me what might keep Afreen busy and ahead of her bills. Till I stumbled on her laptop.

I started it up and looked through the desktop files. There was a portfolio with a number of photos taken in all manner of dress – some demure gaon ki chhori shots, others urbane party girl. Finally, there was a series of positively risqué pictures, of the drape-me-across-the-bed-and-feed-me-grapes variety.

I opened the web browser and looked through the history. I had hoped to get lucky with her e-mail, in case she was still logged in, but that would have proved too good to be true. I scrolled through the other sites she had been visiting, and clicked on one that seemed out of place.

It was an escort site. 'Bollywood actresses, airline hostesses, models, society women and students – all can be yours at Mumbai's premium escort service. Take them to parties, on overseas tours or just for a fantasy night on the town. All your dreams cum true.'

Front and centre was a picture of Afreen. The face was blurred, but I immediately recognized it as one of the shots from the portfolio I had just browsed. It seemed Afreen was one of the showcase stars of the service.

I wrote down the phone numbers and URL and shut down the computer, leaving it as I had found it.

I headed back to office. Once there, I went to Adlakha. 'I need help tracking down a company from its website,' I said.

'What is this about?'

'The Kimaaya murder.'

He looked at me as though he didn't entirely believe me. 'I hope it isn't the Afreen case, because I have just been told we are strictly hands off in that matter.'

News seemed to travel fast in murderous Mumbai. Had Shayak already spoken to him or had it been Ajay? I maintained my poker face and Adlakha seemed to relent.

'You can speak to the digital security team on the second floor. Rishi should be able to do something for you.'

I headed up. Rishi wasn't there, but his colleague Jay was. 'Do you know where Rishi is?' I asked.

'He has taken a half day,' said Jay.

'I'm working on a case and have some tech stuff I needed help with. Pranav Adlakha suggested I speak to Rishi, but I don't think it can wait.'

'Take a seat,' he said, pointing to the empty chair beside him.

'I need to find out who owns a domain in connection with an ongoing investigation,' I said, handing him a piece of paper with the name.

Within a minute he had a name for me: Bobby Gill, as well as a US address and number.

'I can't guarantee that these are the correct details. Often sites like these are registered under false addresses, or to a shell company.'

'How else can I track them down? And quickly.'

Jay gave me a rueful grin. 'We could always call and avail of their services.'

'I don't need to meet the girls. I need to meet the management, as it were.'

'That would be less interesting, but I could trace the phone number on the site to see if I can get you some real contact data.'

'Don't we need police cooperation for that?'

'Not at Titanium,' he said with a smile. 'Just give me an hour or so.'

'There is one more thing.'

'Tell me.'

'What is our policy on hacking?'

Jay's eyes lit up. 'What kind?'

'The e-mail ID of a murder victim.'

'There have been exceptions made in the past, in the course of various investigations, where we have hacked e-mail.'

'But it is not the norm.'

'If it is illegal, it is not the norm at Titanium. But, as I said, exceptions have been made.'

'Okay. Let me give this some thought.'

'Sure,' said Jay. 'You should also know that for something of that nature, we'd need approval from higher up.'

'Meaning?'

'Mr Gupta himself.'

I left him my cell number and went back to my desk.

I had to redirect my attention to the Maaya Island murder, and I rewound to where I was before I found Afreen's body. I checked the file on Madhav Pande once again. There was an address and a landline number. I called, and a woman picked up.

'I'm sorry,' she replied when she heard why I was calling, 'but he doesn't live here anymore. Madhav was my tenant. Two months ago I moved in.'

'Do you have a number or address where I could reach him?'

'Sorry, no,' she said.

I hung up. There must be another way. Madhav was back in the public domain, making media appearances, talking about what had happened. He seemed to be rejoining the ranks of young men his own age. And what did such men do in their spare time? I logged on to Facebook.

There were a number of men by the name of Madhav Pande. But with the aid of an old photograph taken when the stalker was being carted off to court, I found him after a brief search.

Madhav was certainly not shying away from his past. His timeline revealed that not only was he talking about his experiences, he was writing a screenplay about them in his downtime. 'Final act to go!' he had just told his 4,394 friends. And then a month ago: 'In talks with a director about the script!' One of his friends replied: 'Any chance of casting Kimaaya Kapoor in the lead role?' Madhav Pande had hit 'like'.

I took a chance and sent him a direct message.

'My name is Reema Ray and I work with Kimaaya Kapoor. You have a chance to help Kimaaya in her time of need. Call me,' I wrote, sending him my contact details.

And then I packed my laptop and headed home. I had just about reached and slipped the shoes off my sore feet when my phone rang. It was Jay.

'So the cell is registered to the same name from the Whois search, Bobby Gill. Office in Malad.'

I wrote down the address. 'Thanks, Jay. One day, I would like to get the bottom of how Titanium manages to do all these cool things without getting busted.'

'I wish I knew,' Jay replied with a laugh.

A short while later, Rishi called. 'Sorry I wasn't there when you came by today,' he said.

'No problem. Jay was able to help me.'

'He tells me you might need some hacking done?'

'That was just a thought. Will have to discuss it with the bosses. But as I said to Jay, I'd love to know how these things are done within the company.'

'Maybe I could, er, tell you over a drink tomorrow?'

I hesitated, but only for a moment. 'Sure. My schedule is a little unpredictable right now, so I'll give you a call when I know my scene?'

'Great.'

I had just about hung up when I heard another ring. I automatically reached for my cell before I realized that it was the intercom. I rushed over to it. It was Shayak.

'Oh, good. You're home. I'm coming over with dinner,' he announced, not giving me time to reply.

In five minutes, he arrived bearing a basket.

'If you don't mind,' he said. 'I'm famished.'

He quickly unpacked it as I set the table. Numerous dabbas emerged: keema, dal, sabzi, rice, raita.

'Home cooked?' I asked.

'By me.'

'Really?'

'Would I lie to you?'

'Let me try the food before I decide.'

We didn't speak very much as we ate. I had too much on my mind, and Shayak seemed too hungry. By the end of the meal, the world seemed upright again. It was delicious and wholesome and exactly the kind of nourishment I had needed. 'Thank you,' I said, licking my fingers clean.

'My pleasure.'

I cleared the table and turned around to find Shayak staring out the window.

'This Afreen business,' he began. 'You need to stay away.'

So this wasn't just a social call. 'Could I ask why?'

'I wish I knew myself. The commissioner doesn't want us on it. It's that simple. And we have no other reason to step in: there is no client hiring us for the job.'

'I don't understand. How can we solve one case without looking into the other?'

'Stay focused on what you know, rather than what you don't.'

I shrugged. 'I don't think that's part of my psyche.'

'The impatience of youth,' he said with a smile. 'Sometimes I forget how young you really are. Too young, perhaps.' He sat down on the sofa. 'Not every crime committed on Mumbai soil is your sole responsibility.'

'I am so used to being the outsider looking in, making the most of whatever I can grab at, that it is a little hard to compartmentalize.'

'And maybe to take orders.'

'Maybe.'

He nodded. 'By and large, I try not to issue them.'

'What if I told you that Afreen was a call girl?'

'I would have to say that I'm not surprised. And that whatever the facts, I can't change my position. Our alliance with law enforcement is bigger than one case. There are protocols to follow.'

'I find all of this increasingly difficult to understand.'

'I know,' he said with a sigh. He put his head back and closed his eyes. 'This is a lonely business. There are aspects of this I just can't discuss with you, or anyone else.'

'It doesn't sound like you would like to, either.'

'On the contrary. For the first time in many, many years, I feel the price I am paying: having to keep you so far away, despite wanting to do just the opposite.'

Once again, Shayak's lack of artifice sent me spinning. But I tried to stay focused on the words, the moment. 'If you told me what was going on, even without specifics, maybe I could help.'

'Where would I begin?'

'How about with what is really bothering you?'

'Right now?'

'Yes.'

'Not being able to hold you.'

I took a long breath. He wasn't going to make this easy. 'And before you walked through my door?'

'The deep hole I have been digging, to which I can see no bottom.'

'Nothing to do with the Maaya Island murder?'

'No.'

'And you are sure there is nothing I, nor anyone else, can do to help?'

'Not now but in time, maybe. In fact, yes.'

'Why not now?'

'Because you are not ready.'

Shayak the boss was back. I had to remind myself that there were boundaries that should not be breached, but that didn't mean I had to take his word without question.

'How am I not ready?'

'It could be dangerous.'

'Then train me. I already have self-defence skills and I can fire a gun reasonably well, and – '

'You can break into the homes of unsuspecting civilians and escape arrest? Not quite the kind of thing I am talking about here.'

'What is it then? Gang wars and international espionage and political conspiracies deep enough to make Bond blush?'

'Possibly.'

'Possibly which?'

He smiled.

'All of the above?'

'Titanium routinely handles cases that involve the components you just mentioned.'

'And you play all of them close to the chest?'

'Mostly. Got to earn my keep, after all.'

'Ever heard of delegation? Potentially to the newbie in the investigation team?'

'Ever heard the phrase "above your pay grade"?'

'So it comes down to that, does it? On the one hand you complain about being lonely. On the other you aren't willing to share,' I said with a smile.

'There are other things I have to share as well, apart from work.'

'Oh, please. That's such a line. I expected better from you,' I laughed. But I could see he was in earnest. He was bleeding and I was shutting him out.

And yet I had no choice. There was too much to lose, too soon after I had got it.

'I don't do this often. I honestly don't have the time,' said Shayak quietly. 'After a long while, I think I see something worth the effort. I know that at your age, I may have taken these feelings for granted as well. But when you get to where I am, you recognize what is special.'

Special. I shook my head. If it were only so simple.

'Shayak,' I began, my voice shakier than I would have liked it to be, 'I have to prove myself. Not just at Titanium. To myself. To my parents. To everyone who ever told me I couldn't do this.' And then I heard Adlakha's accusations about Shayak using my feelings for him ring in my ears. I knew there was nothing there but malice, but it was a sampler of things to come if I didn't keep my guard up

'I have worked too hard for this, and you've finally given me a chance of getting to where I've always wanted to be. To throw that away would be madness.'

The words came out with a confidence I simply did not feel, and I almost lost my resolve when I saw disappointment staring back at me.

'Fine,' he said, getting up. 'This is the last time I will bring it up. If you ever change your mind, you know where I live. But remember – no door remains open forever.'

I bristled at his words but reminded myself that he was hurt. 'The loss is mine,' I said.

Shayak stepped into the hallway and turned to me. He leaned in and kissed the top of my head.

'Somehow, I doubt that.'

He left me holding the handle of the door, winded and bereft and filled with the certainty that I had just made the worst mistake of my life.

TEN

I awoke feeling shaken on all fronts, fighting for focus, till a call jolted me out of it. It was Madhav Pande. 'I got your message on Facebook. What is this about?' he said abruptly.

'You may have heard about the murder on Kimaaya's island.'

Long pause. 'Yes.'

'I think you can be of help to her.'

'Who are you?'

'I am working on the investigation. My company is employed by Kimaaya.' I kept it vague but banked on the fact that I didn't think that Madhav – no matter how reformed and rehabilitated – would be able to resist such a close connection with the object of his erstwhile affection.

'If I am a suspect, I'd like to say that I was in Pune till yesterday. I can give you names of about twenty-five people you could call to check.'

'I have other questions for you as well. Can you come to our office today?'

'No.'

'Then can I meet you somewhere?'

'If you can make it here in half an hour, I am at Café Kalu.'

As I took directions, I was already pulling on my jeans and trying to tame my mane with a hairbrush. No time to make myself pretty. Half an hour later, when I got to the café, I saw a man tapping away on his tablet, sipping a cup of coffee. He was still very much the man from the courthouse picture, but he had lost the gaunt look and had an air of calm about him.

'Madhav?' I said.

He looked up and nodded. I pulled the chair across from him and sat down.

'How is Kimaaya?' he asked. His concern appeared genuine.

'She is okay,' I replied, reluctant to give this former – perhaps current? – stalker any fodder for fantasy, though apparently I had no compunctions in using his fixation to get information.

'She needs my help?'

'If you know anything about the murder, it might help us solve the case.'

His eyes narrowed. 'How would I know anything about it? You think I am still following her, don't you?'

'I think there is a chance you may know more about her than most, and if your information might help catch a killer, I'd like to know.'

'I haven't got anywhere close to her since my release.'

'Did you know Ashutosh Dhingre?'

'No.'

I had to watch what I said next. I didn't want to mention the paper with the dates found on Dhingre's person to Madhav, but it was still possible that he had known about the marriage and divorce, and he had evidently guessed at her addiction. He could well be the source of the leak.

'Have you ever spoken to anyone about the details of her life?'

'What do you mean?'

'You must know things about her which not many others do.'

'Why would I share our secrets with anyone?' he said with a scowl.

My surprise at his pained words must have shown on my face.

'You don't understand, do you? No one does,' he said.

'I wish you would explain it to me.'

Madhav shook his head. 'I was in love with Kimaaya Kapoor. Head-over-heels, ready-to-give-my-life-for-her, Yash Chopra in love. And in my mind, she loved me back,' he said quietly. 'It might seem unbelievable, but to me it was as real as you sitting in that chair right now. I've been told it's called erotomania.'

I had read about the condition before, in college. It is a psychological disorder characterized by the belief that someone, usually of a higher status and often a celebrity, is in love with you. It is what fuels stalkers the world over, leading them at times to violent crime.

'I stay away from Kimaaya now because I have to. My therapist is helping me through the worst of it, and I am getting better. It might surprise you, but I don't want to feel this way. I want to lead a normal life. To have a job, to find a woman who really loves me. Start a family.'

I felt a sympathy I didn't expect.

'I am moving on, and part of that process has been to accept what I felt in the past and forgive myself for it. But now, as then, I wouldn't do anything to hurt Kimaaya. Not intentionally, not otherwise.'

He had exploded a bomb outside her building – an act I wouldn't consider harmless, even though it hadn't injured anyone. But it was true: Madhav had never caused Kimaaya any physical damage, though fear and intimidation were the consequences of his actions.

'What if it was a question of protecting her?'

'There was a time I might have tried to. But I know that the Kimaaya of my mind is not the true one. The real Kimaaya has done much to cause herself harm. I couldn't protect her, not from herself. And from an outsider – I've grown beyond that, I hope.'

'What about in the past? You may have shared something which may not have been something you'd ordinarily consider harmful,' I said. 'You may have known things that could be valuable to some – and in the wrong hands, dangerous.'

'Of course I knew things about her. I knew about the men she surrounded herself with but I also knew her loneliness, which drove her to seek comfort in ways that were as damaging as my own obsession. But would I tell anyone? No. Part of the whole deal for me was that I had a secret life with Kimaaya. I didn't talk to anyone about her at all. Maybe if I had, someone would have told me I was insane and I would have got help before I ended up in jail.'

His composure was remarkable. It seemed out of sync with the young man I had read about. His therapist must be pretty good.

'Are you including all of this in your screenplay?' I asked.

'My characters are real. The facts are not. Writing about that episode has been cathartic for me. Is it too much to hope that something good comes out of the darkest chapter of my life?'

From a possible liar to a probable one – Afreen's ex-pimp.

Was I in direct violation of a clear directive from Shayak? I told myself that this wasn't necessarily the case. Insofar as Afreen was a witness in the murder of Ashutosh Dhingre, ascertaining her true identity was very much within the purview of solving the Maaya Island murder. What I did with the information I gathered was the key. She could still be the one to have stolen Viraat's watch, in which case she may well be the one who drugged him. Determining that would possibly clear Viraat of murder – a significant step forward.

I had called Vinod to pick me up from the café, and he headed to the address Jay had given me last evening. This was no red-light area: I was at a nondescript office block in a commercial neighbourhood. Outside the building hung a sign pronouncing the presence of Vikram India Impex. What they were imp-ing or ex-ing wasn't clear.

I pushed the door and let myself in. A young woman in salwar-kurta was seated behind a little wooden desk. 'Yes?'

'I am here to meet Bobby Gill.'

'Do you have an appointment?'

'No.'

'Your name?'

'Reema Ray.'

She looked me up and down. Was she appraising my worth as an escort? I wasn't sure what she concluded, but she picked up the phone and told her boss he had a visitor. It seemed like this was as an ask-no-questions sort of establishment. But I would still need an opening gambit.

She ushered me through the wooden door behind her, and there sat Bobby Gill, a big, heavy-set man with unusually pale skin and thick black hair. The air conditioner ran full blast and the room reeked of cigarette smoke.

Another appraising look, of a product that might make it to the market, an assessment of its viability and potential. No tinge of appreciation or otherwise. Either I wasn't Bobby Gill's type or his line of work had left him with no hunger of his own.

'Hi,' I said tentatively. I looked down, hoping to appear demure. Like I might be new to this.

'What can I do for you?' he said, neither warm nor brusque – purely businesslike.

I didn't know how long I'd be able to carry on the charade, but I wanted to get his guard down before I threw Afreen's name into the ring. By now, he might know she was dead, and be keen to disown her.

'I would like to get some work.'

'What sort of work?'

'I think you must understand my meaning.'

'Have you done this before?'

'Once or twice, on my own.'

'Why?'

'I have been trying to get into films, and I need the money. Mumbai is an expensive place to live.'

'Where are you from?'

'Calcutta.'

'Do you know what it involves, doing this full time?'

'Yes, I think so.'

'There are many different sorts of clients.'

'The film industry has prepared me for that, and given me nothing in return.'

It seemed as though this was a story Bobby Gill had heard before. 'Still, this isn't for everyone. You look like an educated girl. You could find other work, I am sure.' He was using his words with care. At once saying what he needed to, without spelling it out.

'I have looked. Entry-level jobs paying 7000-10,000 a month. I couldn't live in a Mumbai slum on that.'

He narrowed his eyes. 'I will invest time and money in you. If you choose to give up in a few weeks, you leave me in the lurch.'

'Is that what you said to Afreen?'

Gill's expression turned stony. 'I don't know who that is.'

'Your website suggests otherwise.'

'Who are you?'

'A friend of Afreen's.'

'From Calcutta?'

Was Afreen from Calcutta, then? I nodded.

'Get out of my office.'

'If you insist, but then I will have to go to the police with what I know. And you wouldn't want me to do that, given that your star call girl is now dead.'

'What do you know?'

Vagueness would be my saviour. 'I work for an investigations firm. We are allied very closely with the police. Your best bet is cooperation with me.'

'How do I know you are telling the truth?'

I gave him my card. 'You can call DCP Ajay Shankaran to verify if you'd like.'

Gill cursed under his breath, and seemed to weigh his options. 'This is just between us for now?'

'For now.'

'Afreen wanted out,' he said at last.

'So you killed her?'

'Why would I do that? This is a commissions game. A dead whore is just as useless as one who doesn't work for me. Plenty of clients requested Afreen for repeats. I was still hoping she'd come back to me. What did I have to gain from her death?'

'You argued.'

'She insisted we take her photos down from the site.'

'Why didn't you?'

'Half the escort sites in the city have pictures of women who have never even worked for them. Models, actresses, you name it. At least Afreen worked for me at some point. Why should I take down her pictures? If you think about it, she was the one who was threatening me!'

'How?'

'She said she had friends who would ensure I paid. She wasn't talking about you, was she?'

'I doubt it. Who else could she have meant?'

'Who knows?'

Prowling through Afreen's life, she seemed, if anything, a little friendless. But I still knew precious little about her.

'Any of her regulars who could have done this?'

He shrugged. 'Not that I know of. But these girls don't exactly share their life histories with me. And she saw clients on her own, too. All the girls do. They think I don't know.'

'Have you heard of a man by the name of Viraat Khanna?'

'No, but many clients use fake names.'

I gave Gill an address.

'Doesn't sound familiar.'

'It doesn't bother you that the girls see other men?'

'Why should it? As long as they are generous with their time when I need it.'

'What other kinds of generosity do you expect?'

'Look, I have better things to do then go about banging whores. I am a family man.'

'So there was no personal animosity between the two of you?'

'Afreen wasn't the only one to have left me. I am not running a brothel here, where women are forced to stay. They all work for me completely voluntarily.'

'Then let me talk to some of the others, maybe someone who knew Afreen?'

'We don't exactly have weekly meetings in our line of work. They are all independent agents.'

He made it sound as though the women had all the power in the world. I knew it to be otherwise. 'There must be someone.'

Gill thought for a minute. 'Afreen worked with me for a couple of years, so it's been a while. But if I remember correctly, there was a woman who had brought her in at the beginning. She left the game herself some time ago, but I think I have her old number. Not sure if it is still valid.'

He pulled out his phone and scribbled. 'Here. Ask her whether I ever mistreated her or any of the girls. But please don't go to the police.'

'I won't – unless I need to. But this is a murder investigation, so don't be surprised if they follow the same leads I did and land up at your doorstep. I have one final question. Do you know Afreen's last name?'

'Nope. And I'm pretty sure I didn't know her first name either.'

When I got back to office, I was summoned by a rather disgruntled-looking Adlakha.

'I have just heard from Shayak's secretary that he is indefinitely detained on some business,' Adlakha said.

'What about our investigation?'

'We follow company policy. Play it by the book. Kimaaya Kapoor is our client. As lead investigator on that,' he said with a sardonic smile, 'you continue as you are. Keep me updated and remember not to meddle in the other murder.'

'What sense does that make when the two cases are connected?'

'What do you mean?'

'We don't even know who Afreen really is. How are we ruling her out as a suspect in the murder of Ashutosh Dhingre?'

He glared me down and I sat there equally determined not to flinch, wondering what I had done to rub him up the wrong way so soon.

'Do we have any evidence that points to her?'

'No, but– '

'I think I said it once already: no buts. If one murder isn't enough for you, or you are unable to handle the case you actually have been given, you could always turn your attention back to the Pratap Puri case.'

I went back to my desk. Almost as soon as I talked myself down from full-on confrontation with Adlakha, I received an e-mail from Shayak fanning the flames of my exasperation.

Reema,

You have full authority to proceed on the Dhingre matter. I hope to be back before long but in case I can't, follow your leads and your instincts. Remember what I said about the other business. Caution is your best bet in this situation.

In the coming days, you may hear things that may surprise you. I trust you will be able to sort out fact from fiction. Be careful whom you rely on. Play it close to the chest and, whatever you do, don't take on Ajay Shankaran. Do not mail me, call me or try to contact me unless it is an emergency. Vinod is at your disposal round the clock.

Best,

S

What the hell was going on? It made no sense. Why would he disappear so suddenly, just when this Kimaaya business was in full swing? No warning, no instructions, except for this strange e-mail. Why didn't he tell me anything over dinner? Be careful whom I trust? Was he referring to the Titanium team as well? I didn't have much of a choice except to rely on the resources I had at hand, and in Shayak's absence, Adlakha was my boss, as he had just made clear. And why couldn't I contact him? What did he expect me to do? It was only my first month on the job, and just last night he was telling me that he would have liked me to have more training!

Amidst all of this, I still didn't have the answer to one long pending question – and one I was fast getting the feeling was critical to this whole business: Who really was Shayak Gupta?

Desperately in need of a friend, I picked up the phone and dialled Rishi's extension.

'Reema here,' I said. 'Wanna get that drink?'

I was pleasantly surprised by Rishi's choice of bar – with beer front and centre, at least fifty kinds from all over the world, in a frill-free, hole-in-the-wall sort of setting just right for my mood. I ordered a Belgian tripel and leaned back.

'You look tired for someone who has just started the job,' said Rishi.

I shook my head and thought of the schedule I had been keeping for the past few days, one that I definitely could not speak about to anyone, particularly after Shayak's most recent advisory. 'Is it always this crazy around here?'

'Ebb and flow. And not everyone works hard.'

'Is slacking off allowed at Titanium?'

'Not encouraged, but thriving nonetheless. Just like everywhere else.'

'What about your schedule?'

'I should probably lie to make myself seem less pathetic, but the truth is that I have the soul of a hacker. I'm always on the job whether I need to be or not.'

'One of those, are you?'

'I try to come up for air sometimes.'

'How long have you been at Titanium?'

'Going on two years now. Started straight out of college, a little guppy.'

'Now you are the shark?'

He grinned. 'Turns out there is a lot of hacking to be done at Titanium.'

Rishi explained what his department did: internal systems and security was a part of it, but they also aided Investigations when the need arose and were the first responders when clients came under cyber attack and wanted systems that were hack-proof, a term he used with much derision.

'Of course, no system is hack-proof. But try explaining that to them.'

'Seriously?'

'Anything can be hacked. It just takes the right hacker.'

'Or does that just mean guys like you aren't doing a good enough job?'

'Whether it is a household safe or a top-secret defence facility, if something is being guarded, someone will try to break in. They'll find a way, even if it takes months or years to do so.'

'You sound as though you approve.'

'I understand the spirit. You can get all righteous and call some hackers ethical and others not, but it really is the same thing at the end of the day.'

'What about electronic surveillance? You guys handle that too at Titanium?' I asked, taking a sip of beer.

'We handle the tech aspects, but the actual footage is Security's baby.'

'And the surveillance on employees? That must not go down well.'

Rishi's eyes narrowed a fraction before he smiled. 'You are staying in one of the company flats, then.'

I nodded.

'I wouldn't worry about that overly. We try to keep it as unobtrusive as possible. I doubt anyone even looks at all the footage. It is more of an insurance policy.'

'Or a veiled threat to anyone gutsy enough to play dirty with Titanium.'

Rishi laughed. 'The machinery that is Titanium takes some getting used to. Lucky for me, I have my own place.'

'How long have you lived here?'

'All my life. I'm an old Mumbai hand. I floated around for a while just after college, spent a little too much time lying about in Goa, but otherwise I rarely feel the need to even leave town.'

A plate of perfect, crisp fries and a bowl of fluffy, buttery popcorn arrived. 'Sorry,' said Rishi, 'but this is about the only food this place has to offer.'

'It's perfect,' I said. 'Would you believe I have never been to Goa?'

'What are you saying, woman!' Rishi said. 'Get your ass over there as soon as you can!'

'It's not overrated?'

'There are many Goas. You can hang about with the tourists, and that experience I would agree is overrated, or you can create your own version of it.'

'And what is yours?'

'Hiking through the hills. Getting lost on winding roads. Drinking too much beer at Sunset Bar in a little spot of the undiscovered south, with a view of the sun going down over the Arabian Sea 365 days a year.'

'Sounds like love. Why did you come back?'

'I needed to.'

'Work?'

'Yup. And I love Mumbai too.'

Rishi started telling me about all his favourite bars in town. 'The great thing about this city is that it has something for you even if you hate all those shiny new clubs.'

'I don't remember telling you that I am new to Mumbai.'

Rishi laughed again. 'Oh, please. You've got noob written all over you.'

He was the second man to have told me that. But unlike Pratap Puri, I got the feeling that Rishi was just trying to extend a warm Mumbai welcome to me.

'Mumbai is always full of fresh blood,' he said. 'It's one of its many virtues for the vampires waiting for a nibble.'

The next morning, I showered and headed to a neighbourhood café for a big breakfast and coffee before striding towards office with a confidence I didn't feel. But I had renewed my resolve to fake it till I could make it.

The good thing about cryptic messages from absent bosses is that they were open to interpretation. Shayak told me I had a free hand in the Dhingre business, and for me that meant investigating Afreen's murder as well. How could I look into one without considering the very real possibility that the two events were connected? And if they were, how much less efficient would it be to examine only half the evidence when the real clues would most likely lie in the intersection between two victims, and the crimes that had claimed each?

To that end, first I spoke to Mrs Dhingre, who said she had no idea if her husband knew a woman by the name of Afreen. I looked through his address book and the file, and found no mention of her anywhere. Afreen herself had denied knowing Dhingre, but I was treating everything she had said with a healthy amount of scepticism.

How could I find out more about the mysterious, tragically short life of Afreen when I didn't even know her last name!

I finally decided to make use of the number Gill had given me for the very unoriginally named Mona, who had allegedly left the escort business after introducing Afreen to it. I made the call.

'Am I speaking to Mona?' I said.

'Uh, yes,' the woman replied somewhat tentatively.

'My name is Reema, and I am a friend of Afreen.'

'Okay,' she said, still wary. I could hear a soft hiss as if she took a drag of a cigarette.

'I'd like to come and meet you today, if that is alright with you.'

'May I know what this is about?'

'It's about Afreen. It's important.'

'Why don't you come to the bar and we can have a chat? Look for Miss Sara. No one calls me Mona anymore.'

My appointment led me to a part of town into which I had not yet ventured. Travelling through the maze of serpentine bylanes, I knew I had entered territory in which anything could happen. I doubted if even the long arm of Titanium could offer me much protection here, in the bowels of Mumbai. Vinod dropped me off with a warning: 'Be careful, ma'am. Call if you need help. I'll be standing outside only.' I told him it wasn't necessary, but didn't think it would make a difference.

I walked down a narrow alley, unaccustomed to but unsurprised by the stares. I kept my eyes down, which served the dual purpose of avoiding potential lewd gestures and of ensuring garbage, spit, excrement and other bodily fluids I'd rather not consider stayed off my shoes. A rat led the way to The Heaven Bar, before it scurried through the narrow passage beside the yellow wall that signalled the start of the establishment. I swung the door open, overwhelmed at once by the tobacco-scented cloud that wafted towards me, almost immediately clinging to my hair, reminding me of nights when brandishing a cigarette was still allowed and still reeked of the romance of new adulthood, or old childhood. Now the wall of smoke hanging in the black air, thick and misty, made me flinch. I heard the crooner's voice wrap itself around a familiar song. My eyes found the person it belonged to, her young face aged by hair a shade too light and lipstick a shade too dark, dressed in tight turquoise jeans and yellow shirt. A chunky gold necklace separated pointy breasts desperate for a lingerie upgrade.

I waited for her to finish. Luckily the place was not yet full. I found a small table in one of the dark corners the bar specialized in and tried to look around without making eye contact with other guests.

'Miss Sara', a board behind the small wooden stage announced.

Mona's new name. Her new job was singing at this bar, and I wondered whether it was much better than working as an escort.

She finished her song and came straight over to my table. There must not be many single women coming to a place like this, and she didn't have to ask if I was Reema.

'Can I get you something?' I asked.

She shook her head, and lit a cigarette. 'You said this was about Afreen? Is she in some kind of trouble?'

'Afreen was murdered.'

Miss Sara gagged on the smoke that had filled her lungs, her bout of violent coughing drawing curious stares from the patrons.

'When was the last time you spoke to her?' I asked.

'God, I don't know. It's been a while. Why? What the hell happened to her?'

'That is what we're trying to find out. We've learnt that she wanted to quit the escort business. Might that be dangerous?'

Miss Sara shrugged. 'Gill didn't try to stop me when I left. Said women like me come and go. But Afreen was more of a draw.'

'Why did you leave?'

She flipped her hair, nonchalant and yet not. 'I met a guy. We were supposed to get married. Turned out he was already married to at least two other women.'

'You didn't want to go back to Gill after you found out?'

'I thought about it. But then I met another guy who said he'd get me playback jobs in Bollywood. I'm a singer – it's what I always wanted to do. Turned out this was all he could get me. But with tips I make enough money here, and I get to sing and don't have to spread my legs if I don't want to. So it's not so bad.'

I could imagine Miss Sara would have been in a different price range than Afreen in the escort industry. She wouldn't be buying herself the designer labels I had found in Afreen's flat even when she was at the top of her game.

'I could have gone back to Gill. He's not a bad sort, you know? But I'm twenty-eight; how long did I have in that line anyway? At least here I am doing something where there is some sort of future.'

'Do you know why Afreen wanted to quit?'

'She met this guy who was going to help her get a role in the movies.' All of Miss Sara's stories seemed to share a theme.

'She did get some roles recently, didn't she?'

'Yeah.'

'He was one of her clients?'

'Yes, but not through Gill, I don't think.'

'Do you have a name?'

'Nope. But I remember her saying something about him being from out of town.'

'Do you know where?'

She squinted. 'No, sorry.'

'How was he connected to films?'

She shrugged, taking a long drag before stubbing out her cigarette gingerly in the cheap plastic ashtray that was a freebie from a whisky company I had never heard of. 'Really have no idea.'

'How did the two of you get involved in the business in the first place?'

'I came to Mumbai to be a singer. Afreen was here to be an actress. But dreams don't always come true, if you hadn't noticed,' she said, lighting up another.

'Not even in Mumbai?'

'Especially not in Mumbai.'

'How did it happen?'

'Oh, it's no effort at all,' she said with a snort. 'There are plenty of people willing to broker and buy sex. Why not take advantage of it?'

'What about your family?'

She smiled. 'Don't go looking for a tale of abuse and neglect in my past. Was my childhood perfect? No, but whose is? I was sick of watching interesting lives lived by others. I wanted to be one of them. I had my chance, and I took it.'

Miss Sara must have seen something in my face that she interpreted as disapproval. 'You can't believe that someone would willingly sell themselves for sex? Not when they have options? Trust me when I say that I was not waiting to be saved. It was just my best bet at the time.'

'But you got out. Even if that meant you had to trade down.'

'My time had come. Maybe Afreen's had too. Maybe it is just that simple.'

'Do you know Afreen's real name?'

'Kavita Ghosh.'

'Bengali?'

She nodded, blowing a puff of smoke out from between her teeth. 'From Calcutta. When I met her, she had just run away from home. There was a police case about it too. She wanted to change her name, change everything. She was a huge Nusrat Fateh Ali Khan fan in those days, so she went with Afreen. Said it reminded her of her first boyfriend, the only man who ever really loved her.'

Miss Sara stood up as she stubbed out her half-smoked cigarette, signalling the end of our interview, and returned to her place in the flickering spotlight.

ELEVEN

I didn't think the motley, bedraggled Calcutta Crime-fighter's Club could help me in faraway Mumbai. The voluntary ranks of the assorted individuals who had come together to fight crime, which I had desperately clung to when infidelity cases threatened to overload my own practice, was an unlikely support system for one now claiming allegiance to the mighty Titanium. But with the ban on my investigating Afreen's death, I couldn't approach Adlakha or anyone else to find out more about the life and times of Kavita Ghosh, whom we knew as Afreen.

So I picked up the phone and called Terrence.

'How have you been?' I asked, hoping he'd ignore the fact that I had not returned his call for days.

'Case is going well, and Mumbai is never boring.'

'No, it's not.'

'What about you? Your murder seems to be getting even more airtime than before.'

'Tell me about it.'

'Any progress?'

'Some. It's early yet.'

'Want to get dinner?'

'I actually needed some help.'

'What about?'

'There is a woman connected with the murder who is from Calcutta. I am trying to find out more about her antecedents and it turns out that she had run away from home to come to Mumbai and a police case had been registered at the time.'

There was a pause on the line. 'Can you tell me why Titanium can't get this information for you?'

'To be honest, I can't.'

'Okay,' he said slowly. 'Do you know which police station?'

'Unfortunately, no.'

'No matter. It will just take a little more time.'

I gave him the name and whatever details I had, which didn't amount to much.

'You aren't making this easy,' sighed Terrence.

'Is it ever?'

'No,' he said with a laugh. 'But this really feels a little like old times, with you chasing impossible cases. The group sort of fell apart after you left, you know.'

I did know, as I had been in touch with Santosh da, my kindly mentor in the CCC. 'Why is that?'

'Maybe we needed your enthusiasm to hold us together.'

'I doubt that.'

'Yeah? Well, all I know is that we haven't even met since you deserted us.'

'I guess I should be flattered.'

'Yup. I'll call you when I know something.'

Maybe I had misjudged Terrence. He had come across as so full of himself, so desperate to get laid that I hadn't looked past it to the sort-of-decent fellow he really was.

I hung up and considered my options. There was one person in the Afreen case whom I could interview without fear of blowback, for he was part of the Maaya Island case as well: Viraat Khanna.

I called Ajay. 'I have a few questions for Viraat regarding the Dhingre murder. Is there any way he can be made accessible to me?'

'I don't see why not. Come by.'

When I got to the police station, I was shown at once into Ajay's room. He sat behind a large wooden desk piled with papers, at the centre of which sat a high-end laptop. There were three cell phones, a wireless router and a modem blinking away.

'I believe your boss is currently out of circulation,' he said.

'So I have been told.'

'Adlakha told me you are the point person on the Maaya Island case.'

'Yes.'

'About the Afreen murder, you do understand that the call wasn't mine to keep Titanium out. My interest is in closing cases, not pointless politics.'

Politics? Ajay tapped on the mouse and it didn't seem like he was going to elucidate. He clearly thought I knew more than I did.

'There is, however, one fact that I think has bearing on the Maaya Island murder and, since you want to see Khanna, I thought you might as well know so we don't end up wasting more time.'

'I appreciate it, sir.'

'Drop the "sir". Ajay.' He looked at me, and I saw a flash of what looked like shyness. Coming from this textbook-filmi police officer, Aviators and all, it was unexpected.

'Viraat did not kill Afreen. We know this because the security-camera footage from his building clearly shows him leaving an hour before she arrived, and returning only after you came in.'

'Where was he?'

'That's the strange part – he won't tell us.'

'No alibi?'

'No, he's clammed up completely.'

'Whatever he was doing was worse than murder?'

'So he seems to think.'

'Is there any way he could have come and gone from the building without being detected?'

'There is a service entrance and lift, but that is also monitored. Unless he ran up twenty-six flights – there are no cameras in the stairwell.'

'Anyone else look good for it?'

'Not at present. My men are going through the footage again.'

I nodded.

'Maybe you can talk some sense into him?' Ajay said. 'Get him to tell us where he was?'

I wasn't sure why he thought I would succeed where he and his men had failed, but I was more than happy to give it a shot.

Ajay called one of his lackeys, who led me to a room bare except for a table and a chair. It was without windows and suspiciously clean. If this was one of the interrogation rooms, it was probably best that I didn't know what most people passing through were subjected to.

Viraat was brought in – haggard, unshaven and trembling. On his heels was his lawyer. Even a rank outsider like me recognized him instantly – it was Satish Joseph, one of the most high-profile criminal attorneys in the country. That explained why Ajay and his men had not made progress on Viraat – with Joseph standing guard, they wouldn't get him to slip up, nor could they lay a hand on him. They must be hoping that I'd fly under the radar and take them by surprise.

Viraat had lost all of the cockiness of our first couple of meetings. The confusion and catatonia were replaced by wear and worry – and withdrawal.

'Thank you for seeing me,' I said.

He looked at me, a little lost.

'I believe you won't tell the police where you were at the time of Afreen's murder.'

'In what capacity are you asking questions about that?' asked the lawyer. 'I was given to understand you are only looking into the murder of Ashutosh Dhingre.'

'If you need any clarifications, you can take it up with DCP Shankaran.'

He began to say something, but Viraat stepped in. 'It's okay, Satish.'

'Thank you,' I said. 'So why don't you tell me what's really going on?'

Viraat ran a hand over his stubble. 'It's complicated.'

'Viraat,' warned Joseph.

'Drugs?' I asked.

His dead eyes didn't react, but the trembling hand had already confirmed what I suspected.

'You were out buying, weren't you?'

'Mr Khanna did not say that,' said Joseph.

'Fine,' I said. 'Hypothetically, if that is what he was doing, is it worse than murder? I wouldn't imagine drug charges would be hard to get out of.'

'There is no evidence yet to implicate me – anything could still happen,' said Viraat.

'So you are playing a waiting game in this police station?' It didn't make sense. Viraat seemed like he wouldn't last another day in lock-up while if history was anything to go by, he could be out on bail with a little cooperation in the right quarters. 'You have to help me understand this.'

I watched a drop of sweat roll down Viraat's face and land on the table. 'Off the record?' he said at last.

'There is no need ...' began Joseph.

'Off the record,' I agreed, cutting the lawyer off.

'If that is what I was doing – and I'm not saying I was – my father would disown me. Without a rupee.'

'So if you can get out of this without admitting where you were, there will be no harm done? Don't you think that's a rather big gamble to take?'

'If I don't, I'll have nothing to gamble with for the rest of my life!'

'Ms Ray,' said Joseph, icy now. 'There are three guards and CCTV footage which confirm that my client was out of the building at the time Afreen came in, and was away till after you entered the flat. Where he actually was, quite frankly, is irrelevant. I see no reason why we should even be held here for a moment longer, do you?'

'What I feel makes little difference to the police, I'm afraid. Particularly since your client was found just a few feet away from the victim on Maaya Island.' I turned back to Viraat. 'About that case at least, is there something you want to tell me – on the record?'

'Look, I really can't help you there,' he said, 'I was just in the wrong place at the wrong time.'

'If there is anyone who can confirm that, it will end all of this. There is no footage to clear you.'

'Someone on the island said he could fix me up with something. I was a little … short.'

So it was drugs once again. 'Who? I need a name.'

'I can't.'

'Why? I am not the police. How I choose to deal with the information is up to me. Your father need not know.'

'If Kimaaya finds out– '

'Kimaaya cannot throw you – or anyone else – in jail.'

Viraat sighed.

Joseph took advantage of the weakness. 'You are under no obligation to cooperate with this woman. And there is no reason to trust her.'

Viraat shot him a stony look before turning to me. He didn't like being told what to do, and it was about to work in my favour. 'It was Raj.'

'The fitness instructor?'

'Yeah. He trains me sometimes when he is in the city.'

'He keeps drugs on the island?'

'Yeah, Kimaaya would freak out if she gets to know. She's absolutely hardcore about her no-drugs policy. Before she invites people, she makes it clear that they aren't to carry anything stronger than alcohol and antacids.'

'He keeps his stash buried in the pit next to where we found you,' I said. Forensics had confirmed my theory that the shard of wood I found was from a box. It must have been Raj's pill receptacle.

Viraat nodded. 'I went to the yacht to get the Scotch and look for my pills. When I couldn't find them, I called Raj.'

'The police told you there was flunitrazepam in your system.'

'Yeah, I guess that's what made me pass out.'

I waited for the penny to drop, but it seemed it would be a while.

'That's not what Raj said he was giving you, was it?' I asked.

'No, he was supposed to give me some E.'

'And then he roofied you.'

I saw the realization creep into his eyes. He jumped up and pounded his fist on the table.

'That bastard stole my watch!'

'I believe he did. Did you have the wine bottle with you when you went out to meet him?'

'I did,' he said ruefully. 'There was a little left from when we decanted, and I remember grabbing it from the poolside bar. I waited in the gazebo for Raj, and I think I left it there.'

I pictured a wasted Viraat taking a slug from that bottle, worth crores, which wine lovers around the world would kill for a little taste of. Poor Ashutosh Dhingre wasn't the only casualty that night.

I called the guards at Maaya and told them to immediately search Raj's room, and then went back to meet Ajay. 'Good news and bad,' I said.

'Good news first.'

'Viraat has finally revealed how he ended up under the hedge on Maaya Island.'

'Has he?

'He met the fitness instructor Raj Rathore, who promised to give him a little something of a pharmaceutical nature. Instead of whatever it is that was promised, Raj slipped him a roofie. My guess is that Raj heard Viraat boasting about the value of the watch he was wearing when he slipped down to the party briefly, and decided to make the most of it.'

'Are you testing your theory?'

'I have asked the guards to search Rathore's belongings.' But I already knew what I needed to – I remembered the well-kempt Raj's ragged, dirty nails the day we questioned him. He had dug up that box in the garden not hours before.

Ajay nodded. 'Though he was our best suspect, Viraat never looked good for Dhingre's murder to me. Now the bad news, please.'

'He is not willing to go on record with where he was at the time of Afreen's death.'

'Why the hell not?'

'Apparently the truth will compromise him in his father's financial graces, and he is willing to wait on the evidence to prove he didn't do it.'

'Then he isn't as stupid as he looks. In truth, apart from the fact that it was Viraat's flat she was murdered in, there is no evidence pointing to him. Any ideas?'

'I think he was out scoring drugs.'

Ajay frowned. 'He's willing to risk a murder charge for this? I'm not interested in a drug bust here.'

'I tried telling him that, but he's more afraid of his father and being disinherited than he is of you and a jail term.'

'I will never understand these people with all the money in the world and no sense at all.'

'Is any of this of much use without the name of a dealer to corroborate the alibi?'

'At least it tells us we need to look elsewhere for now.'

'What about Raj Rathore?'

'If you find the watch on him, we'll bring him in.'

'Would you be looking at him for murder?

'Dhingre could have stumbled upon him while he was stealing the watch. You aren't convinced?' he asked.

'If he had done it, why stick around on the island? Why not take the watch, sell it and disappear? It doesn't make sense.'

Ajay's eyes betrayed little as he assessed me. 'This is your first case for Titanium?'

I nodded.

'Shayak has so much faith in you that he gives you one of the most high-profile cases of the year.'

I felt my hackles rise but held my tongue.

'I can see why,' he said. Ajay looked even more uncomfortable after issuing the compliment than I was having received it.

'Would you like to get dinner sometime?' he asked abruptly.

In shock, I glanced a little too quickly at his hands, which were fiddling with a pen on his desk. He didn't miss it.

'I'm not married,' he said, a small smile softening his unapologetically brusque manner. 'Or otherwise accounted for.'

I told myself to proceed with caution – this was dangerous ground. 'I do not date people I work with.'

'You don't work with me. We just happen to both be working the same case at the moment.'

'Still.'

'Let's not call it a date. Just a meal between unattached associates. I won't hold it against you if you don't want to repeat the experience.'

I said nothing. And then my phone rang. It was the guard at Maaya. 'Madam, we have found a watch in Raj Rathore's room. It was found inside a cavity in the mattress.'

I moved the phone away from my ear. 'They found the watch,' I said to Ajay. 'Anything else?' I asked the guard.

'No, ma'am.'

'I'll have a team over in an hour; ask them to keep him in a secure location till then, guarded at all times,' said Ajay.

I hung up. 'He must have tossed whatever drugs he had into the ocean, or disposed of them by some other means.'

'So how about tomorrow?' continued Ajay, as though we had not been interrupted. 'Maybe around 9 pm? I'll call to confirm tomorrow – I'm sure your schedule is as crazy as mine.'

'Okay,' I said.

I left, having cleared one man on murder and arranged to bring in another suspect, but all shaken up at the possibility of a date. It was time for a distress call to Sohana.

'I need advice,' I said, telling her my problem on my way back to office.

'So many men, so little Reema for them to share.' She laughed.

'Please, Sohana, I'm drowning here!'

'God, you're such a mess. This won't happen over the phone. Give me a call when you're done with work. I'll come over.'

I kept tabs on Rathore's progress till he was in police custody and no longer my headache, and then I called Kimaaya. 'You have heard about Raj Rathore?' I asked.

'Yes, and I am shocked. But I am so happy we can give Viraat his watch back. He's going through so much as it is.'

'You know Raj had drugs on him, at the island?'

'What!'

'Yes. He drugged Viraat.'

Kimaaya let out a sigh. 'Why is it so difficult to find clean people in this town? I even had random drug tests for all staff worked into the contract.'

'He did his best to keep it quiet. He had his stash buried. I'm sure you also heard about Afreen's death,' I said.

'Yes.'

'Do you know anything about the recent films she's been working on?'

'Why don't you speak to Nimisha about this? She'll have a better idea than me,' she said.

I did as Kimaaya suggested, calling Kimaaya's assistant. 'Such a shame,' she clucked. I could hear the TV blaring in the background. She didn't bother to turn down the volume.

'Do you know anything about her career in films? Kimaaya said you might.'

'Sorry to sound so cold, but "career" might be a bit of an overstatement.'

'She had landed a couple of roles of late, or so she told me.'

'A piece of eye candy in a B-grade action film and a lead in a campus love story produced by MTM.'

Manmohan T. Mahindra, with a long Bollywood pedigree but little box-office success in the past decade. Rumoured to be broke, he was suddenly bankrolled for a back-to-college film by an investor, starring forty-something star Adil Khan.

'How did she get the MTM film? Isn't that a big project?'

'Yes, and many known stars were vying for it.'

'Including Kimaaya?'

'No, no. All of these young things.'

'Why Afreen, then?'

'I heard MTM wanted a fresh face.'

'You sound sceptical.'

'If you'd been in the business as long as I have, you'd be sceptical too.'

'I'm sorry Nimisha, but I really need you to be clear about what you mean.'

'What do you think I mean? It could be any number of things – she slept with the producer, she slept with the director, she slept with the actor, take your pick. One or all are possibilities.'

That was way more honesty than I had bargained for. 'Can you get me an interview with any of these people?'

'Sorry, Reema. Kimaaya's never worked with that team. I really don't have any connection with them.'

How much did I doubt that? And yet I had no choice but to accept it, given that Afreen's case was forbidden fruit. I couldn't risk being pushier, and having either Kimaaya or Nimisha raise a red flag.

I made a quick stop at the supermarket after work. It was finally time to debut the new oven. Once home, I stocked the fridge and cupboards, and had just started my prep when the phone rang. Terrence.

'Tell me,' I said.

'Pretty straightforward. Kavita Ghosh, Baguihati. Took part in and won a small-time local beauty pageant two years ago. After that she began to chase the Bollywood dream. Got in touch with some sketchy agent who promised her a shot at stardom. Her parents tried to stop her from leaving town but failed. When she disappeared, they attempted to make a stink in the media with it. There was a bit of a splash in one of the smaller Bengali dailies, but they couldn't make the fraud charges stick.'

'Any information about this agent?'

'I'll send you the details but from what it looks like, it is a fairly standard talent search agency.'

I hung up and mulled over what I had just heard. There was nothing, for the moment, which helped.

So, for now, I would cook. I had started setting things out when Sohana arrived with a bottle of wine and made herself at home. 'What's on the menu?' she asked.

'Quiche Lorraine with rocket, pear and walnut salad.'

'Yum! This is why I needed you here in Mumbai. Want some help?'

'Not really. I hope you aren't on one of your diets.'

The smell of bacon in the skillet was filling the room. Sohana took in a lungful. 'I'd come out of a Master Cleanse for a taste of that.'

I set the bacon aside and handed Sohana the cheese to grate. I then started on the pastry.

'Before we get to the business for the night,' I said, 'I have a favour to ask.'

'Shoot.'

'Would you by any chance know Manmohan T. Mahindra?'

'The producer? No. You know me – I cover all the non-glam stuff. Politics. Crime.'

'Do you know anything about him?'

'All hearsay, so you might want to take it with a pinch of salt.'

I followed nothing of Bollywood gossip, so anything she could tell me was helpful.

'MTM was part of the old-school Bollywood crowd of gangs and money laundering. A few years ago, he had to flee to Dubai to avoid the wrath of some funders. He came back recently and has been trying to relaunch himself.'

'So why was this project so sought after?'

'Because MTM is connected, has had a lot of success in the past and no one really holds these things against you in this town, in this business.'

'Any clue who his mystery backers are?'

'Can't help you there.'

Sohana opened the bottle and hunted through my scanty cupboards and discovered a couple of wine glasses. Meanwhile, I covered my pastry-lined pie plate with foil and poured in some kidney beans before slipping it into the oven to bake. Sohana was appalled. 'Your quiche better not involve rajma.'

'Improvised pie weights. It's to make sure the pastry doesn't puff up.'

She heaved a sigh of relief. 'I should know better than to doubt you when it comes to cooking. With the men, my faith is not as intact.'

'Okay, so I am bad with guys. I am finally going to admit it, so you can stop rubbing it in and help me. There is this man – he's in the police, and is sort of working on the same case as me. He's asked me out.'

'Who is it?'

Though Sohana didn't know much about Bollywood, police matters were very much her domain. 'Ajay Shankaran.'

She raised her eyebrows. 'Not bad!'

'He's not sleazy, is he?'

'Not as far as I can tell. But I don't know him personally. He is doing well for himself in the force and is known to be clean. Not to mention a bit of a hottie.'

'Hmm.'

'But I need details.'

I satisfied Sohana's curiosity as I beat the eggs and cream, grated a little nutmeg and seasoned the custard base.

'So what's the problem?' she asked.

'We are working together.'

'I seem to recall you using that same argument to keep your dishy boss at arm's length.'

'Same logic applies.'

'Not really. If we were all to swear off every person with any connection to our jobs, how are working women to meet anyone?'

'He's a cop. He's got all the power.'

'If he is the kind of guy to misuse it, you should stop seeing him. But to assume he will be some sort of twisted thug seems rather harsh.'

I laughed. 'Back up a bit. I never said he'd act like a thug. Just that power is power. No point in being naïve about it.'

'And which relationship isn't about power play in some form?'

I stopped what I was doing and looked at her.

'Which is why I don't understand why you are shunning Shayak Gupta,' she shrugged.

'I didn't. Not to begin with,' I said. 'Well, first I thought he was a murderer and then, when I realized he wasn't, we had a moment. A brief one, a yummy one, before he offered me a job.'

'Your life is never boring, is it?'

'You'd be surprised.'

'And you are sure that is a road you don't want to go down?'

I thought about Shayak's insatiable need to charm everyone, and was grateful he would never meet Sohana.

'You are smiling, Reema.'

'Am not!'

'And now you are blushing.'

'Lies. Too dark to blush.'

'The word is dusky, sweets. You may be bronze enough to hide your blushes, but that doesn't mean you don't do it, and I have known you long enough to see past the tan. What happened, Reema?'

'One kiss on his yacht.'

'He has a yacht? Are you insane? What are you waiting for?'

'I get seasick.'

'I feel like sticking your head in the oven with that blasted rajma pie!'

'It is way too complicated!'

'Fine, I get it. Shayak is out of bounds,' an exasperated Sohana conceded. 'But no matter how you want to spin it, Ajay is not.'

I retrieved the piecrust from the oven and discarded the rajma, to Sohana's relief. 'Okay. One trial dinner,' I said, layering in the bacon, sautéed leeks and cheese, topping it with the egg mixture, and putting it back in.

'See? Does it feel so horrible to give yourself a chance?'

I ignored the question as I closed the oven door on the quiche and turned my attention to the salad. I still wasn't convinced about any of it.

The next morning, I fell out of bed with a thud. My eyes flew open to see Sohana looming over me. 'Hey, what the hell!'

'You are the most tight-lipped bitch I've ever known!' she screamed.

'What on earth are you talking about?'

Sohana thrust the newspaper under my nose.

'STAR'S SECRET MARRIAGE REVEALED!' it screamed. Kimaaya's picture from a recent society event was splashed across it in four columns.

'We talk till, like, three in the morning, and you don't mention that your hot boss who has the hots for you was married to this woman?'

I could have denied knowing, but there was no point. I swept the hair out of my eyes and read the short piece on the front page.

Kimaaya Kapoor's secret marriage and divorce – worthy of the raciest Bollywood potboiler – has been revealed.

Kapoor, it has been learnt, was married as a young woman to the shadowy and reclusive Shayak Gupta, a former military officer. Why the marriage was kept such a tightly guarded secret for all these years is not known, but with the spotlight on Kapoor for the recent murder of her former assistant on her private island, the relationship – which was dissolved before Kimaaya began to work with the slain Ashutosh Dhingre – is bound to come under the scanner, especially since Gupta is still a business associate whose company Titanium is in charge of Kimaaya's security.

A pointer directed readers to the entertainment supplement, where the story was continued in purple-and-yellow detail. I threw the newspaper down on the kitchen counter as I set about making coffee, slamming the cups down with more force than necessary.

'You know I couldn't tell you this. It concerns an ongoing investigation,' I said, partly because it was easier to address Sohana's mock betrayal than consider the implications of the revelations.

'I get that part. But is this why you won't have anything to do with Shayak?'

'No, Sohana. What difference does it make whom he was married to? I have known from the beginning that he was divorced.'

'That the ex was once the heartthrob of a billion people is not relevant to you?'

'Not really,' I said, not completely honestly. 'Except that it is about to seriously screw up this investigation.' I picked up the entertainment supplement.

KIMAAYA KAPOOR WED AND DIVORCED BEFORE HER FIRST HIT

Kimaaya Kapoor, who broke into Bollywood in the late 1990s with hits such as 'Maaya Mumbai', 'Love in Hong Kong', 'Hello Goodbye' and 'Hero 420' had been married at the time of her debut and soon divorced, a fact that she has managed to keep from her fans and the industry for fifteen years.

Why the secrecy? Industry insiders, not wishing to be named, feel that it is most likely because her chances at success would be much higher if single. Link-ups with co-stars are now part and parcel of promotion of films and, as the fate of recent heroines proves, fans prefer their female stars to be unwed, as it makes them more believable in a romance.

She was married on 26 February 1997 and divorced on 13 July 1999, a few months after she was romantically linked to Suresh Sharma, with whom she had two films in the pipeline. Whether the relationship was the cause for the breakdown of the marriage is not known. 'I had no idea, just like the rest of India, that Kimaaya was married at the time I met her. I feel cheated and betrayed, and grateful that our relationship ended,' said Sharma, who has not been seen in a film since the box-office disaster 'Bhookamp!' in 2008. He and Kimaaya broke up under a cloud of suspicion that he was stopping her from taking plum roles with Abhijeet Bhagat, whom she was later rumoured to be in a short-lived, tumultuous relationship with.

Despite numerous attempts to contact her, Kimaaya Kapoor was not available for comment.

Now all that remain are questions: Did Ashutosh Dhingre know about the marriage, and could it have anything to do with his death? Is this marriage why Kimaaya has chosen to stay single after all these years? And, finally, who is Shayak Gupta?

But that wasn't all. Taking off from where the previous piece left off was another story, accompanied by a picture of Shayak, face shielded by a cap, getting off his yacht and onto Maaya Island.

Next to it was the blurb: 'Who is Shayak Gupta?'

This shadowy figure is someone whom everyone knows, and yet no one knows. Titanium Securities is India's largest private security agency by some distance. As a privately held company, financial data is hard to come by. It provides security solutions to companies and individuals, including many of India's leading cricketers and Bollywood stars and corporates. But it seems an equally popular choice with politicians and for high-profile public events, such as diplomatic visits, large concerts and shows. It is the go-to firm for cyber security. Despite all this, so little is known about the man at the top that his marriage to one of India's leading stars was, till this morning, a secret.

There are whispers of him being ex-military, of a continuing cozy association with the armed forces and politicians. It is not known how he has become trusted by every source of power; his parentage is an absolute mystery, as is any family he may have acquired since the end of his marriage over a decade ago.

The article was remarkable for how very little it actually said. And luckily the picture was not a good one. But I knew that wherever Shayak was, he was livid.

I looked at Sohana. 'This is bad. Very bad.'

Sohana nodded. 'Not sure why it is such a secret in the first place, but this is guaranteed to be in the news forever. They aren't going to let it go.'

I looked at the byline: Prashant Parashar. It was the same on the other two stories as well. 'I need to speak to this journalist.' Whoever gave him this information might have made contact with the killer. He might even *be* the killer.

'Let me make a few calls,' said Sohana, getting on the phone.

I turned on the TV. All the news channels were covering the story. But none of them had any additional information, and several were citing the newspaper article as the source.

'Here's his number,' said Sohana in fifteen minutes, scribbling it on a piece of paper. I tried calling immediately but had no luck. I continued dialling as I got ready for work and headed in to office. Finally, after about the tenth attempt, he answered.

'Yes,' came the voice, short and curt.

'My name is Reema Ray, I am with Titanium Securities.'

There was a pause, and I thought I had lost him. 'Hello?'

'Yes. I have been trying to get in touch with you guys for three days.'

I was confused till I realized he must have been trying to contact Shayak's office for the story. 'You wouldn't have been trying to get in touch with me. I am investigating the death of Ashutosh Dhingre, and believe you may have relevant information.'

Another long pause. 'How have you come to that conclusion?' he said at last.

'I really do believe this conversation should occur face to face.'

'I have an obligation to protect my sources.'

'Mr Parashar, this is a murder investigation, and I am sure you can appreciate its gravity.'

'I will not tell you my sources.'

I fell back on the old line that had been serving me so well. 'Would you like me to involve the police? We are working with them and it would not be a problem bringing you in for questioning. I am, for now, offering you a far more … civilized alternative.'

'Let me speak to my editor and get back to you.'

In five minutes Parashar sent me a text, summoning me to his office at 4 pm. I was in.

I found myself alone at office. I tried my best to order my thoughts, but was struggling. Two murders, Shayak disappearing, Kimaaya's secrets all over the news – we had been engulfed in chaos.

I got a call on my cell from an unknown number; it looked to be an international one. I answered. 'Hello?'

'I'll make this short.' It was Shayak.

'Where are you?' I asked.

'We need this journalist to talk.'

'Already on it,' I said, telling him about the appointment later that day.

'Good. Chances are you will also meet the editor, Shakuntala Padhy. She knows me. Keep your chat off the record. Be careful how much you say – she is great at getting information out of people. About Kimaaya – she assures me she did not speak to any journalists about this business.'

'Okay. Can I contact you?'

'I will touch base with you somehow, as soon as I can. As of now, you are the only one from Titanium working on the Maaya Island murder.'

'I can't do this alone!'

'Why not? I have already seen you solve a murder on your own with a damn sight less than what you have now. Use whatever resources you need. It'll be taken care of. Vinod is yours. For logistics, there is Archana. No one else.'

'Where are you?' I asked again.

'Away,' he said. I was surprised by how distant he sounded. And then he sighed. 'I might need … help, Reema. Soon. Just remember: don't always believe what you hear.'

He hung up and I stared at the phone in exasperation.

I sat in the very intimidating boardroom of the largest English paper in Mumbai. For about ten minutes I was alone, probably by design.

At last two people walked in: a man in a suit, definitely not a journalist and very possibly a lawyer or a particularly uptight management-type, and a pint-sized woman draped in an elegant sari and a string of pearls who wore her power lightly but never for a moment let you forget it – without a doubt, Shakuntala Padhy.

She took a seat, followed by the man. Shakuntala was in no mood to waste time. 'How can we help you?' she asked.

'I wanted to speak to Mr Parashar, as he may have information relevant to our murder investigation.'

'You will have to be more explicit than that,' she said.

'While we are not yet sure Dhingre's death has anything to do with Kimaaya, we cannot ignore the possibility that it might. In light of that, what Mr Parashar revealed in the paper this morning could have a significant bearing on events.'

'You think news of Kimaaya's secret marriage has something to do with this murder?' asked Padhy. Her face gave little away.

'We can't rule out the possibility. How did he come by this information?'

'That, I am sure you know, is confidential.'

I would have to try a different approach. 'Dhingre appears to have recently learnt of this himself, and we would like to know how that came to pass.'

'It does sound like you are considering it as motive.'

'As I said, we are looking into every aspect of this case. Will Mr Parashar be joining us?' I asked.

'Ms Ray,' said Shakuntala, 'the only reason we are entertaining any of your questions in the first place is because Shayak happens to be a close personal friend of mine. But if you aren't going to be open with us, I don't see why we should be open with you. You aren't the police.'

'We are working together with the police; this is by no means an independent investigation.'

'Then why am I talking to a twenty-year-old instead of a uniformed officer? Or Shayak himself?'

'While I don't see why my age is relevant, Ms Padhy, the police can be involved in this if you so desire. And Shayak is away on business, but is overseeing every aspect of my work.'

I paused. She didn't look like she was about to budge.

'I am not withholding information,' I continued. 'I am merely refusing to speculate about motive when we are yet to establish it. I hope you can understand that. If I appear uncommunicative on the essentials, it is merely an occupational hazard. If you know Shayak well, you can gather how little I am authorized to speak about.'

'I don't think anyone knows Shayak well enough to fathom his need to be a perpetual man of mystery,' she said, at last letting slip something resembling a smile. 'Thus the mess he finds himself in this morning.'

'Still, you must understand that it is critical we speak with Mr Parashar.'

She looked at the suited man, and he gave a tiny nod. 'He isn't here,' she said. 'We haven't been able to trace him since this morning.'

'But when I spoke with him– '

'I know. I spoke with him just after that to set up this meeting. But subsequently there has been no sign of him at office or at home, and his cell phone has been switched off.'

'Any idea where he is?'

'No, and I have to say I am a little concerned.'

'Ms Padhy, if Mr Parashar has disappeared, it makes it even more imperative that we look deeper.'

'Why?'

'He has uncovered highly sensitive information that might have bearing on a murder investigation. His disappearance, if that is what it is, can't be a coincidence.'

'It makes him a suspect, doesn't it?'

'It is pointless to speculate, but it certainly bolsters the theory that he has some connection with the case.'

'There was a pen drive,' she said. 'It arrived with the mail a couple of weeks ago.'

'The mail? Snail mail?'

'Yes, it was hand-delivered. It contained copies of three documents with Kimaaya Kapoor's name on them: the marriage certificate, a divorce ruling and a certificate of completion of a course of rehab.'

The three dates we found on Dhingre's person. My pulse quickened. 'No clue as to the identity of the sender?' I had assumed that in looking into Dhingre's death, the journalist had uncovered the information in the paper today. But if someone had sent these explosive personal details to Parashar *ahead* of the murder, that put a different complexion on things entirely.

'No. We even had the tech guys look at it. You can understand how any of those three pieces of news would have been considered gold for our entertainment pages. But all three? It seemed too good to be true, which is why we decided to be as thorough as possible.'

'It was addressed to Mr Parashar?'

'Yes.'

'Do you know why?'

'He is our leading entertainment journalist.'

'He had recently done a few pieces on Kimaaya's career.' I remembered seeing them in Dhingre's file.

'Yes, but that's nothing special. He's written about almost every other actress in town in some context or the other.'

'Did either of you know Ashutosh Dhingre?'

'I didn't. Parashar said he didn't either.'

'Dhingre had a file of stories about Kimaaya, many of which were written by Parashar. Are you sure he wasn't the one who sent the pen drive?'

'Yes, I am.'

'How can you be so certain?'

'Because,' said Shakuntala, 'the information flowed the other way around.'

'What do you mean?'

'When the pen drive came in, Parashar brought it straight to me. He knew it was explosive, and very possibly fake. At first, we weren't sure how to deal with it. Despite all the talk about page 3 and paparazzi in our country, the approach to celebrity gossip in India is still quite immature – if you've noticed, we don't really do a lot of dirty-linen airing that could be seriously harmful to anyone. We know a lot more than we choose to publish. So Parashar would have to proceed with extreme caution, to ensure the documents were authentic beyond a shadow of a doubt.'

I knew what Shakuntala said was true – I had always heard rumours from my journalist friends that were far worse than anything I saw in print. Our stars had it easy compared to their counterparts in the West.

'I told Parashar to move as though it were a hard news story,' Shakuntala continued. 'Only the highest level of information would suffice as verification of these documents. The marriage and divorce papers were easy enough – being matters of official record, corroboration was possible through sources in the municipality and the courts. However, the drug business proved far trickier to establish. We contacted the rehab centre directly and they threatened us with a lawsuit, denying the whole thing. None of Kimaaya's friends would say anything concrete. Though it was pretty well known in the industry that Kimaaya was using something back in her heyday, what it was, when it ended, when it began were not facts we could ascertain. There is an honour code amongst users; no one wants to be the pot calling the kettle black for fear that their turn will come next. So we called Ashutosh Dhingre.'

'You said you didn't know him.'

'We made contact through our columnist Bindu Bisht.'

I remembered her arrival at Maaya Island in a cloud of Chanel No. 5 and faux grief. She had known Dhingre quite well, she had said.

'She called Dhingre in. He didn't try to deny the news of the marriage or divorce – and even if he had, it wouldn't have mattered as we knew by then we were on the verge of getting the proof we needed. On the drug business, he was far more vocal. He said the whole thing was a lie, and that if anyone were to know if Kimaaya had gone to rehab at that time, it would be him.'

'Did you show him the document you had?'

'Yes – said it was fake.'

'And then?'

'He stormed out of here. He called Parashar later to plead with us not to print the story. Said it would destroy Kimaaya.'

'Didn't you find his concern strange, in light of the fact they had parted ways?'

'He said that despite everything he would not watch her be pulled down, after having been with her since she was little more than a child. That she had a good heart underneath it all. Bindu said she wasn't surprised by any of it; he was one of the last gentlemen in the industry and, if Kimaaya had had any sense, she would never have fired him.'

'Is that why you didn't print the drug angle?'

'Of course not. At the end of the day, it came down to too little by way of facts. If the document had turned out to be a fake, we would be hung out to dry. The marriage-divorce story was sensational enough, and we were on solid ground there.'

'Why didn't you wait for Kimaaya's version?'

'We contacted her the night before we ran; she refused to come to the phone.'

'Did she know what it was about?'

'We spoke to her assistant and told her it was urgent. And then we decided, to hell with it. We had government documents, we didn't need anymore verification and we knew we would only get a denial from her anyway.'

'You and Shayak are friends. You didn't contact him?'

'And have the whole weight of the Indian political establishment come down on us before we could go to print? Not a risk worth taking when we had faith in our material.'

'Any luck tracking down the person that sent the pen drive in the first place?'

'No.'

'It didn't strike you as suspicious?'

'Of course. It reeked. Someone was obviously out to get Kimaaya, and we didn't know why. But cold as it may sound, it didn't particularly matter at the end of the day.'

'You didn't have second thoughts after the murder?'

'About running it, no. Timing, yes. We could have gone to print earlier, but it seemed in bad taste. So we waited a couple of days. Wasting any more time seemed foolish. Who knows who else had been sent the same information?'

The murder had only made the story more newsworthy. I wondered how much it would actually affect Kimaaya. Shayak, who prized his privacy and anonymity above all else, seemed to be the one with more to lose.

'No further contact from the sender?'

'No.'

'Could I have a look at the drive? I'd like to see if our tech team has better luck with it than you had.'

'Go ahead,' said Shakuntala, taking it out of her handbag and sliding it across the table. 'We've got what we needed.'

'You'll let me know if Mr Parashar surfaces?'

She nodded.

TWELVE

The murder of Ashutosh Dhingre had begun to feel bigger than what I could see. Tech-savvy snitches, paparazzi, secrets – and a likely connection to another murder. And now, following Shayak's advice to trust no one, I found myself on the outside looking in once more.

I thought I would never have to struggle for information again, with Titanium on the inside track with the police. But that was apparently a qualified association at the moment. So the upshot was that I needed help. Despite Shayak's confidence, there was only so much headway I could make in a new, big city on my own. I needed to turn to someone who, I could say with some degree of certainty, had nothing to do with any of this business.

I called Terrence. 'Are you ready for that drink?' I asked.

'Always.'

I gave him directions to my place, before packing my bag with everything I might need for the next few days, and headed out. I didn't know when I'd be back in office. With Shayak's instructions to act on my own, I thought I would be better off working from home to avoid questions and steer clear of prying eyes.

I picked up some cans of beer and, half an hour later, found Terrence leaning on my doorframe.

'Ray, I knew it would come to this some day,' he smirked.

I reminded myself it was all for a good cause. 'Lose the attitude, Terrence. I called you here because I need your help – and a private place to talk.'

'Private?' The smirk did not dim in its brightness.

'It's about work.'

That got his attention. 'The mighty Titanium needs me again?'

'Come in,' I said.

Terrence followed me in and I went to the fridge and poured our drinks. 'Nice place,' he said.

'Yeah – company flat.'

He let out a low whistle. 'These guys are really taking care of you.'

'It's not bad.'

'If I was in your position, I'd be a damn sight more grateful. A month ago, you were working with Calcutta's saddest collection of crime-fighters, begging for cases for free and you still couldn't get them.'

'That's a little harsh.'

'Well, that's what you can expect from old friends who've seen you before you made the big league. But you made it out of there, so kudos to you.'

And straight into another mess.

'How's the work going?'

'Just getting settled in.'

'With the biggest case of the year.'

'Is that what you consider this?'

'Dude! Don't play dumb. You are in the limelight – might as well enjoy it. And this thing gets better and better. Your boss was married to Kimaaya Kapoor, man!'

'So?'

'Just saying. Some guys have all the luck.'

'Why don't you tell me about your case for a change?' I asked.

He gave me a sketch of what he had been up to – he had followed a man who had allegedly perpetrated a chit fund fraud on 500 unsuspecting families, swindling them of over ₹50 lakh. The victims had rallied together and gone to the police. When they seemed slow on the uptake, they had come to Terrence's agency, and he had tracked the man to Mumbai.

'How much longer do you think you'll be in town?' I asked.

'Do I sense a desire to spend more time together?'

'You're not a very good detective, are you?'

Terrence's smile widened. 'At least another couple of weeks.'

'Do you think you have time to help me with my case?'

'A case – or *the* case?'

'*The* case, if you must.'

'Why would you need my help?'

'Titanium often works with freelancers. It's no big deal.'

'Why is it always like this with you? Even when you want help, you'll make me feel like a fool.'

'You know what this business is like, Terrence. There is just too much I can't tell you. You want in or not?'

'Do I get credit?'

'Where it is due.'

'With your office?'

'With my boss. And you will be compensated for your time.'

'Your boss Shayak Gupta?'

'The very same.'

'And it is for the Maaya Island murder?'

'Yes.'

'You are working on this with freelancers? Why? This is a big case even for Titanium. The dude really hates his ex, doesn't he?'

'In or out?'

'In, Reema. Obviously.'

'Okay. Then we need to get to work now.' I handed Terrence the pen drive and my laptop. 'I am assuming you have read the coverage of Kimaaya's murder and divorce saga.'

'As well as the "Who is Shayak Gupta" piece of trash.'

'So there is only one bit of information on this that you must agree to never discuss with anyone without express permission.'

'Reema, I've been a detective for over ten years now. Since you were still running around in chaddis. Give me some credit.'

'I can't take anything on faith.'

'Are you going to make me sign a non-disclosure agreement, or something else you might consider – though probably falsely – to be legally binding?'

'No.'

'Then you are taking it on faith.'

He was right, and there was nothing I could do about it. I handed Terrence the drive. 'There is only one document on this that has new information, the rest you know.'

'And if I tell anyone about it, I risk a painful death?'

'Something like that.'

'What do you need me to do?'

'I want to know if there is any sign of who may have created this drive, and the source of the information.' Tech was never my forte, and I didn't want to miss anything because I didn't have access to Titanium's manpower.

Terrence plugged it into my machine. 'I'm going to first run a search for malware on it, before I look at the files.' He plugged away for a while. 'Looks clean,' he said.

Then he turned his attention to the documents themselves. When he reached the third one, the certificate from the rehab clinic, he looked up at me with surprise. 'Why didn't this make the paper?'

'Might be a fake,' I said.

He kept working, shaking his head every now and again. 'All these film types are the same, aren't they? Drugs, sex, meltdown. None of them can keep it together. How the hell did anyone get a hold of these?'

'That's what I had hoped you could tell me.'

'I can't find anything that might hint who the author is. But I can tell you that whoever saved these files knew exactly what they were doing. They didn't want to leave any evidence behind and they knew how to do it.'

'How hard is that?'

'Nowadays – not very. There is some pretty common software out there that can help you.'

'But he or she thought to take these measures, so knew the dangers of an electronic footprint.'

'Yes. But having said that, a geeky teenager might have that stuff down.'

'And that's all you can tell me?'

Terrence shrugged. 'I can try to run a data retrieval to see if there are any deleted files, but chances are this is a brand-new drive that has never been used before.'

'I'm not assuming anything. Can you check now?'

Terrence complied, and in a few minutes confirmed what we both already knew.

'So where does that leave us?' I asked.

'You tell me. I'm not asking any questions, remember?'

'For now, I think this is it. But I'll be in touch in case I need anything else.'

I let Terrence out. I was running into wall after wall. I had ruled out our best suspect in Viraat and, while plenty of people had the opportunity and the means to murder Ashutosh Dhingre, motive was less certain. These documents were my strongest angle, and I was running out of ideas about how to make them work.

I took Dhingre's address book and file from my bag. Nothing leapt out as being unusual – it seemed as though Dhingre was just keeping tabs on his former protégée. If this wasn't about blackmail then it must be about ruining Kimaaya. And yet apparently Dhingre was intent on doing the opposite – he was desperate to keep the news of Kimaaya's addiction under wraps. Who else could have it out for her? A Bollywood rival? An angry lover? A disgruntled producer? The list was potentially endless. Where was I even supposed to start?

There was an unexpected upside of being banished from the office – my desk was now my kitchen, if I wanted it to be. And instead of taking notes to clear my head, I could bake.

I looked through my cupboards. It was slim pickings, but I did have enough for brownies. I set all the ingredients on the counter as I greased my pan and preheated the oven. It was something I could bake in my sleep, which was a good thing because the brownies were languishing in the background of my brain as I ran through the details of the case, trying to sort what I knew and keep it separate from what I thought I knew.

The baking, as always, did the trick. By the time I slipped the batch into the oven, I had figured out a way forward. Like the brownies themselves, it was simplicity itself – I would start where I always started: at the source.

But it would have to wait – I had just pulled the fudgy goodness out of the oven when my phone rang. It was Ajay. I had forgotten all about our date that wasn't.

'Are you joining me for dinner?' he asked.

'Yes,' I said a little too quickly to my ear.

He told me where to meet him, and I set out. On the way, I had time to ask myself what I was doing. I was curious about him but there was more to it than that – and I didn't feel comfortable about any of it.

When I arrived at the restaurant, Ajay was seated in the corner, with his back to the room. He had already ordered a bottle of wine. 'Thanks for coming,' he said, pouring me a glass.

I felt unexpectedly at a loss for words. I smiled and held my glass up to his.

'So tell me, how does a woman like you become a private investigator?' he asked without preamble as I took a sip.

I hadn't expected small talk from Ajay, and he didn't disappoint. 'I guess that would depend on what you mean by "woman like you".'

'You know – affluent, urbane, attractive. You could have chosen any profession you wanted.'

'As I am sure you could have done.'

'True. But I asked first.'

'I blame it on an overactive imagination and unfortunate reading habits. And I must have been seriously deluded about the amount of excitement PI work entailed.'

'You regret it?'

'I've had my moments.'

'Where were you before Titanium?'

I told him about my agency, and briefly about the case that threw me in Shayak's path and led me to Mumbai.

'Seems like quite a lot of excitement to me.'

'Only because I've edited out the endless hours I spent tailing cheating spouses,' I said, taking another sip. 'It's your turn.'

'My story is not so different. I must have been seriously deluded about the number of criminals I would lock away as a policeman.'

'Bad day at the office?'

He shook his head. 'We can only do our best. And then we watch the guys get out on bail and, eventually, let off for rape and murder.'

'Are you always this upbeat?'

'I don't know,' he said with a sigh. 'I guess I am just sick of doing so much and achieving so little. Sometimes I feel we are chasing our tails, like we are trying to take down the Amazon with a pair of tweezers.' He gave me a sad smile. 'Don't tell my boss I said that.'

'I'm not on a first-name basis with the commissioner, so you needn't fear. Are private players any better off?'

'When you are Shayak Gupta, I'd say so. You are getting the job done, often because the police have failed and, for the most part, Titanium is pretty good at it.'

Ajay put down his glass and picked up the menu. 'Any preferences?'

'Not really,' I said, surprising myself. I couldn't remember the last time I let anyone else order for me. But as I listened to him talk to the waiter, I realized his choices were telling me much about him.

In fact, all the choices he made through the evening were quite illustrative. The restaurant was multi-cuisine: he skipped through the appealing coastal cuisine section and went straight to the north Indian menu, from which he chose a yellow dal, a mixed vegetable, raita and roti.

'I'm vegetarian,' he said. 'Please order anything else you want.'

'That's okay,' I said. 'I'm very happy eating vegetarian food.'

It wasn't a lie either. I loved vegetables but in my world there were no non-vegetarians – there were the vegetarians and the rest of us omnivores, just as our digestive systems intended us to be.

We chatted as we waited. Despite his lacklustre taste in food, Ajay was good company. He was easy with words, making me laugh with stories of the police station. But as dinner arrived and he poured the last of the wine into our glasses, he abruptly changed tack. 'You are here to talk about the case, aren't you?'

I couldn't lie to him. 'In part, yes.'

He didn't betray anger or irritation. 'It is rather bad timing.'

'Till this is over …'

'Then let me try to speed things up. Any idea why your boss' fingerprints would be at the scene of Afreen's murder?'

I was confused. 'Where?'

'On the bar, under which the body was found.'

The bar – that fancy screen that came to life when Viraat hit it in his frustration. I remembered the water that had danced across the surface when the glass was knocked over. I hadn't had enough time to collect prints before being asked to back off; it was the police team that had worked that scene.

'Perhaps he was there on an earlier occasion?'

'Viraat says he wasn't. I'd ask Shayak, except that he's conveniently unavailable.'

'I'm sure there is a perfectly acceptable explanation.'

'I'm sure. One more thing. Could you explain why a gun licensed to Titanium would be used as the murder weapon?'

'What?'

'The unfortunate facts as they are emerging in this case. The gun that killed Afreen was found in the elevator shaft of Viraat's building. It was a Titanium-licensed weapon.'

'Why are you telling me this?'

'Why not? You'll find out soon enough. People in your office are already being questioned. And you wanted to know about the case,' said Ajay.

I was taken aback by the sudden sarcasm. 'You think Shayak would be shabby enough to kill someone with a gun registered to his company and leave a fingerprint at the scene?'

'So your argument for his innocence is that if he were to commit murder, he would do a better job of it?'

'Amongst others – and I've heard worse. You've worked with him closely enough to know I am right.'

'Be that as it may, too sloppy isn't grounds for dismissing him as a suspect.'

'What about motive?'

'To stop Dhingre from spilling the beans on his marriage. And maybe Afreen saw him do it.'

'How is that good enough reason for a double murder? What did he have to gain?'

'Thankfully, he came clean to me about the marriage before I read about it in the papers,' he said.

'He did?' I was genuinely surprised – and relieved – that he had taken my advice.

'Yup. Otherwise he would have gone straight to the top of the suspect list after that article came out. But that doesn't mean he wasn't protecting Kimaaya from blackmail and himself from scandal. We all know what a private bastard he is.'

I flinched at the words. Ajay's eyes widened just a fraction at my reaction, before the mask fell back into place.

'From what I have learnt, it wasn't Dhingre doing the exposing. He may have only been trying to warn Kimaaya,' I said.

Ajay didn't respond to that one.

'And the fingerprints weren't found at Dhingre's crime scene – they were only found at Afreen's.'

'I don't know exactly what happened yet, Reema, but the evidence is too heavy for me to ignore. And I don't see how an investigator with your skills is so convinced in the face of facts.'

It was my turn to hold my tongue.

'Not that it is any of my business,' said Ajay, 'but is something going on between the two of you?'

'No! He's my boss, and I have great respect for his abilities.' I couldn't tell if he believed me – when I didn't know if I believed myself.

There seemed to be nothing left to say on the subject and for the rest of the evening I tried to enjoy myself: I was entertaining, I asked questions, I made Ajay laugh. And I told myself I did. Ajay was a good, smart, attractive man.

But with everything I heard, I couldn't wait to get out of there. Ajay insisted on dropping me home and, when I finally got to the flat, I fumbled with my phone as I dialled Archana's number. It was engaged, but I kept calling till I got through. 'Why didn't you tell me what's been going on?' I said to her.

'You've heard? How?'

'Never mind.'

'It's not on the news or anything, is it?'

'No.'

'Thank god. It's only just happened! A police team just left and I'm in office trying to sort it out.'

'Who had the gun, Archana?'

'I've been going through the records, but nothing makes sense. I don't know what is happening anymore, Reema.'

'It was Shayak, wasn't it?'

'I don't know.'

'Archana, please. This is my case. I need to know.'

She let out a ragged sigh. 'According to the paperwork, yes. But it just can't be true. He has his own gun and never takes one from office even if he is working on a case.'

'How are these things recorded?'

'It is all part of the requisition system. Forms are filled in on the Intranet.'

'How many people are allowed to use company firearms and ammunition?'

'Anyone who is licensed and passes the internal test. Formal notification also needs to come in from the section head.'

'Which would be redundant in this case.'

'Yes.'

'You'll let me know if I can be of any help?' I asked.

'That is what I should be saying to you.'

'Actually, whenever you get the time, could you go over all the paperwork that has reached you that is in any way connected with this business? Let me know if anything is out of place, however small.'

'Sure. I think I'll be here all night anyhow.'

'Do you want me to come in?'

'No, Reema. I can't let you help me, even if I wanted to. Shayak's orders.'

As I hung up, I realized Shayak had seen this coming, and he had wanted me out of the way when it did. Why?

THIRTEEN

It was time to consider that we were dealing with a professional. Someone who knew what the investigators would be looking for, and was careful to cover his tracks. Someone who knew his way in and around a system – even one as sophisticated as Titanium's.

Obviously Shayak had had an inkling of what was going on when he told me to go solo on this business. Assuming that he had nothing to do with the gun requisition, there were enough protections within the system to make this sort of infiltration quite difficult. Even if this was someone within Titanium.

But by the next morning, I knew we were running out of time as the business had already made the news.

Police are searching for Shayak Gupta in connection with the murders of Ashutosh Dhingre and Afreen. It is a move that comes close on the heels of revelations that Gupta was once married to Bollywood star Kimaaya Kapoor and that they are still on intimate terms. It was on Kimaaya's private island that Dhingre's body was found, leading to speculation of a connection between the actress and the death of her one-time agent. Afreen, a starlet who had also been on the island at the time of Dhingre's murder, was found shot dead shortly after.

Gupta, whose company Titanium is in charge of Kimaaya's security, was present at the crime scene in the days following the murder and, according to sources, was even working towards solving it. Why he is now missing is not known, and whether he is being sought out as a witness or a potential suspect has also not been revealed.

'The police are working to bring the culprits to book, whoever they may be, to the fullest extent of the law. We cannot currently reveal more than this,' said DCP (Detection) Ajay Shankaran.

To law enforcement insiders, the search for Shayak Gupta indeed comes as a surprise, for he is the very man who protects many of the country's celebrities and VVIPs. He is also a close collaborator with the police in a number of other investigations. But in this high-profile case, it seems as though no one is above scrutiny.

I called Archana again. 'How were the details kept out of the press?'

'In part, because it happened late in the evening. And the police have agreed to play it close to the hip till necessary.'

'We don't have much time.'

'No.'

'Do you have any information for me?'

'I did as you asked – I went through every piece of documentation that has been logged into the system since the first murder, and I noticed something odd in the paperwork regarding the construction crew evacuation from Maaya Island. I called the supervisor of the project, and I think he might have some information that may be pertinent.'

I remembered meeting Kaustav Arora on the island. 'Regarding?'

'I'll let him explain it to you.'

In a moment, I received a call from the exceedingly nervous Mr Arora. 'Archana tells me you are the person to report to about the murder?' he said.

'In Mr Gupta's absence.'

'I went through all of the records on the island, and asked everyone about whether they had heard or seen anything as Mr Gupta had asked. We could find nothing earlier. But yesterday, I was going through some other papers and noticed something unusual. Strange, you may call it.'

'Yes?'

'We had interviewed only eighteen people after the murder, and then they were all transported back to Mumbai city by boat. But I just saw the ship's manifest and found that a nineteenth name had been penned in, which the captain had signed off on. The captain remembers there was an extra man on board, whose name wasn't on the list, but he didn't think anything of it at the time, and added him on.'

'Where were you when the men boarded?'

'I was readying the roster for the men helping out with security, to stop the media persons from coming to the island.'

Which Shayak had requested on a priority basis. 'So there was no one to supervise?' I asked.

'No, ma'am,' he said apologetically.

'Do any of the other men remember seeing someone on board who shouldn't have been there?'

'That is the problem – there were a few new labourers who had been brought in to work on the jetty, so there were a number of people whom even the senior workers did not know.'

'Any description of the man?'

'I asked, but no one seemed to remember.'

I took down what details I could – the captain's name and contact information, the ship's name and where I could find it.

'What was the extra man's name?' I asked.

'Lalu Prasad,' Mr Arora replied.

I felt a chill. That was our man, and he had a sense of humour too. Lucky for me, his cockiness made him conspicuous.

'Could you please check the records going back a few days and see whether you spot any similar anomalies in manifests for trips made from the city to the island?'

'If you can wait a moment, I can tell you just now.'

I held on to the phone, tapping my pen impatiently on the notepad before me.

'Here it is.' Mr Arora said after a few minutes. 'The name Lalu Prasad appears on the manifest of the crew going to the island the day before the murder.'

'How are these lists transmitted to the captain?'

'By e-mail, from my office.'

'Who sends them out?'

'I do.'

'How do the names reach you?'

'The foreman gives them to me on paper, then I type them out and send them. I don't remember putting this name in. It's a name you don't forget easily, na?'

'Can you check your sent mail for that day's list?'

'Okay,' he said. 'Give me a moment.'

I waited with growing certainty and dread.

'The list is here but, as I said, the name Lalu Prasad is not on it.'

So we had a hacker on our hands. He or she had had the time to insert the name on the manifest for the trip out to the island – or had an accomplice who could do so. After the murder it was either a question of time, access or nerve: one of them had run out on our perpetrator and he had to risk getting on board and convincing the captain to allow him passage.

'Can you have the mail the captain received sent to me, as well as the original you sent?' I said.

I hung up and considered the significance of this new information. It confirmed that the victim and his killer had not arrived together on the island, for purposes nefarious or otherwise. The killer had come to the island a day in advance, disguised as a construction worker, and had lain in wait. Ashutosh Dhingre, in all probability, had made his way to the island by some desperate measures and had been waylaid.

Which left me with two questions. One: How had the killer known Dhingre was approaching Kimaaya with what he knew? Two: If Dhingre had to fend for himself on the way to the island, what had happened to the vessel by which he arrived; and how could a man in desperate financial straits afford to charter a boat capable of taking him to Maaya Island in the middle of the night?

I called Mrs Dhingre to address the second question, but she seemed as clueless as before.

'No, Reema ji, there is no one we know in Mumbai with a boat. No fishermen here.'

'Are you absolutely certain? It might not be a fisherman.'

'No.'

'It could be someone whose office has a boat for some reason, a rich friend?'

'If we had such a helpful rich friend, would we be in the situation we are in now?'

'What about a tour operator?'

'Tour operator?' she asked, befuddled. 'We don't – what is that you are saying?' she suddenly screamed into the phone.

I heard a faint female voice in the background, and guessed one of her daughters was home.

'Jitin isn't a tour operator, beti. He is a driver. His mother just explained it to me.'

The daughter interrupted again.

'If I don't understand anything, then why don't you speak to Reema ji yourself,' Mrs Dhingre shouted.

I heard the sound of rubber chappals hitting the mosaic as rushed footsteps approached at the other end. 'Hello?'

'Hi, I'm Reema. I'm with– '

'I know who you are. My mother told me about your visit the other day. I'm Lasika.'

'I'm sorry for your loss,' I mumbled.

'What information are you looking for, exactly?'

'I need to know if your father had access to a boat of some kind. It could be a speedboat or a yacht – something he wouldn't have to pay for.'

'As I just told my mother, my cousin Jitin has a boat – or at least the people he works for do.'

'He's not a driver?'

'Uff. My mother is stone-deaf in one ear. He's not a *driver*, he's a *diver*. He operates a tour agency for diving enthusiasts, organizing trips around Mumbai.'

I closed my eyes. How much time had been wasted on this case because of the pesky letter 'r'? Had I only known Dhingre had a nephew with a boat, it would have been the first place I stopped. 'Do you have his contact information?'

She gave me his phone number and the name of his firm.

'Thank you,' I said. 'Have any of you spoken to your cousin since your father's death?'

'His parents. But I don't think he called.'

'Is that unusual? Are you close?'

'He's always been a little aloof. But we are close enough that he should have at least called once, now that you mention it.'

'Sorry,' I mumbled again.

'Why don't you take my number,' added Lasika. 'It might be better to speak to me rather than Mummy if you have any more questions.'

I took it gratefully.

I didn't want to alert Jitin about the purpose of our visit beforehand, so I Googled his tour agency to find out where it was, and then called Terrence.

'Want to come along for an interview?'

'At your service,' he said.

'I'll pick you up in fifteen minutes.'

Once we were on our way, I filled him in. 'You sure this guy hasn't skipped town yet? If I were him, I'd be pretty freaked,' said Terrence.

'We'll find out soon enough.'

We entered Mumbai Mariners Dive Shop in Colaba. Its blue walls were covered with tourists' photos, certificates and posters advertising popular packages. There were two men, one at work on the computer, the other with his feet up, staring into space. They both looked up as the door swung closed in a peal of bells.

'Jitin?' I asked.

The man behind the computer looked at his colleague, who wore cut-off jeans and a black singlet, his shoulder-length hair tied back with a bandana.

'Can I help you?' he said.

'We are here about Ashutosh Dhingre.'

His face was a flipbook of feeling. Fear, disbelief and, finally, determination.

'What about him,' he said.

'He's dead.'

'Yes, I know.'

'Oh? I wasn't sure, since you hadn't been in touch with the family since the murder,' I said.

He was taken aback by this line of attack. 'Yeah, so?' he finally spat out.

'You took him out to Maaya Island.'

'What makes you think that?' he shrugged. 'And why should I tell you anything, anyway?'

'Either you tell me, or DCP Ajay Shankaran will be knocking on your door very soon. Which would you prefer?'

'Look,' he said, finally cracking that cool, 'I may have taken him there, but I don't know anything else about it.'

'You expect us to believe that when he died there that night?'

'I was waiting in the boat. I waited for hours and hours, till daybreak in fact, and then I left.'

'Without trying to find him? You were the only one who knew he was there in the first place!'

'He had told me that under no circumstances was I to get off the boat. He said if I did, the deal was off.'

'And what was the deal?'

'I owed him some money; he was going to write off half my debt.'

'How much?'

'Not much. Like twenty grand.'

'You owed twenty grand or that was the amount he was going to write off?'

'I owed forty.'

Terrence stepped in. 'So let me get this straight: if he lived, you got 20,000. If he died, you got 40,000?'

'Wait, you think I killed my uncle? For 20,000? That's nuts, dude!'

'I think we just established that it was for 40,000. That's a fortune when you don't have it.'

'That's not how it happened. You guys are sick!'

'So is your story, in which you abandoned your uncle for dead.'

'Hey, how was I supposed to know he was dead?' he said, growing increasingly shrill. 'I didn't see or hear anything. I was just following instructions. I tried calling him like a million times but he didn't answer and I had to get to work in the morning.'

'Dude,' said Jitin's colleague from the side. 'You could have come in late. Not like I set the watch by you or anything.'

Jitin rolled his eyes. 'You guys can believe whatever you want, but I'm telling the truth. My uncle called me up earlier in the day, saying he needed a boat. I told him how much we charge for normal tours and that I was out all day anyway, and all of the next. He said I should let him know when I got in, that he had some urgent business that couldn't wait. Then he said where he wanted to go and I was like no way, 'cause I'd lose my job for taking him out there. But when he told me what was in it for me, I thought it was an easy way to get him off my back about paying him the money I owed.'

'Did he say why you shouldn't set foot on the island?'

'No, but I just assumed it would get him in hot water with Kimaaya. She seems so stuck up. All those years they worked together, she never came to his house or to any of the events he invited her to. Every time he'd be waiting, telling us all that she'd make it. Every time he'd make some excuse for her in the end.'

It seemed as though Jitin had suffered his share of disappointments at Kimaaya's hands.

'You weren't worried?'

'Of course I was! But what choice did I have? Even if I had wanted to play the hero, it would have been a bad idea. The jetty was a mess. I had to hoist my uncle – who's scared shitless of water, by the way – onto it and, with no one to help me, it would have been a bad scene on and off the boat, man. And I had to get back before the boat was missed the next day.'

I knew that Dhingre had used the old jetty – we had the footprints to prove it. 'You didn't think you should come forward with what you knew when you heard the news?'

'I was scared. Wouldn't you be, in my position? It wasn't like I knew who did it or anything. So what was the point?'

'And the boss would have fired your sorry ass,' Jitin's colleague mumbled.

'Has your boat been used for fishing of late?' I asked.

'Sure. All the time.'

That would explain the fish scales found on Dhingre's clothes. I asked a few routine questions to confirm the timelines, and then we left. 'Do you believe him?' asked Terrence.

'A story like that? He'd have to be pretty stupid to make it up.'

'He does look pretty stupid.'

'True. But I believe him.'

'So do I.'

At long last, a picture of what happened was beginning to emerge in my mind – the how of Ashutosh Dhingre's murder was being established. Unable to reach Kimaaya over the phone, he had arrived at Maaya Island by boat in the dead of the night to warn Kimaaya of the impending storm likely to be caused by the leaked documents. His nephew helped him onto land, after which he was intercepted by a man – Lalu Prasad – masquerading as a construction worker. It came to blows, and Lalu found the bottle by the gazebo and hit Dhingre over the head with it, and slashed his throat for good measure with a shard of glass. The murderer slunk back to wherever he was hiding on the island – probably in the workers' quarters – and then snuck onto the boat and got back to the mainland.

Now, I needed to find out who Lalu Prasad really was, and why he wanted Kimaaya publicly shamed enough to kill for it.

I dropped off Terrence and sent Vinod to Archana to pick up some cash and other supplies I needed. It was just past noon.

Then I checked my mail. In my personal e-mail, the subject line 'Snuffbox of dim sum' caught my eye. I was about to hit 'delete' thinking it was spam, but it was just odd enough to get me thinking. This was undoubtedly a reference to the murder of Prakash Agarwal, the case that brought Shayak and me together in the first place.

I opened it.

I still remember the place I first held you in my arms. When darkness descends tonight you will be there again, my harbour in this tempest. Fear not the man you find there, no matter how much I have hurt you.

No doubt in my mind, the mail was from Shayak – who thankfully had not chosen poetry as his calling. He wanted to meet me on the *Titania* at sunset, at the coastguard jetty.

That was what the first two lines of his mail meant. The third threw me. Was he afraid that I'd listen to the rumours, to the police version of things, and think he was a murderer?

I had about six hours. But there was much to do in the meantime. As my brownie-baking session had shown me yesterday, it was time to go back to the source – to pay a visit to Kimaaya Kapoor's Mumbai flat.

Compared to the Maaya Island affair, Kimaaya's apartment was a hovel. It was the penthouse of a fairly old building which, like most others in the city, wore a grey and frazzled look despite being some of the most expensive real estate in the world. But this was Mumbai, and the sprawling four-bedroom duplex apartment with a view of the sea was true luxury.

Mrs Pereira greeted me with a smile and then went to fetch Kimaaya. I didn't know how long she would make me wait – I had called, and she had warned me that she was going out and didn't have much time to spare.

I took the opportunity to look around the living space. It was as different as it could be from the open, spa feel of her island getaway, and with an updated, modern vibe – all sleek lines, whites, blacks and greys. It had a softening sort of clutter provided by bric-à-brac, photographs, paintings and carpets, thrown together with artful artlessness. There were no celebrity shots, no awards on show. It felt more like Kimaaya here, more private and intimate.

The lady herself emerged about ten minutes later, looking every inch the star. A blue sheath dress clung to her ample curves, her hair in soft curls around her face softening the smoky eyes and nude lips. She was in slippers at the moment though they would soon be replaced by designer heels, her perpetual accessory to give that much needed lift, and her legs that never-ending illusion.

'Shayak is in trouble,' I said.

'About these marriage and divorce stories?' she asked, slipping on earrings. 'What difference would it make to him?'

It didn't surprise me she didn't follow the news when it had nothing directly to do with her. 'The police have him in a corner over this Afreen business. Somehow it is all connected with the Maaya Island case.'

Kimaaya's face reflected genuine concern. I told her what I could – that there was a very real chance that Shayak would be taken in by the cops.

She collapsed on the couch. 'I don't know why this is happening to me.'

'Not just you,' I said, unable to hide my impatience. 'Did you locate the papers, the original marriage and divorce documents that you said you kept in a safe here?'

'Sorry, I forgot.'

'Can you check now? See that they are all intact?'

'Wait here,' she said.

'Actually, if you don't mind, I'd like to see where the safe is.'

Kimaaya shrugged. 'I guess everyone in your office knows anyway. Follow me.'

I trailed behind Kimaaya through the hallway to a large bedroom with picture windows opening out to the Arabian Sea. She led me into a dressing room the size of my flat. She squatted to remove a floor tile, revealing a small safe.

'When was the last time you accessed this?' I asked.

'Before I went to the island, to put some jewellery away.'

'I'd like to check for prints before you open it.'

She moved aside as I dusted for prints. I lifted the latents and handed her a pair of latex gloves. 'Go ahead,' I told her, 'put these on.'

As she went through the contents of the safe I scanned the prints and compared them to Kimaaya's, which I already had on my machine. They were a match. They were also the only prints I found.

I looked up to find Kimaaya pulling a folder full of papers out from underneath a stash of small bags and jewellery boxes. She rummaged through them and found the rehab certificate. It looked exactly like the scanned copy I had on the pen drive. If I had any doubt about its authenticity, I could forget about that now. Further down in the stack were the marriage certificate and the divorce decree.

'It all looks exactly like I had left it.'

I took them from her and knew that looking for more prints would be a waste of time, but I did so anyway.

'The only prints on the safe are yours,' I said.

'I told you: whoever it was that got those documents couldn't have got them from here.'

'Oh, I'm pretty sure your safe was the source. These three items are together in only this one place.'

'So you are saying this man has been in my house?' she said in horror. 'Is it someone I know?'

'We can't rule anyone out at the moment.'

'I feel so violated! How could this person have gotten past all the security?'

'They knew exactly what they were doing, and were in no rush to do it. It probably happened while you were out of town at some point.'

'How do I know they didn't take anything else?'

'Have you noticed anything missing?'

'Not really, but it's impossible to keep track of everything.'

'Of course anything is possible, but it seems they knew what they were looking for and where to find it.'

'Such a disaster!'

'Kimaaya, right now I need you to think of anything that might help Shayak. Anything about this that you haven't told me yet?'

'I really can't think of anything,' she said offhand. 'What I do know is that he'll find his way out of this mess.'

'What do you mean?'

'When you've known Shayak for as long as I have, you expect him to get into trouble – usually because he is off saving the world. He'll tell you very little of what is actually going on but no matter how impossible it seems at the time, you'll always know that he'll come out of it okay.'

I was amazed at how cavalier she could be with Shayak's neck on the line.

'You're surprised? Don't worry, Reema, I've done my share of worrying about Shayak when he was in the army, in the early days. It didn't take me long to realize that nothing was more important to him than work. He was always in the business of putting the needs of others before his own and I must warn you that while it seems very romantic and noble at the beginning, it gets old very fast. Even if you think you aren't as self-centred as me.'

'This has nothing to do with me.'

'Are you sure about that? I haven't seen him look at anyone the way he looks at you in a long time.'

I shook my head.

'You don't seem very convinced yourself. You'd be crazy to turn down Shayak. Believe me, I know,' she said.

'If you feel so strongly about him, why didn't it work for you?'

'Because too much time had passed and damage had been done before I realized what I had thrown away all those years ago. Shayak is a real man – he isn't a chocolate-faced child who will take my tantrums because he wants to shine in my reflected glory. He wants a home and someone to share it with. Besides, Shayak isn't one to revisit old mistakes.'

I remembered his words in my apartment – that the door would remain open for only so long.

'Shayak has made it amply clear that he believes, no matter how good he is to me as a friend, that as lovers we were all wrong.'

Why was she telling me any of this? 'And you?'

'I have been through enough wrong relationships to know how wrong feels inside out, upside down and in between. Ever since I got cleaned up I've been trying to change his mind, and it is finally over for me. I am ready to move on.'

'With Pratap Puri,' I said.

Her eyes widened. 'How did you know that?'

I shrugged.

'Tell me.'

'It was the little things, really.'

'Like what? Not even Shayak has it worked out. He knows there is someone. But …'

'You aren't the only one noticing reactions,' I said with a smile.

'I can't have given it away. How many times have I warned Pratap to be more careful!' she said, exasperated.

'Don't be so hard on him. One of your guests overheard someone having sex the night of the murder,' I said, 'and that got me thinking.' Kimaaya's room had been above Sandhya's. As for partners, with Viraat out cold on the lawn and Raj away from the house in the servants' quarters, it could either have been Shiv or Pratap. With everyone noticing how Pratap was preening for Kimaaya, it seemed he was the most likely, and if you added to that his hunt for divorce settlement fodder against his wife, it became the obvious scenario.

'Uff. Busybodies, all of them.'

'I don't think it would have come up had a man not been murdered.' I tried hard to keep the irritation out of my voice. It was not my place to judge Kimaaya for her self-absorption or anything else. She was single and had every right to look for happiness. So who better to find it with than her billionaire neighbour? What was a little divorce between lovers?

'Anyway, I guess it doesn't matter. We'll be making it public soon enough,' Kimaaya shrugged.

'What about his wife? And all the other women he is seen with?'

'The other women are a ruse – one I am sure he enjoys very much,' she said drily. 'He didn't want his wife to know, so his solution is to flirt with every woman he meets.'

He did a good job of it, too. 'She doesn't mind his many girlfriends, but she'd mind just one?'

'Oh, she minds all of it. But she doesn't have any evidence of anything, beyond what is reported on page 3. Pratap is careful – almost diabolically so,' she said with a gleam of admiration.

'Is she looking for it?'

'I'm sure she is.'

'And he is looking for an opening to divorce her without being the bad guy.'

She shot me a look, but wouldn't confirm nor deny it. 'Quite a piece of work, that one. So holier-than-thou. You'd think she never did anything wrong or stupid in her life.'

Was it possible that the man at the breakfast café I saw her with was a detective? It still wouldn't explain the awkward attempts at conversation they were making.

'She doesn't suspect anything is on between you two?'

'I sometimes wonder.'

'You really don't know why she left early the night of the party?'

'No, but she and Pratap had been fighting from the moment he came back to town that day.'

'Do you know about what?'

'Pratap had a big work announcement coming up and he wanted her to host an event, but she refused.'

'What sort of event?' I asked.

'Why don't you read about it for yourself,' said Kimaaya, walking out of the closet and into the bedroom. She picked up a pink paper from her bed. 'It's like what he is setting up on the island, the electricity stuff, but on a larger scale.'

I had eyes only for the picture that accompanied the piece, featuring Pratap and the man from the café. It all became clear. 'Do you know when the event is?' I asked.

'It's tonight. That's where I am going, in fact. I'm the brand ambassador for the project.'

'Can you get me in?'

'I don't think so.'

I wasn't to be deterred by her refusal. 'It's important,' I said.

'It starts in an hour, and it's strictly formal. You can't go in looking like you are. The Prime Minister is coming!'

'Introduce me to the head of security and I'll hang about outside with the rest of the thugs and dishevelled journalists.'

Kimaaya sighed.

'It's for Pratap. And Shayak too.'

'I can't believe I am saying this,' she said, rolling her eyes. 'Fine. Come along.'

I kept the visit, as promised, brief. This was a detour, one I really didn't have the time for. But it would be another piece of the puzzle in place – and help out one of Titanium's star clients.

Kimaaya had dropped me off and disappeared, saying she would be making her entrance shortly, with more fanfare. The press conference was about to start; the party would follow in the grand ballroom next door. The media was present in full force. Not just the mainline news but the business and entertainment news as well. This evening promised everything.

Luckily for me, with such high-powered VIPs in attendance, it all happened precisely on schedule. It was standing-room only by the time Pratap entered, as he took a seat at the top table. He was quickly followed by his CFO and his CTO. His Chief Technology Officer. The man from breakfast with Poonam. The man of the awkward conversation. The man of the black-file-left-behind.

The din rose and abruptly fell when the lights went out and a 3-D holographic projection filled the front of the room. This was Pratap Puri's game changer. The technology that promised green, clean energy to one village to start with – and potentially all of rural India if it went according to plan. This was his trump card ahead of the initial public offering slated for early next year. Pratap Puri had everything riding on this, his big gamble. He could have sat on his money, grown it safely and securely without tempting fate. But he dreamt big, of creating a second fortune.

I sat it out – the presentation and the questions that followed. Once again, it was kept tight ahead of the arrival of the Prime Minister. I waited till the crowd had thinned out before approaching Pratap.

He did not look happy to see me. 'I thought I made myself clear – you are a ghost here.'

No hint of scandal could sully his day. If only. 'You'll want to hear this.'

I didn't give him a chance to stop me. I launched straight into it, keeping my volume as low as possible while making sure I was being heard. Pratap's jaw clenched and skin paled as he heard about the breakfast meeting and my suspicion that his CTO and wife had conspired to steal company secrets that could jeopardize everything.

'What do we do?' he said when I was finished.

'You need to call Adlakha now and give him an update. This is not the time to be squeamish. If you move now, all may not be lost.'

I couldn't wait any longer. On my way out there was Kimaaya, basking in the glow of a 1000 flashbulbs. It was a world away from the woman who confessed her regret to me over losing Shayak just an hour ago.

In that moment, I knew she was right – Shayak was not built for this, to stand beside her in the spotlight. He craved shadows and shelter and calm away from the madness of his work. This Kimaaya was just right for Pratap Puri, hungry for a legacy.

Whether Poonam Puri saw it that way was another matter entirely.

FOURTEEN

I was on my way to the car when I read a message I had received mid-press conference from an unknown number. It was Shayak, with further instructions.

'Third room from the right. Bring Vinod.'

Amongst the rush of cars and security coming and going from the venue, it took longer for Vinod to find me than usual. I felt the panic rise. I couldn't be late – not tonight.

'I need to get to the *Titania*,' I told him. 'Fast.'

On the way, I was forced to consider that I was taking an awful lot on faith. How did I hope to get into a protected zone like the coastguard facility where the *Titania* was docked without Shayak? What if they stopped me before I could enter the secure compound?

But when we got there, the uniformed men waved us through. 'How?' I simply asked.

'I've told you before, ma'am, this is sir's city.'

'They know you?'

'I have been lucky to drive sir for many years now.'

'Even on his top secret assignments?'

I saw his smile in the rear-view mirror. 'There are some rooms or offices here?'

'Yes ma'am, on the side there.'

It seemed to be an administrative block of some sort. I looked for the third door. There were no windows.

'Vinod ...'

'I'll be right outside ma'am.' Then, wordlessly, he handed me his gun. Vinod clearly was much more than a driver. I only hesitated for a moment before taking it and slipping it into my bag.

'Thank you,' I said, getting out.

I walked into the dingy room and there he sat, in the light cast by a naked yellow incandescent bulb hanging from the ceiling. I didn't know why we were here but one look at Shayak's tired, drawn face was enough to convince me that things were much worse than I imagined.

I stood before him and took stock of his desolation. His mouth tried on its sardonic smile but didn't quite make it. 'You are upset with me for disappearing,' he said.

I didn't say anything. I found that I couldn't.

'I'm sorry. None of this should have happened. Not now, not when I haven't even begun to ...' He ran his hand through his hair. 'The pressure is getting intense, Reema. If something were to happen to me, there are things you need to know.'

'What are you talking about, Shayak?' I interrupted. 'Why would something happen to you?'

'The police are coming for me.'

'I know. But I thought we could fight it. Clear it up.'

'They have enough to get me.'

'I don't understand.'

'I might not be able to help it. Ajay has stalled it as long as he could.'

'What's going on?

'I don't know how much I can tell you. There might not be a lot of time, Reema, and you are going to be on your own soon.'

'All the more reason for you to be honest with me.'

'First tell me you are equipped to handle this on your own.'

'Go rogue? I thought I already had.' I told him about shifting base from office to home, enlisting the help of Terrence. On my part, it was no sacrifice. It was Shayak who had kept telling me that we should try to work within the system. My own experience with authority hadn't always been good, and I chose to operate at its fringes.

'It is going to get far lonelier before this is through,' he said.

'But why are the police after you on these ridiculous charges, all of a sudden, if you always work together?' I asked.

'I have made things a little uncomfortable for some people in power in the past few months,' he said.

'Still not making sense. I need you to start at the beginning.'

'I don't know where that is.'

'What is the source of your influence with almost everyone who counts, and what is the cause of the sudden animosity?'

Shayak stared me straight in the face, and did not look inclined to share.

'If this is in any way pertinent to the investigation into these murders, I need to know, Shayak.'

He closed his eyes. 'It's a long, complicated story and there are no shortcuts.' He poured us both some more water, biding his time, collecting his thoughts.

'So much goes under the radar of the common man in this city. Outside the realm of politics, there are forces within the administration that want things to be handled quietly, efficiently. Titanium is the natural choice.'

'Why?'

'Our low profile helps no end. And generally, I was one of their foot-soldiers for long enough to know how they like things done.'

'What do you mean?'

'I was an intelligence agent.'

'RAW?'

He shook his head. 'It was a clandestine wing of the military that was set up before my time. The closest equivalent I could give you was the National Security Group. The task was to do whatever was required in whatever situation was presented to us. I grew to lead it and, on many occasions, that meant I reported to none but the highest offices of the country.'

That explained his deep web of contacts. 'Why did you leave?'

'I can't really tell you the operational details, you have to understand that.'

'I do.'

'It was my first ever job. When I began, I was green and willing to do whatever it took to prove myself. Eventually, what they were asking got to be too much. I believed I could do more actual good – and less harm – outside the establishment.'

'It was an amicable parting?'

'Amicable enough that Titanium's bread and butter are government – often military – assignments,' he said. 'Very few people know what I have just told you within or outside of the company; I trust you will keep it to yourself.'

'Of course, but there must be plenty of talk.'

'Till they have a confirmation, it doesn't really matter.'

I could see I would get nothing more specific out of Shayak yet. And still it explained so much. Everything, in fact, about Titanium. The secrecy, Shayak's long disappearances. And why putting Shayak Gupta's face in every newspaper in the country could have devastating consequences.

He took a sip of water. I waited for him to continue and, at last, he did. 'You remember the shootout at the warehouse?'

'Yes.'

'Your journalist friend was right: I was there. Titanium was called in to investigate, as the police suspected a connection to a case we had worked on some time ago.'

'Tell me about the old investigation.'

'No one inside Titanium has heard what you are about to hear. Remember the blast in Worli two years ago?'

How could I forget it? It had been a powerful explosion. Fatalities had been low because it had occurred in a deserted building, but two policemen and three civilians who had been passing were killed. The strength of the device had sparked fear and, with the spectre of serial blasts always looming over the city, it had caused panic.

'What no one knew was that the bomb was made from explosives from the Ordnance Factory. The police decided to bury this piece of information and, when a terrorist outfit took responsibility for it, things played right into their hands. An investigation was launched, the usual suspects rounded up and a suitable fall guy obtained.'

'Any explanation of how the explosives were acquired and by whom?'

'Before we got that far in the investigation, I was stopped by the then commissioner from moving ahead. By the time Ajay was appointed, the trail had gone cold. But from what we saw, this was someone we hadn't dealt with before. It was not the Mumbai gangs or any of the other terrorist groups that Titanium or the police were familiar with.'

'Motive?'

'The building was being used as a temporary hold for seized drugs. About 250 kg of drugs had been found in a succession of lorries coming in from Goa, and the entire consignment disappeared following the blast.'

'A high-intensity explosion to steal drugs? That hardly seems efficient when a bribe in the right quarters would probably have sufficed.'

Shayak shot me a smile. 'Exactly what was bothering me about it. More so, because one of the officers killed, Ajay's predecessor Daanish Alam, was one of the brightest to have entered the force in some time. He was moving up fast, had a reputation for incorruptibility and was taking the gangs head on.'

'So the drugs ...'

'Merely an added perk. In all likelihood, Daanish had been the real target, and the bomb and drugs served to diffuse that.'

'What did Daanish know?'

'That's the problem. He knew too much about almost everyone in Mumbai. He was relentless. But the methods, the explosives – it all pointed to someone we weren't familiar with. That, coupled with the drugs haul, led me to believe that whoever was behind those shipments must also be involved with the blast. But then we were called off the case.'

'Why?'

'The commissioner said they had caught the people behind it, who belonged to the terrorist outfit that claimed credit.'

'But?'

'I didn't buy the story and couldn't let it go. Daanish was a good man, and a friend. I knew that if someone had taken such a risk to kill him, what they were hiding was a serious affair. But I got busy, and it was only earlier this year that I started following up on leads.'

'What have you learnt?'

'I matched the explosives to an ordnance factory in Goa. The lorries smuggling drugs were coming from there, and I was able to confirm that they were loaded in Goa itself. But as soon as I started asking questions, I got another call. This time not from the police, but from a minister. The message was clear: Back off, no conditions.'

'But why were you called in after the recent shootout in that case?'

'Special request from Ajay. No one was supposed to know. But of course, it got out. As what I am now considering direct fallout of that, one of our most sensitive operations in the Middle East was cancelled, and I have been overseas bringing our team back to safety as soon as I could.'

Thus his dropping off the grid. 'And how is any of this related to Afreen's murder?'

'It may not be connected at all – I think they found a good way to get rid of me.'

'But someone chose this moment to get scared enough to go through all this trouble to frame you.'

'Yes, but we have too little to establish why.'

'Your sources can't tell you who it is that ordered you off?'

'No, and that is what frightens me.'

'So how do you suggest I proceed?'

'I am at a loss. I have been working with extreme caution, as I'm sure you've noticed, so as not to precipitate this situation. But now the die has been cast. All I can suggest is that you concentrate on solving the cases you have.'

'That includes Afreen's murder?'

'Yes,' he said. 'Since I am the prime suspect,' he added with a smile. 'I was wrong about that.'

I nodded. 'I'll need the material on the shootout as well.'

'No. I won't burden you any further, and there is no evidence of a connection. Besides, there isn't much material that's not in my head.'

'How useful.'

'Maybe I'll be out in time to be of some real help.'

'Out of where?'

'Lock-up. Jail. Wherever they stash me.'

'You can't go to jail!'

'And maybe I won't.'

'Why don't you run?'

'That will achieve nothing apart from creating an illusion of guilt. And don't forget that I am hardly a friendless, anonymous Mumbai man. I'll be dealt with quickly and fairly.'

'How can you be sure when you don't even know whom you are up against?'

'Ye of little faith.'

'What if you are wrong?'

'Then I have you on the outside. You'll find the real killer and get me out.'

Shayak smiled and I felt the panic rise to choke me. He didn't miss the fleeting fear, and he reached out to run his fingers across my cheek.

'I'm asking a lot of you.'

'Too much.' I stood up and I turned away. I heard the chair scrape the floor as he stood up.

'I know you,' he said, his mouth dangerously close to my ear, hands on my shoulders.

'No, you don't.'

'I know what I need to know. You're strong, you're smart, you're independent. You don't need me for this.'

He turned me around. There were barely six inches between us. He was still too far. But the anger I felt was like a wall between us.

'Break it down to its littlest pieces,' he said.

'And then it is as easy as pie?'

'The more I tell you, the more occluded it will all get.'

I shook my head, and took a ragged breath. 'Fine.'

'Attagirl. Now quickly,' said Shayak, 'tell me what you know.'

I told him about clearing Viraat, nailing Raj for the theft of the watch and even the progress I had made in the Pratap Puri affair.

'How about that,' he said. 'You've already solved three cases.'

'Don't patronize me,' I said. 'You still haven't heard about the Afreen business.'

He didn't seem surprised that I had pursued it.

'I only went as far as I needed to establish her identity.'

'I'm sure,' Shayak said dryly.

'She ran away from home in Calcutta to make a name for herself in Bollywood. Work was impossible to find, and she became a call girl. However, her luck was turning, thanks to a sugar daddy of some kind.'

Then I heard the door open and the sound of footsteps on the hard cement ground. I stepped back but didn't turn around to look; I already knew who would be standing there.

'Ajay,' said Shayak.

'Sorry to have to do this,' he said.

'Let's get it over with.'

Shayak moved towards him as I stood rooted to my spot. When I finally turned around, my eyes met Ajay's and I saw surprise there, and a hint of something else. He didn't handcuff Shayak but simply led him away, a constable trailing in their wake.

I waited till I heard their car pull away before I exited, turning off the light and closing the door behind me as though I was doing nothing more than leaving office for the day.

And then, with terror in my heart, I walked into the night.

FIFTEEN

In a fog, I got out of the lift in my building to almost stumble upon Terrence squatting on the ground, back against my door. 'What are you doing here?' I said.

'I've been trying to call you for an hour,' he said.

I had switched off my phone on entering the warehouse, and had forgotten to turn it back on. 'What about?' I said, fishing through my bag for the keys.

'I may have learned something about Afreen that could be of help.'

'Come in.' We walked in and I threw my bag on the sofa, collapsing beside it.

'I wanted–'

'Shh. Just wait.' I couldn't think yet. I put on a pot of coffee and ordered Chinese from a nearby restaurant. Then I went into the bathroom and splashed water on my face. I watched myself in the mirror till I felt emptied of emotion. Then I went back out, poured the coffee and took a seat. 'Now talk,' I said.

'Afreen recently wrote to her parents.'

'How do you know this?'

'My guy met them.'

I had no idea Terrence was still pursuing that angle. 'She apologized for what had happened, and said that she was working in films, thanks to her new friends, and had seen the way to her truth. Used those words over and over again.'

'Strange.'

'Hindu girl adopting a Muslim name, quoting what sounds to me like scripture,' said Terrence.

'I've heard that phrase before.'

'Been hanging about in church of late?'

'No, it's not that.' Where had I come across those exact words? It couldn't have been so long ago. The more I tried to remember, I knew, the harder it would be. 'Anyway, go on.'

'Well, her parents were thrilled to hear from her at all. They wrote back, asking her what she was doing and when they could visit. She replied to say that she didn't have a place for them to stay but after this new film she was working on, she should be able to afford a nicer flat, so they should wait awhile.'

'Did she say anything else about these friends of hers?'

'No. Couldn't you ask the crowd at Maaya Island?' Terrence suggested.

I shook my head. 'None of them know her very well. She was so out of place there.'

And then it came to me, the mention of Maaya Island jolting my memory. 'I *have* heard that expression before! In a conversation at Kimaaya's place between two women. It sounded like one was giving the other a message from someone else. Something about remembering the way to the truth.'

'Which women?'

'That's the thing – I didn't see them.'

'Any guesses?'

'I think it is safe to assume one of them was Afreen.'

'Spreading the good word?'

'No, I don't think that was it. It sounded like a veiled threat almost, and most likely it was Afreen being intimidated.' She had seemed so scared, so uncertain during our conversation that day after the lunch with Bindu Bisht. 'It sounded like someone was reminding her about a debt of gratitude.'

'Any idea what it could have been about?'

'No.' I ran a tired hand through my hair and gave it a tug.

'Coincidence?'

Shayak believed in coincidence, I did not. 'I don't think so. We need to find out where these two cases overlap to make sense of any of it,' I said.

But before I came to any conclusions, it was time to pare it down to just the facts. 'The journalist Prashant Parashar definitely had made contact with Dhingre, and now in all probability has disappeared himself. Let's start there,' I said.

'Right.'

I grabbed a piece of chart paper and started to write in big block letters. 'Dhingre was not at the island to blackmail Kimaaya – he was there to warn her. The journalist was the source of the information that came from a person I believe may be the killer.'

'What about motive? To destroy Kimaaya's career?' said Terrence.

'Why? She was hardly a threat to anyone at this stage. And if it was about putting her out of commission, why not attack her instead of her has-been agent?'

'What about her stalker guy? He could have unresolved issues.'

'He has an alibi for Dhingre's death, and has no connection to Afreen.'

'So who else could it be? Nothing else makes any sense.'

In the light of Shayak's latest revelations and his being framed in Afreen's murder, there was a possibility that needed to be considered: What if none of this was about Kimaaya at all? What if it had nothing to do with secret marriages and divorces, or blackmail and extortion or Bollywood? What if it was about bringing down Shayak?

The marriage data was leaked. Not to harm Kimaaya but to put the spotlight on Shayak. To make him India's most famous face. To expose him and thereby to compromise the covert operations that depended on his anonymity. Dhingre was killed only incidentally, to stop him from going to Kimaaya with what he knew, which could potentially have prevented the scandal.

Then why kill Afreen? She must have known something. But not about Kimaaya – about Dhingre's killer. About Shayak. Was it something she had seen?

I was suddenly certain. 'None of this is about Kimaaya,' I said, telling Terrence what I could about Shayak's arrest.

'Well, that changes everything,' he said.

'But I can't figure out how Afreen fits.'

'What do we know about her?'

'Call girl who wanted out. Starlet just making it in Bollywood. One of her clients, or perhaps a boyfriend, got her a big break.'

'Who is he? A producer? This is Bollywood we are talking about. This guy could be all kinds of criminal.'

Her film was being produced by Manmohan T. Mahindra. He was an industry veteran, but had seen better days.

'This is all just speculation,' I said. Right now I needed to focus on the concrete, otherwise I would be lost again. 'We'd be better off looking at the solid, incontrovertible facts.'

'How was Shayak framed?'

I told him about the fingerprint and gun. 'Someone must have planted a serious amount of information in what must be one of the most secure systems in the business.'

'Which tells you what?'

'That this – at least some part of it – was an inside job.'

'Shit, man,' said Terrence. 'You'd think Titanium would be above this.'

If any of Titanium's special assignments for the government were compromised due to an internal breach, the ramifications could be catastrophic – for much more than Shayak and his company. 'I need you to hack an e-mail account,' I said.

'Child's play. Shoot.'

I gave him the two e-mail IDs I had for Pranav Adlakha.

'Who is this guy?'

'My boss.'

'Why him?'

I told him what I could, though it was all circumstantial. Pranav Adlakha seemed to nurse more than a little resentment against Shayak, not to mention the fact that he would know exactly what sort of incriminating evidence to plant, what would be required to create a case against Shayak and how best to go about it. He had access to all aspects of the system, would have known about Kimaaya's safe and her security arrangement. And then the fact that Shayak had given this case to me instead of his far more experienced investigator.

'I doubt you'll find much in his e-mail,' said Terrence. 'He'd have to be smarter than that.'

'Then what do you suggest?'

'Get me into the office and let me play around on his computer.'

'Impossible. That place is a fortress. Without some major clearance, I'd have no hope. And with everything that's going on, forget about it.'

'Can't the boss man get it done?'

My silence told him what he needed to know.

'Lover boy has left you out in the cold, has he?'

I tried hard to hide it, but his words bristled. 'Kind of hard to help when you are in lock-up,' I said. 'Can't you hack it remotely?'

Terrence gave me a look of undiluted shock.

'What?'

'You want me to break into the Titanium system? These guys keep every corporation in the country secure.'

'I have been told that nothing is un-hackable.'

'Some are less hackable than others.'

'Do it, Terrence. I know you can.'

'I won't get arrested, will I?'

I would have liked to have been able to issue a categorical 'no' but with Shayak in jail, who was I to say? So I qualified my answer. 'Not if you do it right.'

Terrence gave me a glare that smacked the happy-go-lucky air straight out of his face. 'Give me something to work with here.'

I closed my eyes. I called Archana. When I hung up, I had a name and a number. 'Neeraj Surana – the man who built the current Titanium system. Heard of him?'

'Of course I have.' Neeraj, Terrence informed me, was something of a prodigy. By age eighteen he had hacked several government websites, had almost been arrested and received job offers from leading IT firms. He turned them all down to drop out of high school and start his own company. 'It would be great to work with him,' Terrence said.

It was late, but I called Neeraj anyway. He heard me out.

'You want me to do what?'

In half an hour, Neeraj, who looked not a day over fifteen, was seated in front of me.

'You want me to do what?' he repeated.

'Hack Titanium.'

'You do realize I have nothing but the word of a woman I have never met before that one of the tightest security systems I have ever set up has been breached?'

'Shayak trusts you. I was told to go to you and no one else.'

'And I can't contact Shayak in any way for confirmation of this story?'

'No.'

He shook his head. 'How do I know you even work with Titanium?'

'Terrence here doesn't. I do. Have you met Archana?' I asked, dialling her number.

'The admin woman? Yeah, she made me sign a bunch of forms, took my fingerprints and practically asked me to piss in a cup.'

'Archana,' I said, 'I have Neeraj Surana in front of me. He is afraid to proceed without some form of official communication about what we discussed earlier.'

'Put me on speaker,' said Archana.

'Go ahead,' I said.

'Neeraj,' said Archana, 'Reema Ray is authorized to act on Shayak's behalf for the moment.'

'Even if that means breaching Titanium's own security mechanisms?'

'Even if it means blowing up the building.'

Neeraj's eyes widened and, with an incredulous shake of the head, made it clear what he thought of all of us.

'How do I know this won't come back to bite me in the ass? Where's the paperwork?'

'There's no time for that.'

'Then I don't think I am comfortable– '

'If we double your hourly rate would you care so much?'

'Hell no!'

'Then get to it.' With that, Archana hung up.

'What precisely do you want me to do?' Neeraj asked.

'We think someone inside Titanium is somehow involved with the murders of Ashutosh Dhingre and Afreen. This person has manipulated requisition forms, altered e-mail communication and has almost certainly been monitoring and perhaps doctoring surveillance footage. We need you to find out who it was.'

I shared the mail sent to Arora where Lalu Prasad's name had been inserted, and the requisition for the gun. I gave him an approximate window when our man Lalu was on the island, if that might help him determine whether the security tapes had been tampered with in some way.

'That's days of footage,' he said.

'Yes.'

'I'm the only one authorized to see this?'

'Apart from us, yes, for the time being.'

'Then screw the footage. Even if it was doctored, it won't tell us much. Let me get to work on this other info.'

Half an hour later, another pot of coffee on, Neeraj was still shaking his head. 'I can see where the intrusions occurred. They definitely did. But I can't say where they are originating.'

'They are from within the system?'

'Knowing what I know about the system, I would say yes. But at this time, that is an educated guess. Someone with exceptional skills – and I mean skills to match mine – could have cracked it from the outside. Especially the e-mail tampering. But this gun requisition is tricky. Plus, if you look at the serial numbers and all the additional information this person needed to have, it seems the most likely scenario is an inside job.'

'If I give you a username, will you be able to see its activity?' I asked.

'Sure.'

I scribbled Adlakha's account information and passed it to him.

'Adlakha?' he said, his surprise evident.

'You know him?'

'I worked with him when we were setting this up.'

'He knows about this stuff?'

'Actually, no. He knows very little about anything of a higher tech profile than signing in to e-mail. He's old school.'

'Why did he work with you then?'

'He briefed me about Titanium's vulnerabilities, and which sections of company data needed to be closely guarded. He picked up where Shayak left off.'

Shayak involving Adlakha in ramping up security meant two things: Shayak did *not* share my suspicions about the investigator, and Adlakha had all the information he needed for an attack. 'That means he'd know, in theory, how to work the system, maybe in collaboration with a hacker?'

He shrugged. 'It's possible.'

'Check it out,' I said.

'Right.'

In half an hour, Neeraj gave me another negative. 'I can't find anything here. If Adlakha is working with a hacker, he didn't give him access to his account.'

'In other words, it's unlikely?'

'I'd say it doesn't make any kind of sense. But I only know what you've told me.'

'Any other ideas?' asked Terrence.

'I can't really keep throwing names out at random,' I said, the frustration creeping up on me. 'It's a huge company, and I've been there only a couple of weeks.' There were half a dozen offices on the fourth floor belonging to senior Titanium staff, and I didn't even know their names. Then there was Archana, who seemed to have her finger on the pulse of the organization. Except that Shayak seemed to trust her above all else. Till I could speak to Shayak, anything I would say would be guess work; without foundation and irresponsible given the circumstances.

'Give me something more to work with and I'll do my best. But there is nothing here to identify your virtual intruder,' said Neeraj.

'Fair enough,' I sighed. 'Thanks. I'll call you if I can think of anything else.'

SIXTEEN

It wasn't easy getting a foot onto MTM's set. It was my persistent badgering and dire warnings regarding the fate that would befall Shayak without Kimaaya's utmost cooperation that caused her to direct Nimisha to do the needful. It turned out to be nothing more inconvenient than making a phone call.

On the floor were scenes of far greater chaos than I had ever imagined, and far fewer – zero, in fact – stars hanging about in their dressing gowns, sipping Bellinis at an inappropriate hour. It was kind of dingy around the corners and, with the cameras quiet, dimly lit. A few extras hung about but mainly it was the production crew.

This would have been Afreen's new project. Her big break.

I had arrived before the cameras started rolling for the day. Spot boys were serving hot tea. Samosas were piled onto a tray, and I had to fight my growling stomach and stay seated. I was directed to Manmohan T. Mahindra's office, and made to wait.

Mahindra finally walked in. A lackey trailing in his wake got an earful about something that had nothing to do with his job; he poured two cups of tea for his boss and me, and left.

Mahindra seemed to have embraced every cliché about suspect Bollywood producers without any trace of irony: he was a hulking figure in a safari suit and photo-sensitive glasses that were dark despite his being indoors for some time. He had a thick gold chain around his neck and a tika on his forehead. He barely looked at me.

'Yes!' he barked.

'I am Reema Ray. Nimisha from Kimaaya Kapoor's office spoke to you about me.'

'Yes, yes,' he said, scrolling through messages on his phone. 'What you wanted? An audition, no?'

Was that what Nimisha said to get me in? 'Actually, I need to speak to you about Afreen.'

I had his attention. 'Are you with some media?' he asked.

'No, I am investigating her death.'

'Police?'

'No. Private investigator.'

'Accha.'

'I was wondering if you could tell me anything about her?'

'Meaning?'

'Anything, really. What was she like?'

'Sweet girl, but nervous, very nervous. First big role and all.'

'How was she selected for it?'

'Meaning?'

'Did she audition for you?'

'Are you implying that there was some improper business?'

'No– '

'Is this a sting operation? Like how you media got hold of Shakti bhai?'

'I am not with the media.'

'Get out!' he shouted.

I tried to hold my ground.

'Get out now before I throw you out!'

I exited hastily, cursing his bizarre behaviour. But I was far from done. I looked around for an inconspicuous spot away from MTM's glare, hoping to get lost in the melee. Once I found a suitable corner, I lounged around with my teacup, trying to blend in. A few moments later, actor Adil Khan strolled on to the set. He looked like he could do with a couple more hours of sleep, or a couple of months in rehab. Director Anupam Khattri was furious, but didn't say a word. Perhaps because it was Adil who had convinced MTM to come on board and was rumoured to have arranged the funding, it appeared he could get away with anything on set. Or maybe this was how it always worked.

Adil retreated to his vanity van and came out after fifteen minutes, not looking ready for anything, apart from perhaps a fight sequence.

'Madness, isn't it?'

The words came from beside me: a man, quite a bit taller than I, a head of unruly dark brown hair hanging down to his shoulders, a beard covering half his face. He was dressed in a faded T-shirt, well-worn skinny chinos and blue rubber chappals that had survived at least a year or two beyond their throw-by date. Despite the casual attire, he was well groomed. There was a tattoo on the inside of his right wrist, a Japanese character. It looked familiar, and not just because of six months of college Kanji, but I couldn't recall what it meant. His skin was swarthy, so it was hard to tell his origins – he sounded British but looked like he could be from anywhere.

'Can't argue with you there,' I said.

'It's a mad industry. You are not an actress, are you?'

'No.'

'You should keep it that way.'

'Why?'

'This is pretty tame compared to what I have seen, and I am new here too.'

'You look familiar. Are you sure I haven't seen you in anything?'

The man doubled over in laughter. 'That will be the day! I'd be just another British villain speaking ridiculous Hindi.'

British, then. 'So, no relation to the film industry at all?'

'Just a curious onlooker. But you really do fit the part. I'd run for my life. Never know when you'll be waylaid. It might even be contagious.'

I smiled. 'I think I must be immune to this particular disease. I wonder if this film will even get made.'

'Oh yes,' he nodded. 'It might take a few years and will probably do quite badly, but it'll get made.'

'I heard that young actress who died recently was supposed to be in it.'

'Yup,' said the man, face grim. 'But this is Mumbai, and it stops for no one.'

With that, he moved on to have a word with Adil Khan.

I saw the boy who had brought tea earlier. 'Who is that?' I asked, nodding to the stranger.

'That is George sa'ab.'

'Who is he?'

'How should I know? I only serve tea.'

'Is he part of the production crew?'

'No.'

'Where is he from?'

'Outside.'

He moved on, bored by my questions. I heard 'George sa'ab' talking to MTM in flawless Hindi. As I got close enough to hear what was being said, MTM turned around and his eyes settled on me. I took that as my cue to exit.

Where had I seen that man? I got home and hit Google first thing.

'George' and 'Manmohan T. Mahindra' threw up nothing. There was precious little written about the film and there was no mention of a George anywhere, not even on MTM's older projects.

Then I thought of his conversation with Adil Khan, what I knew about the film's financiers. I entered 'George' plus 'Adil Khan'.

No wonder he looked familiar – I must have seen his photograph in any number of lifestyle pages, possibly in the magazine I used to write for. George Santos, current guru to every mover and shaker in Mumbai, who had rehabilitated a string of disillusioned foreign millionaires through his enlightenment programme run in a camp tucked away in the farthest reaches in south Goa. There were several pictures of him arm in arm with film stars, including Adil.

He had no website, but I found a blog written by someone who had been through one of his workshops. George Santos' motto? 'See the way to the truth.'

The very same words Afreen wrote to her parents, the words I had overheard between her and the mystery woman on Maaya Island.

The pieces of the jigsaw were finally coming together. I was inches away – I could feel it. And, somehow, George was also part of this picture.

But I couldn't function at full capacity on an empty stomach, so I opened the fridge to put together a hasty lunch. I threw together a simple salad and piled ham and cheese on bread and, while it toasted, I worked on a vinaigrette.

I dug through my cupboard and there it was. On my bottle of light soy was the character I had seen on George's wrist. I knew it was familiar; it must have been this strange synaptic connection that had fuelled my food urge. I almost never put soy in my salad: though I knew it would provide the perfect salty counterpoint to creamy avocado and sweet pomegranate, it was the tattoo that had triggered the inspiration. I took a picture with my phone and searched for matches online: it meant 'sunset'. How trite.

I pulled out the other ingredients for my dressing. Rice wine vinegar, sesame oil and chilli. Quick didn't have to mean bad. As the oil made contact with the vinegar and formed beads, it all hit me with the force of too much wasabi up the nose.

Clarity had arrived, as usual, all at once, cutting through the fog of memory and meaning. No matter how rewarding the meal had become, it was time to abandon it. I called Ajay. 'I can prove Shayak wasn't at Afreen's crime scene.'

'How?'

'By showing you there is no way *that* fingerprint was actually on *that* bar.'

'Once again, how?'

'I can demonstrate, but I need access to Viraat's flat. In your presence, of course.'

'I really don't have time for this, Reema.'

'It will take ten minutes, if that.'

He sighed. 'Meet me there in an hour.'

I got there before Ajay and waited outside the flat. When he arrived, I saw that he still wore the face he had on the night he arrested Shayak. As far as he was concerned I was Titanium, and that made me the enemy. For now, at least.

He was brusque as he opened the door. 'Now, what do you want to show me?'

I walked over to the bar, my evidence kit in hand.

'I don't know what you think we missed,' he said.

'You missed nothing. Your team simply found something it shouldn't have.'

'I won't pretend to know what you mean by that.'

'Let me show you.'

I opened the kit and took out the dusting powder, brushes and transparencies.

'Press your whole palm on the surface of the bar, please,' I said.

'How?'

'Just press down with a moderate amount of pressure.'

Ajay did as I asked.

'Perfect,' I said. He raised his hand and crossed his arms. I quickly brushed powder over where his imprint should have been.

'What do you see?' I asked.

'Not much,' he said.

'Exactly.' I then took the transfers and scanned them. 'See this?' I said, as the first image opened on my laptop. 'There is absolutely no ridge detail available here. Only a broader sort of smudge.'

'Why?'

'Because this screen has been specially treated with a product designed to repel both water and oil. And as you know, fingerprints are the traces left behind by our body's natural oils.'

'I've never heard of such a screen before.'

'The coating has been designed for numerous purposes, mostly industrial. It is used on touchscreen surfaces to reduce the smudges and smears that appear with use. This being a cutting-edge professional bar, designed for handling by many people while displaying high-definition advertising images, it has received that treatment.'

'How did you figure this out?'

'Viraat spilled a glass of water on it the day Afreen died. It behaved very oddly. It didn't hit me then but when I considered that highly improbable fingerprint more closely, it eventually came to me.'

No need to mention the moment of epiphany over a salad, or beads of suspended fluids dancing in my vinaigrette.

'Try it again at a different spot,' said Ajay. 'This time with your own prints.'

'This is no magic trick.'

'I know. I just need to be sure.'

I wiped away the residual powder and repeated the demonstration.

Ajay stood there, jaw clenched. 'You know I still can't release Shayak. Not on the basis of this alone.'

'Why?'

'The gun.'

'But doesn't this prove someone is trying to frame him?'

'It's not enough.'

'Even though anyone could have fired the gun that shot Afreen?'

'Reema, you don't know how these things work.'

A phone call from the right person was far more powerful than evidence from a nobody. 'Ajay,' I said, exasperated, 'I think I know exactly how it works.'

I got back home and reassembled my makeshift team of Terrence and Neeraj. It was time for the gloves to come off.

I first turned to Neeraj. 'How do you feel about hacking the e-mail ID of a murdered woman?'

'Like it is something that might land me in jail.'

'What if the same rules apply as yesterday?'

'Double pay? I'd say the fastest way to my heart is through my wallet.'

I gave him Afreen's e-mail ID.

'What am I looking for?'

'Anything that connects with Shayak Gupta, Titanium, Kimaaya Kapoor, Ashutosh Dhingre or George Santos.'

Terrence raised a brow. 'George Santos?'

'Yes. You are from Goa, right?'

'Originally, yes. Lived in Calcutta all my life, though.'

'What do you know about him?'

'Spiritual, self-help type guru. There is plenty of information in the public domain.'

'Seeing as how I do my best to avoid the gossip columns, I apparently missed it all.'

'Give me half an hour and I'll put together a document for you.'

I turned my attention back to the chart paper, which was now overrun with what would look to an outsider like random neural firings, when I received a call from Shakuntala Padhy.

'Prashant Parashar has surfaced,' she said.

'Where has he been?'

'He says he was being held in a house somewhere on the outskirts of the city.'

'Can he identify his captors?'

'He says there were two men, but he didn't see their faces.'

'Can I meet him?'

'I am with him at his home. Why don't you come over now?'

I took directions and hung up. 'I need to go,' I told Neeraj and Terrence.

'This will take me a while, so I'll be here,' said Neeraj.

'Do you have anything yet?' I asked Terrence.

'Not much, but I will soon.'

'Can you mail me if you find anything of interest? I'll read it on my phone.'

In the half hour it took me to reach Parashar's residence in Andheri, I received a mail from Neeraj marked 'Urgent'.

Your girl received some pretty unfriendly mails from an unknown sender I have not yet been able to identify, digging for information on what was going on at Maaya Island the day after the murder. No sign that she replied. Sender's bases covered pretty comprehensively.

My pulse quickened. Here at last was a definitive link between the two murders. Afreen either knew something – or someone believed she might know something – about the death of Ashutosh Dhingre. The conversation I had overheard was surely someone trying to get information from her – using George Santos' motto as emotional leverage. Now if I could only figure out what it all meant.

At the home of Prashant Parashar, I composed my thoughts as I waited at the door. Shakuntala let me in and led me to a small living room. There sat Parashar, a small man wearing a blue half-sleeved shirt and baggy khakis, feet bare. His wet hair told me he had showered but he had not shaved, and his grey-peppered beard sat uneasy on his face and contributed to the general air of shell shock.

Shakuntala introduced us. 'He was abducted not far from our office the day you spoke,' she said.

'Can you tell me anything about where you were taken?' I asked.

'It seemed like it was the middle of nowhere,' he began. 'For much of the way it was quiet and took a long time to get to. My head was covered with some sort of bag, so I had no idea where I was going. The only thing I can tell you for sure is that before we reached our destination, we were travelling on a highway for some time.'

'Did you see your assailants?'

'No. Not then or later. They were very careful. I thought from their voices that there were two of them, but mainly it was just one guy staying in the house.'

'How did they restrain you?'

'I was tied,' he said, holding up raw, red-ringed wrists. 'But I also think I was drugged. There are periods of time I can't really remember.'

'How did they release you?'

'Same way they abducted me – drove me, bag over my head, to an empty field off Navi Mumbai. I called Shakuntala who had me picked up.'

'They were nice enough to give your cell phone back?'

'Fully charged.'

'You want to tell me how you really came by that pen drive?'

He looked contrite. 'Someone had contacted me by e-mail after I had written a piece about Kimaaya being dropped from one of her film projects.'

'What did they say?' I asked.

'That they had information that would give me the scoop of the year. At first I thought it was a hoax but I kept getting these mails and then, when I showed an interest, the person said the information was mine on condition that I didn't seek out the sender's identity. And that we didn't contact Kimaaya before publication.'

'Did you?'

'No – the only thing we were concerned about is the authenticity of the information.'

'So what you wrote in your article about not being able to reach Kimaaya for comment ...'

'Wasn't true.'

I stole a glance at Shakuntala. Her lips pursed for just a second, displeasure quickly filed away for another time.

'Then why did they abduct you?'

'To tell me that if I spoke to you or any other investigators again, I would be sleeping with the sharks or something to that effect.'

'That's a lot of effort and time for a threat.'

Parashar shook his head. 'I am as confused as you are, but I really wasn't in a position to ask them about their motive, or to expect them to answer.'

'Did they mention me by name?' I asked.

'No, now that I think of it, they didn't.'

They had known within moments of our conversation that we were planning to meet. The killer had also known Dhingre was on his way to warn Kimaaya.

'Had Dhingre called you before heading to Maaya Island?'

'Not just before, but he kept calling, threatening to tell her everything.'

'Where is your cell phone now?'

He held it up.

'I wouldn't use it if I were you.'

His eyes widened.

'How did they treat you?' I continued.

'What do you mean?'

'Did they feed you?'

'Yes.'

'What sort of food?'

'Uh … bread and cheese. Maggi. Roti-sabzi one day. How does it matter?'

'What about water?'

'Yeah, they gave it to me when I asked. Tea too, a couple of times.'

'Are you sure you never heard or saw anything that might tell us where they held you? Think hard.'

Parashar looked uncertain. 'It's all so hazy ... but there was a phone call, during which one of the men said something about being near the Paras Hills food factory.'

'Paras Hills?' asked Shakuntala.

'Yes,' replied Parashar.

'You know where that is?' I asked.

Shakuntala nodded. 'It's right next to a piece of land that was acquired for a factory which then went under dispute. It was in the headlines quite a lot about six months ago. About an hour outside the city.'

'What else is out there?'

'Some factories, fishing villages, not much else. It's an uninspiring stretch of coast. Industrial run-off and politics have ensured its unsuitability as a home for resorts or luxury housing, even though it is on the water.'

'It could be worth a trip,' I said.

'Are you sure that's a good idea?'

'I'm pretty sure it is not.'

From what it sounded like, the abductors had merely wanted Parashar out of the way to obscure the source of the information they had leaked. Someone had panicked when they realized he might be speaking to me. When his silence had no more value, they had released him.

Ordinarily I would have called in reinforcements – armed reinforcements – to scope out the place. But I didn't have good information – and it definitely was not enough to put both myself and Vinod at risk.

In the absence of Titanium's long arm, I would have to work smart. I went back again to that whispered conversation on the island, and the bridge that had been built between Parashar and Dhingre at the intervention of the newspaper, which had prompted Dhingre's desperate measures to protect an unreceptive Kimaaya. 'Shakuntala,' I said, 'would it be possible to bring in Bindu Bisht?'

'Why?'

'She is holding a piece to this puzzle. I can't tell you more than that right now.'

She nodded and made the call. 'My office, 6 pm,' she told me, striding off.

SEVENTEEN

'Quite a piece of work, this George Santos,' Terrence said as I walked in. 'Guru for all seasons. Spiritual, corporate, relationship – he seems to have an answer for everything.'

'Who is he?' I asked.

'No one seems to be clear about that. British expat. Has lived around the world according to various interviews, and was a regular in the Goa 1970s scene in his youth. He only settled down there in the past few years, during which time he has been doing the rounds of the Goa-Mumbai celebrity circuit. Everyone who wants to be anyone goes to him for these transformational workshops he holds at his retreat.'

'What is he selling?'

'Enlightenment.'

'God man-style?'

'He leaves God out of it. His focus is on self-awareness in "all its many facets", cutting through all the bull that holds us back from becoming our best self.'

'Jeez. Where does he fit into our picture?'

'Adil Khan met him while researching a role he had a couple of years ago.'

That still didn't explain how Afreen fit in. 'Anything about Afreen and Adil, or George?' Mona aka Miss Sara had mentioned a sugar daddy who helped her get her break. Could that be George?

'There is nothing on her. But she would be too small a name to be mentioned in any of these puff pieces.'

I turned to Neeraj. 'Anything from Afreen's mail that can shed light?'

He shook his head. 'She doesn't seem to have been much of an electronic communicator.'

'Nothing on Santos?'

'Nope. Not much of anything except e-mail forwards, spam and those strange mails I told you about.'

'Can I see them?'

Neeraj pulled up a file. '*He expects your loyalty. Answer your phone. Reply to this mail. Anything to prove your commitment.*'

And the next morning: '*What is happening out there? What do you know? If you don't respond, expect a visit.*'

A visit – and a threat. 'Run a search for Bindu Bisht and George.'

'Coming up.'

What he found was not just any article but an experiential narrative of a week in a workshop with George. I skimmed through it and learned how he was surrounded by celebrities in search of self-discovery, foreign patrons who had given up on raves in favour of finding the path to their 'best self', sporting the latest designer resort wear and chowing down detox food – organic, of course. It was eastern exotica meets western self-help set against a deliciously luxe backdrop. And Bindu Bisht had signed up for the full package.

'Yes, I know George Santos. So does half of Mumbai.'

Bindu was seated before Shakuntala and me, in the editor's office. She was right too: the part of Mumbai in which Bindu moved was Santos' happy hunting ground.

'Somehow, Bindu, you have a connection with a number of elements of this case,' I said. 'I am just trying to understand them.'

'What are you going on about?' she said with a wave of the hand. Gone was Bindu's veneer of decency; she had no time for me or my questions.

'You were acquainted with Ashutosh Dhingre, a fact that Shakuntala leveraged to verify explosive information, making you one of the very few people who knew Kimaaya's secrets before they were printed in the paper.'

'Yes, I was at the meeting.'

'And you also know George Santos, who is somehow connected to Afreen.'

'She was one of his many students.'

'Did he get her the role in the MTM film?'

'It's possible.'

'What was he? Her sugar daddy?'

Bindu laughed. 'George doesn't need to sleep with two-bit starlets.'

'So he did it out of the kindness of his heart?'

'More likely a favour for someone.'

'And you wouldn't happen to know who that someone might be?'

'No.'

'It was you who mentioned to George this information about Kimaaya, which is how he knew about it before it made its way into the paper.'

'Definitely not.' Her outrage seemed like it might be genuine.

I changed course. 'George asked you to visit Maaya Island to remind Afreen what she owed him.'

Bindu had a pretty game poker face, but even she couldn't conceal her surprise at this.

'That was nothing, just a message delivered,' she said at last.

'He wanted to know what was happening on that island. Why do you think that is?'

'He didn't tell me any of that! He just said that he was expecting a call from Afreen and was annoyed at not having heard anything.'

'So annoyed that he had to send you to make contact? That didn't strike you as suspicious?'

'I was going to meet Kimaaya anyway. This was just one more reason to make the trip.'

'Bindu, I think you can be a little more helpful than that,' said Shakuntala.

'Look, as far as I know, the only thing connecting George and Afreen is this film he is helping Adil make.'

'George is the producer?'

'No, but he is involved somehow. You really should be asking him these questions, not me.'

'Did he say why he wanted you to send this message?'

'He only said he needed to know what was going on, that he wouldn't have asked if it wasn't important. He couldn't go himself as he was in Europe then.'

'Are you sure about that?'

'As is the rest of the world. He's been delivering talks around the globe that are being streamed live online. When we talked, he said he was in Germany somewhere.'

'But I met him on the set soon after.'

'He must have got back subsequently.'

'You took it as a matter of course that he would call you from overseas to go have a chat with a perfect stranger on his behalf?'

'Not a matter of course, no, but also not a matter of murder.'

I would check his tour dates, but I didn't doubt Bindu's words, nor did it really matter where George was. Even if he was involved, he wouldn't have been the man who wielded the wine bottle or pulled the trigger. His sort seldom were.

Once home, it didn't take long to confirm that George had just returned from Zurich the night before we met. The days of the Dhingre and Afreen murders, he was in Berlin and Paris respectively.

'Neeraj,' I said, 'I need something more on this man.'

'Permission to hack?' he said.

'Need you ask at this point?'

'Enough said.'

After a few minutes, Neeraj turned to me. 'It's the strangest thing,' he said. 'George Santos' digital life is harder to breach than a jail.'

'So not very hard,' Terrence laughed.

'I thought he had no website?'

'That's true, but that doesn't mean he has no presence online.'

'And you can't get into it?'

'It's taking more time than usual. And what I am seeing are sophisticated defences.'

'How sophisticated?'

'Very. And they seem familiar. I'm pretty sure I've seen them before.'

'Where?'

'Coincidentally, when I was working with Titanium, ramping up their security about a year ago.'

'What does that mean?' I asked.

'I think these safeguards were created by the same person.'

'Are you sure?'

'The code is not generic, and it is fairly distinctive. I have never seen it aside from these two occasions.'

'Is it good?'

'Yes, very.'

'Unbreachable?'

Neeraj grinned. 'If it were, would I have been called in by Titanium to improve upon it?'

'Why did that happen, exactly?'

'Of course I wasn't privy to specifics, but I was told that there had been leaks to do with confidential information.'

'Was the source of the leak ever identified?'

'From what I gathered, no. But they wanted to ensure defences were in place.'

'Is there any way of finding out whether there were any incursions into the system recently?'

'We would have known. I've set it up that way.'

'How about attempted incursions?'

'That is trickier. The system might catch it, but a smart hacker might be able to get away with it.'

'Can you look for anything, red flags of any kind, in the past month?'

'Believe me, I'm already on it. I want to know if my fortress has been breached as much as anyone. But it will take time.'

'Have you taken a closer look at the gun requisition and e-mail to the captain?'

'Next on the list,' said Neeraj.

'Take a few hours of downtime. Go home. I'll check in with you first thing tomorrow.'

I had barely surfaced the next morning when my phone rang. It was Vinod to tell me Archana needed him in office and that he would be reporting after noon.

I pottered around the kitchenette for a while before calling Neeraj to see if he had anything new. 'Hope I didn't wake you.'

'Nope. I've been up all night and your hunch was right – there have been a number of attempts to breach Titanium's system in the past month.'

'What do you know?'

'It happened over a period of time and the digital pathway is not the same, nor is it clear. But what puzzles me is that these attempts should have been spotted.'

'Have the safety mechanisms been compromised?'

'Must have been, or else reports of these breaches should have been sent to both Shayak and me. They were attempts to get into highly classified files. What exactly is the content of the files is information I cannot access.'

I would bet anything that they were pertaining to Titanium's defence projects. 'So this was a sophisticated, concerted effort?'

'Undoubtedly.'

'One that would require intensive work and deep knowledge?'

'Yes.'

'From a hacker like yourself?'

'*Like* me. Yes. And I can tell you that the gun requisition was sent from Shayak's user ID, though not from his computers at office or home. And the tampered email had the same source.'

I closed my eyes. Words I heard not long ago came back. *The soul of a hacker.* I opened them when I heard the ping of new mail and saw a message from Shayak's mail ID.

'Plot no. 8, Shantinagar, beside Paras Hills Food Factory. Meet me there at 10 am.'

'Neeraj, I'll have to get back to you,' I said.

Had Shayak been released? I tried calling his number; it was switched off. Even though Ajay had made it clear that he was not an ally when it came to this case, I tried his number repeatedly but it rang out. Either he was indisposed or he was screening my calls.

I had to act fast. If Shayak wanted to meet at Paras Hills food factory, he must have a lead on Prashant Parashar's kidnapper – most likely our murderer. I looked at my watch. I had only about ninety minutes to get there. I cursed my luck – to not have Vinod at a time like this was not ideal. When I couldn't reach Archana either I gave my phone a good shake to make sure it wasn't playing tricks on me.

I had to get moving, and a taxi wouldn't do. I called Sohana and in fifteen minutes was at her house, starting her ancient blue hatchback. She had been to the area a couple of times to cover the land unrest that Shakuntala had told me about, and gave rough directions.

'It's just off the highway, so you shouldn't have a problem.'

I was still unfamiliar with Mumbai, let alone a village an hour away. Using the phone as GPS, I got started. But as I reached the outskirts of the city, I lost network. Thankfully, Sohana's directions proved easy to follow and there were road signs showing the way. And yet, the closer I got to my destination, the more uncomfortable I became. I was far from the Mumbai I knew.

I finally hit a huge construction site which was the nearest landmark Sohana had been able to recall. Soon I saw a cluster of factories, all abandoned. And then a dilapidated sign for Paras Hills Foods. There was an unpainted boundary wall right beside it. I parked the car and approached a heavy-duty metal gate, which was unmanned and unlocked. I pushed it open and walked in.

It closed behind me with a click. The moment I heard that sound, I realized my deepest fears had been correct: I had walked into a trap. I was inside a high-tech hideout for a high-tech war, and my little lock-pick set wasn't enough to get me out of it. That mail I received was fake. I would not find Shayak inside. No one knew where I was except Sohana, and she would have no reason to come looking for me. It was too late to call for reinforcements – and it struck me with cold certainty that my phone had probably been hacked and my network killed to prevent just such a thing. Probably why I couldn't reach either Shayak, Ajay or Archana.

I scanned the perimeter. The wall was at least ten feet tall, with barbed wire looping around the top. It was electrified.

There still was not a person in sight. But there were cameras everywhere. My isolation was an illusion.

With no turning back, I could only forge ahead. I walked towards the building: a one-storey affair with shuttered windows. I approached the door, turned the knob. I had little doubt that if I didn't enter voluntarily, I'd be forced to soon enough.

I was in a small, sparse room with a set of functional sofas. The windows I saw from the outside were for show: on the inside they were boarded up and the only light filtered in through tiny recesses to allow ventilation. The air was heavy with the salt smell of the sea and a strange, oppressive, chemical odour.

One of the doors opened and out walked Rishi. 'Gotta give you credit, Reema, you were getting awfully close.'

I shocked myself by managing a smile. 'I've been dancing around you this whole time.'

How could I have not put it together sooner? It was only this morning, while speaking with Neeraj, that I finally worked it out. I had no excuse except that I had been blinded by my dislike for Adlakha. Once I realized it was an inside job, my judgement had been hijacked by Adlakha's reluctance to let me in, his resentment, his standing in the way of the Afreen investigation. And yet, all he had been doing was following orders, a concept I had no regard for. So I ignored all the signs that had pointed to a technologically-inclined mind being behind this, which Adlakha clearly was not.

'Get moving, Reema,' said Rishi.

My mistakes flashed through my mind one after another. Even if Adlakha could have paid an accomplice, wouldn't he have done a better job of planting a fingerprint? Instead Rishi, the tech genius who had no idea about forensics, had been slipped up by popular science – the ease with which fingerprints are found in crime shows. An investigator of Adlakha's experience wouldn't make such a rookie mistake. Shayak's print was not taken anywhere near that bar. It was lifted from somewhere everyday – like from the Titanium office or a doorbell – and carefully controlled, scanned and planted into the police forensics report digitally.

'We could stay here,' I said. I was mirroring his eerie sense of calm. But when he shot me back a small, cold smile, I began to fear that Rishi was far more – to put it bluntly – psycho than I had suspected.

Every piece of evidence we found in this crime was digital – except the two very real dead bodies. And behind it all was Rishi. No matter how good he was behind the computer, he was out of his depth in the real world. When it came to a tiny smear on a treated, oil- and water-repellent surface, his hack was easy to catch.

'Walk out of that door over there,' he said, pointing to a side exit.

As I complied, I weighed my options. I could try to overpower him – he wasn't very large and I had the skill to do it. But he was surely armed. He was being very careful to keep me in front of him. He had a plan.

I opened the door and walked out to find myself on a deck. There was a speedboat in front of us.

And there it was: the muzzle of a gun leaving a cold circle against the back of my neck.

'Get in,' he said. 'We're about to take a trip.'

I looked around. It was just me and Rishi, the boat and the sea. 'There's no audience here, Rishi. Must we resort to tired clichés?'

'Forgive me if the quality of my conversation isn't up to your standards. Perhaps we could try silence instead.'

I got in – I had no choice – and was filled with dread at what I saw: a long length of rope and a military-grade knife.

'Pass me your cell phone,' he said. 'Slowly.'

I reached into my pocket and did as I was told. I heard a small splash as he chucked it into the water. With it sunk all my hopes of being tracked down.

'Kind of pointless, since you commandeered it anyway.'

'No harm in extra measures. Sit on the floor,' said Rishi.

Once I was restrained, breaking free would be far more difficult. 'Rishi, I thought we were friends,' I said, kneeling before him.

'Yeah, well,' he said. 'If you had stayed out of this, maybe we could have been. But when Jay got you Bobby Gill's number, I knew you'd figure things out soon enough,' he said.

'You weren't in office that day because you were busy putting a bullet into Afreen.'

'And so it is. A half day. That's all it takes,' he said, bending to put down the gun and pick up the rope.

In the second he was distracted, I rested on my palms and kicked back in the direction of his kneecap as hard as I could.

He let out a scream of anger and pain and, as he lost balance, I made a mad scramble for the gun.

But I hadn't done enough damage for, even flat on his back, Rishi had recovered and grabbed the weapon, pointing it back at me.

'Don't even think of it,' he said, breathless. 'Sit down now or I shoot you right here.'

'Why don't you just get it over with?'

Rishi didn't respond.

As he got back to work, I asked myself why he hadn't killed me already. We were in the middle of nowhere; wasn't this as good a place as any to get the job done?

Rishi tied my hands with a rope, this time making sure he had a firm grip on the gun. 'Wrap this rope around your legs.'

I did as I was told, keeping it as loose as possible.

'Nice try,' he said, quickly tightening them with one hand before putting the weapon down and tying the knot.

Rishi started up the boat, pulling away from the shore before opening his laptop. The way he was bumbling about, it was clear he didn't know what he was doing.

I could smell fuel, and surmised that the jerry cans which I had seen at the back carried a supply. I didn't know how far we'd go in this vessel or whether Rishi was planning to make any stops along the way, but I was fairly certain we'd be heading in the direction of Goa. Somewhere in the vicinity of Sunset Bar.

That was, if Rishi didn't get us lost at sea first. He looked thoroughly confused as he stared at the controls – and that confusion was what I was counting on to save me.

An hour later, I was convinced that Rishi had no idea what he was doing or where he was going. He had made a couple of pained calls to someone – given where we were and the size of the device I assumed it was a satellite phone – and continued to look at his computer in a bewildered fashion.

'I might be able to help, you know,' I said.

'Why would you do that?'

'Getting lost at sea isn't on my list of things to do today.'

'I am assuming that neither was getting abducted by a disgruntled colleague.'

'I don't think "disgruntled" quite covers it.'

'Just a turn of phrase.'

'You're unhappy at Titanium?'

'Do my actions strike you as those of one who is content?'

'Most people would just leave.'

'Sarcasm doesn't suit you, Ray.'

'I have been told otherwise. And you didn't answer the question.'

'Why should I when it is so much more fun this way?'

'Whom are you working for?'

'Why do you assume I am working for someone?'

'I'm right, aren't I?'

He shrugged. 'In a loose sort of way.'

'It's George, isn't it? And we are going to meet him at Sunset Bar.'

He looked at me, clearly surprised.

'I bumped into your friend,' I said. 'He had an interesting tattoo on his wrist. A man in the sunset of his life, creating a second career for himself in a little spot of undiscovered south Goa, with a view of the sun going down over the Arabian Sea, 365 days a year,' I said, quoting Rishi's words back to him.

I saw a flash of annoyance pass over my captor's face. 'Sometimes we all talk too much,' I continued. 'Why take me to him?'

'Why do you think?'

And then it dawned on me. This was never about me – just like Dhingre's murder had not been about Kimaaya. 'You are using me as bait.'

'Took you long enough.'

'No one knows I am missing.'

'They'll be told in time.'

They thought Shayak would come for me. 'You've got it all wrong.'

'Do I? There is a lot one can glean from hours of surveillance tapes.'

'You've been watching me?'

'Only incidentally, at first. But once Shayak made a few stops by your place, I knew you'd come in handy.'

I remembered that tender forehead kiss in the doorway, in full view of the security cameras. 'Why, Rishi? With talent like yours, you could make a fortune without the capital crime under your belt.'

'Hackers like me aren't after a fortune.'

'So you infiltrate the Titanium system for the thrill of it?'

'You might say that.'

'At the behest of a gang of Goan gangsters?'

'Sometimes you need a pretext. And I wouldn't call them gangsters.'

'Sorry, George Santos is a spiritual guru.'

'You're not bad, Ray, but don't get ahead of yourself. George is but a small piece of the puzzle, much like me.'

'What am I missing?'

'George is a part of the whole, but he is pretty much legit. I worked for him as a security consultant. Took up the job after I dropped out of college, before he told me about this opportunity at Titanium.'

'Who is calling the shots?'

'It was my plan,' Rishi said, suddenly on the defensive.

'Why?'

'Boredom. For the joy of the hack. Because no one loved me when I was a little boy. Take your pick.'

Rishi's bravado really did not seem like an act. It would have worried me had I not seen the chink in his armour. 'Was that really enough reason to kill two people?'

'Ray, you think you've figured this all out but what you see are the trees, not the forest.'

'Tell me about this grand plan of yours. How did killing two people benefit anyone?'

'The deaths were a transactional necessity, not an end in themselves. Dhingre was never meant to die. Afreen was collateral damage; at a convenient place at a convenient time.'

'You had to stop Dhingre from approaching Kimaaya with what he knew about the stolen documents.'

'The wheels had been set in motion. It was important nothing got in the way. I couldn't let Kimaaya stop publication.'

'All to discredit Shayak.'

'And Titanium.'

'Then with Afreen you were killing two birds with one stone. She refused to help when called upon to do so, and was a good starting point to frame Shayak.'

'If she hadn't been so skittish, she would have lived. But she knew too much, and couldn't be trusted anymore. There is a lesson in there for you.'

'George wanted information.'

'She clammed up. I wouldn't have moved so fast, but after Dhingre died ...'

'You had upset some people with the way things were going, and needed to make amends, clean up after yourself.'

He shrugged. 'If I helped smear Titanium, I'd be set up for life. I'd never have to work for anyone again.'

'What was your prize?'

'What difference does it make?'

'Just curious.'

'I might not have wanted a fortune, but this would give me my independence. I could use my talent how I saw fit.'

'It always boils down to money.'

'I don't expect you to understand.'

But Rishi was distracted. He was fussing around the controls. I could tell from his expression that it wasn't looking good. Not only was it approaching darkness, it was eerily overcast.

'Don't you think it is a better idea to anchor for the night?' I suggested.

'Did I ask you?'

'There is no need to be rude. You clearly don't know what you are doing here.'

'I've made a call. Help should be on its way.'

'You've lost contact with them, haven't you?'

Rishi didn't answer, but when he cut the engine and looked around listlessly, it told me what I needed to know.

'Your bosses weren't happy with the way you did things, were they? When it became clear that the charges against Shayak wouldn't stick, you suggested your latest, messy fix by way of this abduction drama. And then you were saddled with a bum boat with bum GPS and bum instructions. To get rid of both of us in one go.'

'Shut up!' he screamed.

It was just a theory, but his anger told me I had hit close to home. 'Rishi, you can either let me help or you can screw this up all on your own.'

'Do you know how to sail this thing?' he asked, surly yet rapidly approaching desperate.

'I know a little about navigation.'

'At sea?'

'Not specifically, but the principles are the same.'

'We don't have reliable maps.'

'You have a satellite phone. We can find our own maps.'

'That might not help. Something seems wrong with the wheel,' he said.

'What do you mean?'

'It doesn't seem to be responding.'

'Why don't you have a look below?'

'I guess I'll have to.' He gave me a long glare before disappearing into the cabin.

I couldn't hear anything but when he came up ten minutes later, Rishi was even paler than before. For a good minute or two, he sat and stared out before coming to some sort of decision. 'You have two choices: either we both make it out of this alive, or only I do,' he said.

'Didn't I volunteer to help just a few minutes ago?'

'We need to get to shore. Something is wrong with the wheel, but the rudder thingie below deck seems to be responding. You'll have to navigate while I manually steer.'

'Okay.'

He got ready to go below.

'If you want me to help navigate, I will need my hands,' I said.

'No you won't. This is where we need to go,' he said, pointing to a location on the map on the southern coast of Goa, close to Palolem.

'I'll untie your legs so you can come up here and use the onboard compass, since the GPS seems to be malfunctioning. Try anything funny and I'll know.'

I waited till he was gone a few minutes before setting to work. I kept shouting directions to Rishi as, with my back to the laptop, I used what minimal functionality I had in my fingers to unplug the satellite phone and dial Shayak's number. In his panic, Rishi must have forgotten it was there, for I didn't think he'd knowingly leave it within reach.

It was slow going as after pressing each digit I had to turn around to make sure I had got the right one. But I finally made it, and hit 'dial' before squatting to the ground so I could press my face up against the device.

Then I heard footsteps – Rishi was on his way back up. I quickly stood up. But he was back on deck before I could get into position.

'What do you think you are doing?'

'I was having some trouble and I was going down to call you.'

He took a step forward suspiciously before he noticed the phone. He lunged towards me.

In that moment, the world slowed down. I looked for his gun. It was not pointed at me, and that was all that mattered. This was the only chance I would get.

I took a step back and scissor-kicked with all my might, hitting him square in the head as he reached out towards the phone. Both of us went down hard. As I slammed against the deck I heard, rather than felt, a bone give way. The pain was intense but I couldn't, in that moment, identify its source. It was with a far greater sense of horror that I watched the phone skid towards the railing. Even before I heard the ominous plop into the darkening waters, I knew there was nothing I could do. My hands were, quite literally, tied.

I looked over at Rishi at my feet. For one moment, I thought I had killed him. But as I calmed down, I saw he was still breathing. I didn't know how long I had before he came to.

I gritted my teeth through the pain, struggled to my feet and saw the knife sticking out of his back pocket. I turned around and picked it up with my bound hands, every movement excrutiating. I didn't think I would be able to cut through my restraints without aggravating the injury, but I had no choice. I realized the pain was originating in my right arm, somewhere up near the shoulder. I carried the knife over to the front and positioned it on the driver seat, pointing towards the rear of the vessel. I sat on the handle to anchor it, manoeuvring my hands into a position to cut through the ties. It was slow going and a few nicks were unavoidable, but I finally felt that release of pressure that told me I had worked my way through at least one part of rope.

I tugged frantically, ignoring the agony. I had, I hoped, enough adrenaline racing through my body to keep me standing, keep me fighting.

Without a phone, there was little I could do. But at least I was alive.

I grabbed the rope Rishi had removed earlier and first bound his legs. I had to hunt around for the rest of it to tie his hands and, when I got back, he was stirring. I dealt with his arms as quickly as I could. I stood up and he looked up at me, pained and angry.

'You're lucky I haven't thrown you overboard,' I said.

'How will you get out of here without a phone?'

It was time to think low-tech. The compass on the dash told me which way was East. I knew if I headed anywhere towards the mainland, I'd eventually catch sight of a fishing boat or some other vessel that could help us. But with the malfunctioning steering wheel, that would involve letting Rishi go below deck or leaving him here on his own, and I didn't know if I could take that chance, given that the knots I had managed to make with my diminished capacity were hardly rock steady.

I went below to see what I could do, and it became clear why Rishi had left me on deck. There were all manner of sharp corners with which to cut through restraints. I made some effort at navigation, but between my arm and lack of experience, I was soon frustrated. I closed my eyes and slowed my breathing in an attempt to clear my head and battle the rising fear. And then I heard a noise.

I ran back up on deck. In the distance, I could see a helicopter. Whether my people were in it or his, it was all over.

EIGHTEEN

As it drew nearer, I saw that it was a Titanium helicopter and Shayak was hanging out of it, gun trained at us.

'Don't shoot!' I screamed above the whirring of the blades, certain he couldn't hear me. 'I have him in restraints!'

Whether he heard or saw what he needed to, he put the weapon away and threw a rope ladder down to me.

I had climbed one of these before, and it required more upper body strength than I could muster at the moment. I pointed at my arm and hoped that he'd be able to see me, and guess the rest.

It seemed he did, for he quickly began the descent, a harness dangling from his hip. Once on board, he first tightened Rishi's restraints.

'You're hurt,' he said, turning to me.

'My arm – I think it is broken.'

'Anything else?'

I shook my head.

He put the straps around my waist and tightened the buckles. He then lifted my good arm around his neck and put one of his around me in an iron grip. 'Hold on,' he said.

Using his one free arm, Shayak got us both up that ladder. As soon as we made it to the top another man headed down, and I watched as he cut through my clumsy knots and escorted Rishi up to the chopper.

'He's had a nasty blow to the head. He passed out briefly too,' I told Shayak.

'All the better,' he said, glaring at Rishi.

'He needs medical attention.'

'As do you – and maybe a psychiatric evaluation as well.'

Hours later I was still in a hospital bed, much against my wishes. 'I don't see why I have to stay here,' I said.

'You have a broken arm and a minor concussion. Either you stay here or insurance won't cover it,' said Shayak.

Which was bollocks invented to get me to shut up. 'Fine,' I said, 'then it is your job to entertain me.'

'You need sleep.'

'I need to know what happened,' I said.

'I've been locked up in a cell for the last few days. Shouldn't I be saying that to you?'

'First tell me how you got out.'

'It all happened this morning – and I believe I have you to thank for it.'

'Really?'

'That's all Ajay had to say to me. He looked rather put out about it as well. Care to tell me what happened?'

I told him about the fingerprint on the impossible surface which could not have hosted one. 'But Ajay didn't look convinced when I showed him.'

'He can be prickly when he is wrong but he eventually comes around.'

'How did you find me?'

'That is the wonder of Neeraj. He realized my e-mail account had been hacked and found the mail asking you to come to the factory. I couldn't reach you by phone, so I set out. When you called from the satellite phone we were able to trace the call and get the coordinates.'

'How is Rishi?'

'Alive. Soon to be incarcerated, I hope, for a very long time thanks to you. How did you put it all together?'

I told Shayak about the string of electronic evidence; the stowaway Lalu Prasad, the signs that all pointed to an insider; my initial suspicions about Adlakha; and, finally, my encounter with George Santos which pointed me in the right direction.

'George was the connection between Afreen's murder and Dhingre's,' I said.

'Rishi told the cops she was one of George's most fervent disciples. George merely helped Afreen out as a favour – and then expected her to spy on the investigation on Maaya Island.'

'Which she refused to do.'

I had all the essential pieces, but questions still lurked. 'I really would like to speak to Rishi.'

'You've earned that right,' said Shayak. 'Soon.'

'What's wrong with now?'

'The police are in with him.'

'We still have nothing to connect George to these crimes. If what Rishi says is true, he was at the very least complicit.'

'You can have a go at him too – he's on his way here now.'

'How did you manage that?'

'Threatened with arrest from the ashram or a trip to Mumbai, he chose wisely.'

When I finally came face to face with Rishi again, I was pleased to note that he looked far worse than I did. He had a couple of broken ribs and compound fractures to his leg, both inflicted by me.

'Reema, it's almost nice to see you after the ugly mugs the police have been throwing at me,' he said.

'Why, Rishi? And don't give me all that soul-of-a-hacker crap again,' I asked.

'Must we really do this?'

'Do what?'

'The whole grand reveal? Try to humanize the sociopath? So melodramatic, don't you think?'

'Is that what you think you are, Rishi, a sociopath?'

'Hell, yeah. Don't need a psychology degree to figure that one out.'

The smile on his face told me I should believe him.

'You can't choose your ending,' said Shayak. 'This is a double murder investigation. So we'll need those answers, whether or not it suits your idea of a good story.'

'I'm done for anyway, so why should I tell you anything?'

'Cooperation can only help you at this point. Tell us who wanted to take Titanium down, and you'll be doing yourself a favour. I don't think you were acting alone.'

'I think I liked her question better,' said Rishi.

'So let's start there,' I said.

Rishi looked bored as he began. 'Alright. Cue tale of terrible childhood. I come from a long line of military men. My father could imagine no other future for me. He thought my passion for computers was a juvenile obsession, and he pushed me to take the UPSC exams, to join the NDA. I got through, but I refused to go. And he gave me the thrashing of my life. After years of watching him do the same to my mother, whenever he was on furlough, and to me, I had had enough. I took off for Goa.'

'Where you met George.'

'He was disgruntled ex-army himself, so we had something in common. And he had work for me. My mother died soon after I left, and there was nothing to bring me back here till

I heard about this opening in Titanium, and I thought it was the chance to come back to Mumbai and do the sort of work I always dreamed of doing – hacking.'

'It was also your shot at revenge,' I said. 'You knew Titanium was working on defence contracts.'

'I'm sure it was one of my father's rages that brought on the heart attack that killed my mother. So yes, revenge did cross my mind.'

'If you have stolen any information pertinent to ongoing military operations, you're looking at a death sentence,' said Shayak.

'I could have if I just had a little more time. But the man I was working for first wanted to take you down, Shayak. Whatever you did to piss him off, you shouldn't have.'

'Who?' asked Shayak.

'Never met him. Contact was made a few months after I joined. Communication was through a different person every time, some low-level operative who knew nothing more than what he needed to. The brief was simple: compromise Titanium without making it clear that the organization was the target.'

'How did you learn about the connection between Kimaaya and me?'

'Soon after I got started, a couple of years ago, she came to your apartment. There was something in the way she looked at you, when she was leaving.'

Shayak's jaw hardened. 'That footage was not meant for your eyes.'

'Yeah, well. Go figure.'

'Then what?'

'I found out about the safe Titanium had installed for her, and decided to go on a treasure hunt. The certificates were just sitting there, waiting to be discovered.'

'In a secure vault.'

'Secure is as secure does. Remember, Reema, what I told you about notions of unhackability. Not even at Titanium,' he said, with a look of pride.

'You thought a personal scandal like this would be enough to take me down?' Shayak said with a sneer.

'To hurt you long enough to deliver the fatal blow.'

'Which you hoped would involve blowing Titanium's most senstitive operations.'

'Something like that.'

'But it wasn't as easy as you thought it would be, leading to two senseless deaths,' I said.

'The plan was a good one. But that Dhingre was a busybody. Afreen was unfortunate, yet unavoidable given that she wasn't cooperating. It seemed a convenient way to deal with her and frame you.'

'Why was George sending her messages to provide information about Dhingre's death when you were around?' I asked.

'I guess trust has just gone out of style,' he said. 'They wanted to corroborate my version of events.'

'How did you lure her to Viraat's flat?' I asked.

'Much like I got you to Paras Foods. A fake SMS about a date. I knew Viraat would be out because the first thing he did when he got out of the hospital was call his dealer. I had his phone tapped just in case he knew more about Dhingre's death than he was letting on, having been within earshot and all.'

'And you had tapped Prashant Parashar's cell, too?'

'Long before I sent him that pen drive.'

Shayak and I returned to my room and awaited George's arrival. Vinod came bearing coffee that thankfully didn't taste like dishwater and a tiffin box filled with homecooked food. I nursed my cup with worshipful reverence.

'So Rishi went from one mess to another in an attempt to clean up after himself, all to make me one of the most notorious faces in the country,' Shayak said.

'At the behest of someone with enough influence to have a trumped-up murder charge hanged on you.'

My mind had already raced far ahead. 'It all connects with your Goa case, the drug hauls and Daanish Alam's death. The answer is hidden in George Santos' extended universe. And I guess that's as good a place to start as any.'

'Not so fast, Reema. You have a lot of healing to do. Your arm will take at least a month of complete rest.'

'But this isn't resolved – not really.'

'You've solved two murders and cleared my name.'

'Only to open a bigger can of worms.'

'We'll move on to that in due course. Don't worry – none of it will magically go away.'

But I already had an idea. 'George will be here soon. If he really isn't an accessory to these crimes, we might be able to use him to our advantage.'

'What do you mean?'

I ran my thoughts by him. His instant answer was a vehement 'no'. I had as long as it took for George to arrive to change his mind.

He walked in to my room, clad in white kurta and pyjama, the same worn chappals on his feet, beard neatly trimmed. He gave Shayak a nod. 'You've got to know I didn't have a clue about this, boss.'

'A little difficult to believe, George.'

'You two know each other?' I asked.

'We've met once, at a party. I wasn't sure George would remember me.'

George gave a nervous laugh, as if to assure Shayak he was unforgettable. And then he turned his attention to me.

'Wait a minute – you're that girl from the film set!'

'Right. That's when I figured out there was some connection between you and Afreen,' I said. 'It was you who brought her in to the Adil Khan project. That is why you were demanding her loyalty in the form of information on the investigation into Dhingre's death.'

'She needed a favour to get her into the film industry. I don't usually do this sort of thing, but it was at the request of a particular friend.'

'Who was the friend?'

'A hotelier in Goa. He introduced her to the ashram. He was a regular of hers, and many of my ashram guests stayed at his hotel. It was an innocent request, one that I was happy to help with.'

'You were the producer?'

'No! Oh no. I made a couple of calls for Adil to help him get financing.'

'Why were you pumping her for information if you had nothing to do with any of it?'

'A favour to another friend.'

'Who?'

He smiled. 'You can't expect me to give up all my secrets so soon.'

Shayak was stony faced. 'Rishi says it was you who told him about the job at Titanium. Who put you up to that?'

'It was a while ago.'

'Don't give me that crap,' said Shayak, finally losing his patience.

'Look, I thought it was a random tourist who had come for a drink to the bar. Got talking with Rishi and me one night.

The next day he swung by and told me about this opportunity at Titanium. Now I realize it was a set-up.'

'You really expect us to believe that?'

'I make my living not asking too many questions about people. But now that I think about it, the method makes sense. There are a certain set of people who rely on me to give them assistance from time to time. I don't really meet them face to face – I only ever meet the messenger.'

'What sort of assistance?'

'I think of myself as a connector.'

'So basically you are a fixer?'

'You might call it that. But I don't have blood on my hands. I try not to know what my associates are up to.'

'Ignorance doesn't protect you from the law.'

'I beg to differ. What exactly are you accusing me of? Getting Rishi a job interview? Helping Afreen out with a role in a film? Go searching, as I am sure you will, boss, and you will find me guilty of nothing more than some tax evasion, probably not more than your average business man.'

'Money laundering?'

He shrugged.

'If that is true, help us.'

'Why would I do that?'

'Because if you don't, we'll make it our mission to find something on you and, trust me, you don't want Titanium as your enemy. If it is only tax evasion, as you say, at the very least we can arrange a deportation. It won't even take more than one phone call.'

I wasn't sure if Shayak was bluffing, but George's sudden pallor told me he had bought it. 'What do you need?' he said.

'We'll let you know, in time,' said Shayak.

'It sounds like you aren't leaving me with a choice.'

'More or less. For now, we only want you to return to Goa and act as though everything is okay. Which it is, for now.'

George nodded, and left us.

'So does that mean I will be going undercover?' I asked hopefully.

Shayak shook his head – but it was more out of exasperation than anything else. My spirits lifted.

'Is that a yes, then?'

He left the room. Yes.

I woke up to a dark room. I could hear voices. Loud voices.

It took me a moment to remember where I was: Shayak's apartment. Just for the day. After which Sohana was kidnapping me until I got better, for the sole purpose of vegging out in front of her TV and the promise of beer.

I scrambled out of bed and turned on the light, looking at myself in the mirror. My right eye was still a little swollen, my arm in a sling adding to the rough-and-tumble look. I didn't have any of my things so making myself presentable wasn't an option. I ran a brush through my hair, straightened my crumpled T-shirt and headed for the living room.

There was Shayak, staring me down. Pratap and Poonam Puri had both swung around to face me, arms akimbo. 'Why are you out of bed?' asked Shayak.

'What, and miss all the action? What's going on here?'

'Shayak is trying to resolve our situation, as it were,' said Pratap.

'Can I help?' I must have been giddy from the pain meds because otherwise Poonam's death glare would have sent me scurrying. 'I think you've done quite enough,' she said.

'I don't believe you've formally met,' said Shayak.

'No introductions required,' she snarled.

'Don't blame Reema, she's just the messenger,' said Pratap.

For some reason, I was smiling.

'Sit down,' said Shayak, more gently. Perhaps he was afraid that it had all finally caught up with me.

I took a seat. 'What did I miss?'

'You were right about everything,' said Pratap. 'Poonam was stealing company secrets through my head of tech and hawking them to the highest bidder, hoping to inflict deep damage before our IPO.'

Poonam rolled her eyes. 'You left out the part where you were cheating on me and planning to leave me.'

'You know as well as I that our marriage has been over for a long time.'

'Here we go again,' said Shayak.

'I was merely protecting my interests.'

'You thought I'd leave you wanting? Don't you know me better than that at least?' I saw what appeared to be a genuine look of pain in Pratap's eyes. It seemed Poonam had registered it too for her anger deflated and she sat down. When she spoke next it was with a mix of sadness and bitterness.

'Jasmine tea,' she said, raising the delicate blue-and-white china cup before her. 'The good stuff, at least, is the result of tea leaves being mixed with jasmine buds till the tea itself takes on the fragrance of the flowers. Marriage is just like that. Bad marriages, too. For years I slept next to Pratap, inhaling the perfume of his deceit till it became a part of my fibre. I could have cheated right back, like so many scorned spouses, but I knew I could do better than a cheap lay. I wanted to really make him bleed. Tell me, given a chance, would you do any different?'

'Poonam,' said Shayak, 'you know how I feel about this stuff. But it's time to let go. Pratap has agreed not to press charges and to honour your pre-nuptial agreement which, you have to admit, is hardly harsh. Neither of you have been at your best in this business, and this is a chance for both of you to make as clean a break as possible and move on.'

Poonam shook her head, angrily wiping away a tear that had escaped. 'You know he is just going to turn around and marry your ex-wife. You are okay with that?'

'I'm happy for them, Poonam. The only thing about this situation that upsets me is the two of you tearing each other up in this way. And that I don't like being lied to,' he said, directing his attention to Pratap.

'What do you mean?' he said.

'For starters, you should have looked elsewhere for your witch hunt against Poonam.'

'I didn't lie about anything! She had been behaving so oddly, I thought she could be having an affair.'

Poonam, looking exhausted, stood up. 'I'm going home.'

'So you'll look over the papers?' asked Pratap.

'You'll drop the case against me?'

'Yes.'

'Then I'll look at the papers.' She walked out.

Pratap shot Shayak a cheeky grin. 'Thanks, man.'

'Don't thank me,' said Shayak. 'If I hadn't known you for so long, I would have punched you in the face and advised her to hang you out to dry.'

Pratap laughed. 'That's a load of bull and you know it. Shayak Gupta stand by a criminal? Never.'

'When the victim is pathologically incapable of keeping it in his pants, my standards are prone to change.'

The insult didn't seem to affect Pratap one bit. He turned to me. 'It wasn't an accident that we met in the nightclub that night, was it?'

'Nope.'

'Why were you following me instead of my wife?'

'Just testing a theory.'

'Which was?'

'Your wife was clearly not cheating on you. So why were you so keen to prove that she was?'

'Hey, it turned out she wasn't cheating on me – she was just plain cheating me!'

'Anyhow, I'll admit I was wrong. I shouldn't have wasted my time following you. You were the client, and your motives were none of my business.'

'That's a rather noble admission. Maybe you should have continued following me for a while longer. Who knows, right?' he said with a wink.

Shayak rolled his eyes. 'Okay, Pratap. I think it is time you left now,' he said. 'Unless you want to sample Reema's self-defence skills first-hand.'

Shayak let Pratap out. When he returned, his face was strangely haunted.

'What's wrong?' I asked.

'It's going to be dangerous, what we have to do in the coming months.'

'I'm ready.'

'No you are not. Before you begin we'll have some fairly intense training.'

'Bring it on.'

'The stakes are high. Everything that Rishi and George have told us points to an outfit that operates much like a terrorist cell, using people who know little about the overall operation to get the job done. These are people who work smart, with deep resources and network. They'll stop at nothing, and their intentions are currently far from clear. If you want to back down I'll understand.'

'Not for a moment. So I will be going undercover?'

'We have a lot of work to do before that. We have to find out everything we can about George Santos before coming to any kind of arrangement with him.'

'And we need to determine how the Daanish Alam murder and the warehouse shoot-out tie into this.'

He nodded. 'It's a long game.'

It was hard to contain my excitement. No matter what the danger, my moment had come. Till two months ago I had been playing at detective. Now I was the veteran of three murders and an attempt on my life. Finally it felt right – the risk and the sacrifice. This job was no longer what I did, it was who I was.

'I'm in – on one condition.'

'What's that?'

'No more boats.'

ACKNOWLEDGEMENTS

I would like to thank everyone who read, appreciated, critiqued and helped spread the word about *The Masala Murder*. I hope you stay with Reema for this, and all her future adventures.

The team at Pan Macmillan India, new and old. Pranav and Shiny. Saugata and Pallavi. Thank you for your hard work and commitment to make these books better.

My friends at *The Telegraph*, for some stellar support.

Finally, a shout out to Debjani, official first reader; Shradha, launch genie; Shabari, Lakshman, Maitri and Venky, the best customers ever!